# Vortex

## by Matt Carrell

### Author's note

This book is a work of fiction. All characters portrayed herein are fictitious and any resemblance to real persons, living or dead, is purely coincidental.

### Linden Tree and Matt Carrell Books

### Copyright © Mattcarrellbooks 2014

### ISBN - 9781494805814

The right of Matt Carrell to be identified as the author of this work has been asserted by him in accordance with the Copyright, Designs and Patents Act 1988 of the United Kingdom. You may not copy, store, transmit, reproduce or otherwise make available this publication (or any part of it) in any form, or by any means without the prior written consent of Mattcarrellbooks (mattcarrellbooks@gmail.com). Any person who does any unauthorised act in relation to this publication may be liable to criminal prosecution and civil claims for damages.

# CHAPTER ONE

**When the rain stops...**

   Piruwat Angsorn ran a hand through his thick mop of greying hair and stared in awe at the seething chaos of Bangkok's traffic. Once again his eyes were drawn to the illuminated display perched high above the junction, ticking down the seconds until the lights changed. The clock turned from red to green three times, but the car was barely a hundred feet closer to the junction of Asoke and Sukhumvit Road. Only the green-jacketed motorbike taxi riders made any progress, along with the occasional *tuk-tuk* dodging from lane to lane, to speed an unwary tourist towards another gold shop or designer outlet. The passenger would be offered a once in a lifetime bargain and the driver, a healthy commission for delivering another eager punter. For most of the other travellers that night, patience was running short, but Piruwat couldn't have been happier. It gave him a little longer to luxuriate in the plush leather seat of the huge Toyota Land Cruiser, watching the city unfold in front of him. He'd never seen so many people before; his village was little more than a network of dirt tracks with fewer than thirty houses. This was his first visit to Thailand's distant capital.
   Stroking the smooth wooden finish of the car's interior with rough calloused fingers, he eased himself still lower in the soft hide of his seat. Piruwat examined his cracked, dirty fingernails and the deep brown face reflected in the car window. The locals would pick him out in a second, as a farmer from the poor northeast of the country. A westerner might guess his fiftieth birthday was behind him but outdoor life had taken a heavy toll in Piruwat's thirty-seven years. The plaid shirt was new and the jeans were a passable copy of genuine Levis, but there could be no mistaking a man who made his living planting rice and tending tobacco plants.
   "*Mai pen rai.*" Never mind... he chuckled to himself. Instinctively he stroked the amulet, the *Phra Kreuang* he picked up at his village market three weeks before. The vendor promised him good luck and as Piruwat stared down at the face of the Buddha, he

promised himself that the seller would share in his good fortune. Things were destined to change, the poem told him so and it had been right up to now.

Piruwat owned a Toyota too, but it was a thirty-year-old pickup truck and much of the vehicle had been replaced, more than once, with parts salvaged from the scrap yard. It got him to the market once a week, as long as he didn't push it too hard. That was the first thing on his wish list, a new truck, or at least a second hand one that still had its own documentation and hadn't been scavenged piece by piece. He'd have to spend a little on the house too, maybe an extra room for his two daughters, they were getting too old to share with their brother. There were so many things he could do with his newfound fortune, so many choices. He never had choices before.

Piruwat smiled again as he picked up the heavy crystal glass from the sleek wooden holder at the side of his seat. He raised the tumbler to his lips and took another sip of the iced Jack Daniels Black Label the driver poured for him as he got into the car. It couldn't have been more different to the harsh bite of his usual Songsam Thai whisky. He knew he'd never have a car like this one, but he might be able to treat himself to a decent bottle of *farang* liquor from time to time.

As the traffic ground to a halt once more, a face appeared at the window, a tiny girl who couldn't have been any older than his six year old daughter, Pim. The girl brushed her long black hair from her face with a thin, dirty hand and looked up at Piruwat with huge brown eyes. She offered one of the garlands many drivers hang over their rear view mirror for luck. Piruwat reached into his pocket to find some change but as he started to lower the window, the car eased forward and picked up pace. The young girl was left standing by the road, her expression unchanged. She often tapped on a hundred windows before anyone bought a garland. But she was already an old hand at the trade. As the Toyota pulled away, she stepped back onto the sidewalk and waited for the traffic lights to bring her the next batch of potential customers.

Piruwat settled back in his seat and stared out at the frantic, bustling streets of the city. Shoppers poured out of the vast Terminal 21 shopping centre, most heading for the Skytrain, knowing a taxi would just have to take its place in the largely stationary traffic of Sukhumvit Road. The farmer took another long hit of the whisky. He was in no hurry, things never moved that fast in his village and he was determined to enjoy every second of his trip. The pedestrians looked gloomily at the sky and their pace quickened as they fled the humid streets like a single being, heading for the stairs and the air-conditioned sanctuary of the Skytrain line that runs the length of Sukhumvit Road. A few raindrops hit the window at Piruwat's cheek and he too stared at the darkening sky. He was new to the city, but no stranger to a Thai rainstorm. He could almost count down the seconds until the heavens opened and a wall of rain hit the street. The lights changed once more before the Toyota passed through, but by the time the car crossed the junction, water flowed inches deep in the gutter and passers-by fought to raise their umbrellas against the deluge. Piruwat was a good Buddhist, and would never take pleasure in the misfortune of others, but he knew he was a very lucky man. Sipping from the crystal glass, his hand closed over the precious slip of paper in his trouser pocket.

    Three weeks had passed since the game. He went to the temple that day with offerings for the monks. Piruwat prayed and knelt in silent contemplation for nearly fifteen minutes. He picked up the small wooden container of *kau cim* sticks and thought about the question he wanted to ask. That night he'd be playing *Hi-Lo* with *Kuhn* Karapong and his friends and the farmer wanted to know if luck would be on his side. He shook the box gently until a stick fell to the ground. Painted crudely on its side, was a number that had never come up for him before and he was anxious to check its meaning. A smiling saffron-robed monk beckoned him towards the row of boxes where he would find the poem matching the number on the stick. The verse was short and simple.
    *"The spring is here, yet it still rains. When the rain stops, joy comes. The sun and moon gradually rise. The old gives way to the new. To see through this is like going through the Dragon gate. The God and Buddha aid you. "*
    Piruwat had driven his battered Toyota to the game that night, through a rainstorm just like the one now drenching the streets of Bangkok. As he reached Karapong's house he saw that

stone dragons guarded the stairway to the front door. The original part of the house was a traditional bamboo, stilt construction, raised to guard against flooding and to keep vermin from the living areas. Karapong had recently built a huge extension in modern style, including a vast terrace commanding a panoramic view of the valley below. Underneath was an air-conditioned garage for his brand new Mercedes.

Piruwat thought about how he could get to the door without being soaked to the skin. He decided to make a run for it… then the rain stopped. The dragons… the rain… there could be no doubt about the meaning of the stick, the poem could not have been clearer. When the rain stops, joy will follow.

*Kuhn* Karapong greeted each of his guests as though they were long-standing friends and a young girl was on hand to wash the feet of each of his visitors before they were ushered to the *sala* where the game would take place. There was plenty of beer, several bottles of Songsam and a selection of regional delicacies betraying the host's birthplace of Chiang Mai and his enormous appetite. The table was laden with *tord man plaa, sai kok* and *por pea gung*, easy snacks to eat without distracting the players from the game. Karapong eyed the food and the assembled gamblers as though he could not decide which to devour first.

Piruwat had few expectations of winning before his visit to the temple. He brought five hundred baht and his main concern was to ensure he got his fair share of food and whisky before his pockets were empty. As usual he started cautiously, with low stakes and simple bets, more often than not guessing correctly whether the combined total of the dice would be higher or lower than 7. With each roll of the dice he stroked his amulet and prayed for good luck. As his pile of cash grew, his confidence rose and he began to place more money on outcomes with higher odds. In less than two hours he started to believe the message of the sticks, he'd won four thousand baht and his luck was in. Had he left the table, it would have been disrespectful to the spirits who were smiling on him. More than that, he felt at one with the dice. As Karapong rattled them inside the wooden cup, Piruwat could see the dice turning and ricocheting off one another. As his host slapped the tumbler on the table, Piruwat felt his hands drawn to the bets he should make. Occasionally he must have misinterpreted the spirits who guided him because Karapong would gratefully sweep his stake from the board. More often, and normally when he bet high, his host strained to look nonchalant as he paid out on a winning bet. Piruwat was embarrassed by his success, the pile of baht in front of him grew higher with each throw of the dice and his fellow players stared in awe. He placed higher stakes and chose more improbable bets, he was anxious his host should not lose face in his own home. To lose a little of his winnings would ensure both men could leave the table with honour intact. Yet the dice continued to fall for Piruwat.

As the clock struck midnight, the farmer sat with a little over twenty thousand baht at his elbow. The farm might generate such a sum in a month; he'd won it in just a few hours. The new day gave his host the opportunity to call a halt to the game and the players started to say their goodbyes. Piruwat had no idea how to deal with his good fortune. It would be disrespectful to offer a tip to his host but he was anxious to make some sort of gesture. Only as the local garage owner bade farewell did the idea strike him. The man handed Karapong some baht notes and received a slip of paper in return. Piruwat had forgotten that in addition to the *Hi-Lo* games, his host offered odds on the lottery. Not the official government version but the parallel underground lottery. Choose three digits that match the last three of the number drawn on TV twice a month and Karapong paid five hundred-to-one; choose two matching digits and the pay-out was still a healthy fifty-to-one. The farmer could make a gesture without embarrassing his host.

"May I play too?" he asked as the garage owner departed.

"With your luck *Kuhn* Angsorn, I think it would be better for me if you did not," Karapong replied.

"As you wish," Piruwat said, embarrassed by his clumsiness.

The older man smiled and gripped the farmer's shoulder.

"My little joke, I would be delighted to have the chance to win a little of my money back."

Piruwat relaxed and returned the man's smile.

"How many numbers, *Kuhn* Angsorn?"

"Three," the farmer replied.

"And your bet?"

Piruwat paused, "Two thousand," he answered, reaching eagerly for the wad of notes in his trouser pocket.

The farmer took the paper Karapong offered and wrote the number 795 on one side. As his host returned the signed slip, he handed over two thousand baht. Honour was partly restored in Piruwat's mind.

Piruwat barely thought about the ticket in the days that followed. He bought half a baht of gold, a little over a quarter of an ounce, with most of his winnings; it's the Thai way of saving for a rainy day. Piruwat owed his brother two thousand baht since the previous harvest and the men shared a full bottle of Songsam to celebrate its repayment. His wife and children were able to replenish their threadbare wardrobes and the rest went into a small tin behind the hearth in their house with the lottery slip he received from Karapong.

Two weeks later, Piruwat saw Aiee; his neighbour's daughter, running through the village. Twice a month she sold roughly copied sheets listing the winning lottery numbers. He paid the five baht, more as a kindness than because he wanted to check the numbers. Nonetheless he couldn't resist taking a look. He ran to the house and frantically dug out the tin. His fingers trembled as he looked at the numbers again. The farmer's mind raced and for a moment he thought maybe it was the first three numbers he needed to match not the last. The winning number was 876795. It was the last three on which he'd bet and Karapong owed him one million baht.

Piruwat drove to see Karapong without even telling his wife where he was going. He couldn't bear to raise her hopes without confirmation of his luck. Karapong was waiting for him; he too had seen the numbers and knew the bet was won.

"*Kuhn* Angsorn, I am honoured to be visited by a man who is so clearly blessed by the spirits."

Piruwat relaxed, since he'd expected the man to be hostile.

"*Kuhn* Karapong, it is I who am honoured."

"My friend, I am pleased for your win and I am anxious to get you the money as quickly as possible. I have been in contact with my partner who is in a position to pay you immediately. Will you be taking your family with you?"

"*Kuhn* Karapong, my family does not know about the ticket. My wife would have been angry if I told her about the wager. She will know nothing until I return with the money." He paused for a moment, confused by the question. "Taking them where?"

Karapong smiled and slapped the farmer on the back.

"You will be on the bus to Bangkok this afternoon but you must hurry. I will tell your wife you had to travel on urgent business. She will be thrilled when you return."

"Bangkok?"

"My partner is in Bangkok, we have never lost such a bet before. I am sure you understand we do not keep such a large amount in the village."

Piruwat smiled again and shook his host's hand. Of course, he should have thought about it. Who would keep a million baht in their house?

As promised the man was waiting at Mo Chit bus station in Bangkok, wearing a black suit and a red tie, exactly as Karapong described.

"*Kuhn* Angsorn?" he asked, without offering the traditional *wai* greeting one would expect from a chauffeur.

"I am Angsorn," Piruwat replied.

"*Kuhn* Karapong's partner has been detained in a meeting but looks forward to meeting you shortly. I have been instructed to take you to the Amari hotel in the city centre. There is excellent seafood and my employers were sure you would wish to celebrate."

Piruwat just wanted to get his cash and head back to his family, but the driver opened the door and gestured for him to get inside. Having poured his passenger a generous measure of whisky, the driver got back in the car and they began their slow progress though the streets of Bangkok. The poem came back to Piruwat… the old gave way to the new, just as it predicted. By the standards of the wealthy of Bangkok he was still a peasant, but soon he would be heading back to Isaan with one million baht in his pocket. He would not be boastful of his good fortune but gradually the other villagers would understand he was a man of means, a man to be respected. There are many things in Thailand that can win the respect of one's peers, the most effective of course was money and soon the farmer would have a great deal of that.

The Toyota picked up pace, left the main road and headed east on a small *soi*. Piruwat turned to check he wasn't imagining things. As they passed a sign for the district of Klong Toey he noticed that once again they passed under an arch framed with dragons. The poem again… the old would give way to the new. Piruwat was in no doubt things would never be the same for his family, he'd never had such luck with *Hi-Lo* or the lottery, nor had he visited the capital of his country and it was certainly the first time he'd ever ridden in such a magnificent vehicle. He'd tasted JD Black Label before but, as he swirled the last of the amber liquid in the crystal glass, it occurred to him that it was usually a little clearer than this one. There'd been no strange white residue in the bottom of the glass. He wanted to ask the driver about that, and why they were now heading further from the main roads when the man had explained he was going to a city-centre hotel. He wanted to tap on the screen that separated him from his chauffeur but as he yawned, he couldn't summon the energy. His arms felt heavy, he could barely keep his eyes open and as the car drew to a halt on the dockside he drifted into a deep sleep.

Piruwat was right that life for his family would never be the same again, he was right that his luck had changed completely. The chauffeur opened the rear door and pulled the slumped body of the farmer from his seat. It was no real struggle to drag the man to the edge of the dock. It took a few seconds to go through his pockets, to find the once precious lottery ticket and the small fold of baht bills Piruwat had brought to Bangkok. The driver removed the farmer's watch and searched briefly, and in vain, for any other valuables. Satisfied that, should the body be recovered; it would look like a street robbery, there was only one thing to do before he dropped the limp body into the river. The driver pulled out his knife and drew it firmly across Piruwat's throat. It was a practiced move, the man knew exactly how the blood would spurt from the wound, and he was anxious not to soil his clothes. Seconds later, there was a splash and the driver returned to his seat in the Toyota.

## Welcome to the firm

The rain had eased to a gentle warm drizzle by the time Prem Boonamee had navigated the final few kilometres of Bangkok traffic and arrived at the warehouse. Nonetheless, he was anxious to avoid the puddles as he stepped from the car in his expensive leather loafers. First he had to fumble for the electronic key card in the box under the dashboard. The alleyway was deserted but Boonamee was a careful man and checked in both directions before he slid the plastic card into the mechanism and keyed in the passcode. The door slid back and in seconds the car was in its space. Boonamee returned to the alley and hailed a motorbike taxi for the short ride to his apartment near the Park Lane mall in Ekamai.

The passcode was changed every month. It was Song's idea to match the latest six-digit code to the last set of numbers drawn for the state lottery.

"So lucky for some," he said as he gave Boonamee his latest assignment. "But not for others."

Boonamee's boss suffered from a mild obsession with the lottery. Unsurprising, as it was one of the reasons the two men made such a very good living. Four years passed since they met at the house of a mutual friend. Boonamee lamented to his neighbour that there was little money to be made selling air conditioning units and the man agreed to make the introduction to Song. The job sounded straightforward albeit with a small amount of risk.

Only a fraction of those who tune in twice a month to watch the government lottery draw have ever bought a ticket. The vast majority place their stake on the parallel underground lottery. Boonamee's job was simply to sell as many tickets as he could and pay the occasional winner when a gambler got lucky. He had to be wary of the police, the schemes are illegal, but he was comforted by the knowledge the local Chief took ten per-cent of the profits.

Song encouraged Boonamee to recruit a network of agents with whom he could split his commission. It took no time at all to realise sexy, outgoing girls were the best bet and in a matter of months, he had eight working for him. He'd slept with three of the girls but still needed to make a conscious effort to match a face with a name when he went to collect their cash every week. Finding women was never a problem for Boonamee. At five feet ten he was tall for a Thai, his hair was always immaculately coiffed and he'd acquired a taste for genuine brand name suits, rather than the cheap copies many of his friends were obliged to buy. His bedroom wall was adorned with an original poster for the movie Bangkok Dangerous with Nicholas Cage. He'd watched it more than a dozen times and convinced himself he was the spitting image of the main Thai actor, Shahkrit Yamnarm. A steady stream of girls played along with his fantasy.

Pom was different. She'd worked at the petrol station where he filled his car and clearly ran the place. It never occurred to him she might be interested in him or in the line of work he could offer. He wasn't quite sure how he got that first date, he mentioned a restaurant across town and she said she'd always wanted to eat there. In a matter of days he was besotted, finding any excuse to drop by and see how she was doing. When she complained about how little she was paid at the petrol station, he told her about the lottery. Three weeks later she was his best selling agent. Life was sweet, the cash was rolling in and he'd fallen for the sexiest woman he'd ever met. It was obvious the first time they spent the night together that he was far from being Pom's first boyfriend. He suppressed the pangs of jealousy and enjoyed the fact that wherever they went, all eyes turned to watch his girlfriend. Prem Boonamee thought he was the luckiest man alive.

Pom sounded elated when she left the message that changed everything. He was in the shower and didn't hear the phone ring; otherwise he might have had the chance to talk to her one last time.
"Prem, it's me. I can't believe it but some of the tickets I sold have won big money. It's amazing, the guys are here now and they promised to give me a huge tip. Phone me back, they want to know when you will bring the cash. Please call me, this is so exciting."
Boonamee grabbed the folder with the bets for the month as he went on-line to check the winning number. As he found the site

and cursed the slowness of his connection, the phone rang again. It was no surprise when he saw the name on the screen.

"It's Song," said the familiar voice.

"Yeah, I saw that it was you."

"Have you checked the numbers you sent me?"

"Doing it now," replied Boonamee; still wrestling with the manila folder and cursing the spinning icon that told him the page was still loading. "Is there a problem?"

"Your girlfriend sold three winning tickets. How the fuck does that happen? If you hadn't sent me the numbers before the draw I'd think you were cheating me."

"What makes you think she's my girlfriend? She's just another sales agent." Boonamee replied with panic rising in his gut.

"Don't play me for a fool Prem. I know things about you, you don't know yourself. I make it my business to know about the weaknesses of my associates."

"Song, you know I didn't cheat you. It's simply bad luck… for us at least."

"Prem, we don't have bad luck. I can live with paying out a few thousand to those Isaan pigs you live amongst, but this is two million baht. Didn't you read the small print, we don't pay out sums like that."

"What do you mean you don't pay? The guys are sitting in her office at the petrol station."

"Not my problem."

"You're going to walk away from it?"

"Of course, and you will too if you have any sense."

"And leave her to it?"

"If she's just another sales agent, why would you care?" The voice taunted him now.

'I can't do that."

"Up to you. Prem, you are a valued employee, but there are plenty more where you came from. Dump the girl, get in that piece of shit you call a car and head for Bangkok. In three days time make sure you're sitting at the outside terrace of the Bangkok Baking Company on the corner of Sukhumvit Soi Two at four in the afternoon. If you're there, I have another job for you. If not, *chok dee kap…* good luck."

"But… I can't just…"

"Up to you. This phone is going in the river in thirty seconds, so unless you're there in three days time, we won't be speaking again. I suggest you do the same with yours." The line went dead; Boonamee was left staring at the screen.

He had a pretty good idea how much Song made from the lottery and there was no need to walk away from a loss, however big. He did because he could. It was just another way of showing how powerful he'd become. As the main man in the syndicate, as far as Boonamee knew, Song was insulated from the people who bought the tickets. The only two people in the firing line were he and Pom. Only they were known to anyone locally. Had he been smarter, he'd have kept it all at arm's length, but Pom was his girl and he'd shared a glass or two with a few lucky gamblers as he handed over ten or twenty thousand baht. Usually a winner picked up no more than a few hundred, having wagered fifty on guessing two correct numbers. He knew a big win was bound to happen sometime, but why did it have to happen to him… and Pom?

He couldn't walk away from her, but if he stayed her problem would become his problem. The phone rang again… Pom. He let the message go to voicemail. For a second he thought about playing it back, but then pressed delete. Boonamee removed the battery and placed the phone on the floor. With two sharp strikes of a claw hammer it was in pieces at his feet. Boonamee picked up his car keys, pausing only to think of the quickest route to the main road and the highway to Bangkok.

Boonamee had gone to the Bangkok Baking Company coffee shop three days later as Song instructed. He sipped his coffee and waited. A girl in a traditional Thai outfit winked at him as she walked past, returning to work at the massage shop next door. Three sunburnt *farang* paused to ask for a light as they headed for the bars of Nana Plaza in the next *soi*, cursing him in a foreign language as he waved them away. A pretty young waitress buzzed around him, constantly checking whether there was anything else he needed.

His watch showed twenty past four when a motorcycle taxi rider appeared at his side.

"Prem Boonamee?"

"That's me."
"Who are you waiting for?"
"Song."

The man dropped a small package on the table and turned away without another word. Inside was a pay-as-you-go mobile, with one number in the contacts list and one name - Song.

Three years had passed since he fled Korat. Boonamee owned a nice apartment and a Kawasaki motorbike, made use of Song's fleet of expensive cars whenever he needed them and a procession of willing girls helped to keep him amused. Boonamee still thought often about Pom. For a few months his friends said she carried on working at the petrol station but then all of a sudden she disappeared. There was talk she went to work as a dancer in Pattaya. Sometimes he dreamt about her. She'd appear from nowhere... angry, he'd explain he had no choice; there was nothing he could have done to help her. After all, he could never have found two million baht. She carried on working for a while so she must have found a way out somehow. Now he could make it up to her, he had plenty of money. If she was still in debt, he could deal with that, she just needed to tell him how much and who he should pay. They could go back to the way it was before. The dream always ended the same way. She'd smile and step into his arms... that perfume, that mane of beautiful black hair, that soft, warm, supple body. It would envelope him and he'd collapse against her, so grateful to have another chance... a chance to put it all right. Then he stepped back to look at her, to tell her he loved her and that everything would be OK. That's when he felt the sharp pain in his heart, that's when he saw the knife. He'd clutch the gaping wound a centimetre below his rib cage and start to feel himself drifting away, he tried to cling on to consciousness but something told him it was over and then he'd hear a voice.

"Oh my Buddha, so much blood. I've never seen so much blood."

When Boonamee woke from these dreams his body was bathed in sweat. Sometimes there'd be a girl in his room and he'd scream at her to leave, whatever the time of night. Then he sat and meditated until the terror subsided. More than three years passed since he'd last seen Pom and the dreams were less frequent, maybe even a little less terrifying when they did occur. In his waking hours he still thought about seeing her again, maybe he could still put it right.

Since he'd left Korat, Boonamee's life had changed beyond recognition. The provincial lottery hustler threw himself into his new job in the capital and was starting to reap the rewards. At the outset it wasn't that different. The lottery network in Bangkok was far bigger than that in Korat, where he'd met Pom. The formula was identical; one man controlled a network of foot soldiers who sold the tickets. Boonamee managed the flow of cash between each network and Song. If anyone failed to meet his targets, Boonamee paid them a visit.

At his side for each of these trips was Kong. Korean, with maybe a smattering of Thai blood somewhere in his ancestry, he was at least a hundred and fifty kilos with no discernible gap between his head and his shoulders. Every exposed inch of flesh was covered in tattoos, some of which clearly dated back to when he was a great deal thinner. The dragon on Kong's calf was as swollen as the man himself. Boonamee idly reflected that his own trouser belt might fit round the man's thigh, as long as it didn't need to be fastened. There was little to do on these visits apart from introduce himself, explain Song's disappointment to the terrified agent and then leave the guy alone with Kong for five minutes. There would be minimal violence, there was no point in putting a source of revenue in hospital, but the visits were invariably motivational and revenues always rose again in the weeks that followed.

Business was good and Boonamee could almost convince himself he was a law-abiding citizen. At the very least, when he delivered the envelope once a month to the local police captain, he could claim that he and the forces of law and order were on the same side. He planned a visit to his agents in the north of the city on the day he got an urgent message from Kong. Within twenty minutes he was at the warehouse, where another Thai dressed all in black stood impatiently next to a powerful Kawasaki motorbike, not unlike his own. A casual acquaintance of the Korean might believe he had a single facial expression; the aggressive glower implied an act of random violence was imminent. It was the look Kong employed ninety-five per cent of the time, essentially to maintain his hard man image. Nature had regrettably seen to it that, when the Korean smiled, his face took on the imbecilic quality of a man who recognised a joke but could never really fathom its meaning. As Kong threw him a helmet with a full-face visor, Boonamee was treated to one of those rare smiles. This time he could sense an uncomfortable gnawing sensation in his gut, the feeling that there might be a joke and Kong was fully aware of how it would be played out.

"Song says you are to take him to Bang Rak, he has to follow a guy who has done business with the boss. He needs a really good rider."

Boonamee nodded in recognition of the compliment and threw one leg over the seat of the Kawasaki. The stranger did not even acknowledge him, but took the pillion seat of the bike with an easy athletic grace. Within minutes the men were speeding down Surawong Road towards the river. His passenger told him to wait by the entrance to the Mandarin hotel. Nearly forty-five minutes passed before a black Lexus pulled out of the hotel car park into the *soi*.

"That's the car."

The limousine took the turn for Silom Road and quickly headed back in the direction from which they came. Boonamee easily weaved through the traffic to make sure he was rarely more than a car or two behind.

"Pull alongside, I want to see who he's with."

Boonamee eased the bike up to the side of the Lexus and watched the countdown to when the lights would change. The clock showed twenty seconds. At twelve he felt his passenger pull something from inside his jacket, at eight he heard a metallic click and at four the rear passenger window of the Lexus exploded in a hail of automatic gunfire.

"Get out of here now."

Boonamee didn't need to be told twice as he gave the bike full throttle, they entered the junction, scattering pedestrians who were yet to clear the crossing. He didn't have time to think about what was happening, his flight reflex kicked in hard and he wanted to be as far away from the Lexus as possible. He turned sharply into a *soi* and sped to the junction with Surawong Road.

"OK, slow down, we're clear. No need to attract attention."

They were only a few minutes from the warehouse and Boonamee knew the advice was sound. The man flicked up both their visors and in seconds the assassins appeared to be no more than a couple of friends on an afternoon jaunt. Kong was waiting as they arrived at the warehouse; the man in black dropped the weapon into a drum by the door and grabbed a set of car keys from Kong's huge hand. In seconds he was gone.

Boonamee's heart pounded furiously as he stared at Kong, unable to come to terms with what had just occurred. The man threw him an envelope. There was five thousand baht in cash and a note from Song.

"Welcome to the firm."

The murder was all over the newspapers the following day. One of the victims was a prominent Bangkok businessman. There was endless speculation as to why he'd been killed and the internet was alive with rumours his wife had hired a hitman, largely because of the second passenger to die in the hail of bullets. Police originally reported it to be a very beautiful young woman, immaculately dressed in the finest designer clothes. The ID card in the victim's handbag and the penis discovered at the post mortem, beneath La Perla underwear, both indicated the police report was mistaken with respect to their gender. The businessman clearly liked ladyboys and he and his new friend were now dead. His betrayed wife was the obvious suspect. A police spokesman confirmed they'd located the motorbike used in the attack and were confident of finding the perpetrators.

Boonamee sat in his apartment, stupefied, realising that Song had set him up. He'd had no idea he was taking part in a hit. Now he was firmly on the other side of the law. There was no going back.

Just two weeks later he and Kong went to visit Kook. He wasn't one of Boonamee's agents but Song explained that Kook had been skimming thousands of baht from his lottery takings for months. There was no way the man could repay the stolen money, but they had to send a signal to the wider network that this was unacceptable behaviour. Boonamee explained the error of Kook's ways and went to step outside so Kong could do his party piece. The huge Korean blocked the door. Mercifully, it was the handle of the small automatic pistol he was holding that pointed towards Boonamee.

"One in the balls, one in the head," Kong said with the nonchalance of a man ordering lunch.

Boonamee took the gun and shrugged.

"Right; one in the balls, one in the head."

It took four shots before Kook stopped squirming.

The dreams still plagued him, less often perhaps. Occasionally he felt the wetness of his sheets and thought it might be real blood, only to realise he'd lost control of his bladder as he dreamt. In the day he tried to shut out the thought of Pom and he abandoned the idea of ever making it all up to her. At night he hoped the dream would not come.

Kong did most of the dirty work, but Song insisted on Boonamee keeping his hand in. All the orders came direct to him from Song and the Korean did pretty much as he was told. Most of their work was low-level thuggery, keeping the troops in line and occasionally taking care of an ill-advised newcomer who mistakenly believed he could operate on their territory. Citizens of Bangkok are used to the regular reports of street killings and no-one pays much attention unless the circumstances are unusual or a foreigner is involved. After the motorbike hit, there were only two occasions when Boonamee and Kong's activities hit the headlines. Uncharacteristically, the Korean had become very attached to Min, a go-go dancer who worked on the third level of the Nana Plaza entertainment centre. He arrived at her club to propose that she leave the bar and come to live with him. Henrik was forty-two years old, Danish, completely bald and one hundred and ten kilos in his khaki shorts and flip-flops. Regrettably he had his hand inside Min's bikini top when Kong arrived. The Korean's strength was pretty impressive in itself; he appeared to lift the Dane over the rail with only a modicum of effort. What was truly admirable was his aim. The ground floor of Nana is always teaming with customers and ladies eager to make their acquaintance. Henrik's body appeared to shatter on the only three square metres of floor that was not occupied. The *mamasan* ensured that Kong was spirited away from the scene and with no other customers in the bar or by the third floor rail; it was a simple matter for all those present to agree that the man had jumped. Suicide was recorded and to Kong's chagrin, Min fled the city. He would never know that she soon turned up in Pattaya and imaginatively changed her name to Nim.

Kong was also the key player in the second incident but that was planned meticulously. For four days, the two men checked their target's routine. At eleven p.m. each night she stopped her tiny Fiat 500 outside the gates of her home in an exclusive suburb of Bangkok. It took a few moments to locate the button on her key fob, then another four or five seconds for the gates to swing open. On the final day of their assignment, Kong drove a fourteen-ton ex-military truck down the quiet residential street and crushed the Fiat against a Hyundai four-by-four parked forty metres further down the road. The Korean dragged the lifeless form of a Cambodian lorry driver into the driver's seat. The man had been fed alcohol and drugs for much of the day and his heart had only given out less than an hour earlier. Boonamee's motorbike was on hand to ensure they could make their escape before the alarm was raised. The papers were full of the story the following day. The wife of a highly respected Bangkok policeman had been killed, by a driver who was out of his head on *yaba* and Thai whisky. Boonamee had personally killed four men since Kook and never again took more than two shots to do the job.

Boonamee was back in his apartment less than an hour after Piruwat Angsorn's first and only trip to Bangkok had ended in the murky waters of the Chao Praya river. As he closed and triple-locked his front door, Boonamee threw his linen jacket over a chair and kicked off the leather loafers. A quick flick through the TV channels showed, as ever, there was nothing to watch. He took a long swig of Jim Beam, direct from the bottle, and headed for the shower.

The call from Song had come at two that afternoon. The job should have been Kong's, but with only two days to the Queen's birthday, Mother's Day was almost upon them and the giant Korean had gone home to spend time with his family. Boonamee was shocked when Kong made the request, he never really thought of him as having a family.

Boonamee left Nana Post Office minutes before his phone rang. He'd dutifully sent toys to his nephews and nieces in Korat and then used an ATM to transfer cash to their parents. As he turned back onto Sukhumvit Road he spotted the stall. It was mainly aimed at tourists, but he chatted to the vendor occasionally and the man often stocked some exquisite knives. Boonamee's mobile rang as he pocketed his purchase. The edge was razor sharp but it was the handle that caught his attention. The workmanship was extraordinary.

Song explained about the farmer and repeated the words Boonamee had heard years before.

"We just don't pay out on bets like that."

Boonamee wanted to ask why Song didn't leave Karapong high and dry for the bet, like with Pom, but he knew that was pointless. This time, they would deal with it in a different way. He thought about the farmer in the back of his Toyota, he watched him in the rear view mirror and it was obvious the man could barely contain his excitement. Then there was the confusion as they turned off the main road and stopped at the dockside. Boonamee's timing was impeccable. That was when the barbiturate kicked in and the farmer fell into his final sleep. It was a last minute instinct to slit the man's throat. As Boonamee drove off and recalled the moment he started to feel a pang of regret. He'd thrown the knife into the river after the body. It wouldn't be easy to get another knife like that.

A few minutes after midnight, Boonamee switched off the lights and headed for bed. His stomach was tight and his head started to throb. It wasn't the whisky. It was the certainty that sometime before he woke he would dream of Pom… of the knife and the blood, so much blood.

# CHAPTER TWO

## The Beach

Rawai Beach featured in every one of Andy Duncan's oldest and fondest memories. Late afternoon was his favourite part of the day. The Andaman sea was almost still as the sun completed its slow descent. The waves subsided, the sea lazily caressed the beach with each ebb and flow of the tide and the horizon turned a startling shade of bright orange. Andy wanted the sky to be clear at water level for the final dramatic exit, but a scattering of light fluffy clouds would add to the effect. Their far side reflected the sunlight, the near side would be inky black and sinister. He'd recall his metalwork teacher showing him how to mould steel. Heating it until it glowed, so it could be twisted and hammered into shape then plunged into ice-cold water. In a second the metal was stronger than before. He liked to imagine the same thing happening as the sun looked to have disappeared into the ocean, spreading a long inviting path of light towards where he stood on the beach. It was always a magical moment, then the light was gone and he first noticed a chill in the air. As a teenager, Andy Duncan believed everything he could ever want was there on Phuket island. The sea, the surf, and the most magnificent beach he'd ever seen. He had no real conviction the world beyond could possibly have anything to offer him.

A couple of times each year, right up until he started university, Andy's father would tear himself away from his office in Hong Kong, and their housekeeper would join them for a family holiday on Thailand's Phuket island. As each day of the trip passed, Victor Duncan would spend more and more time at his computer; certain that, in his absence, the investment firm he worked for in Hong Kong would collapse. He couldn't conceive how they could function if he were not in near constant contact. The truth of course was that the dependency operated the other way round.

Andy spent his days at the beach, usually at the surf school at the far end of Rawai. Steve was always busy, making running repairs to his surfboard, scraping or painting the hull of his boat or teaching another class of hopeless *farang* how to run the waves. Nonetheless he was the calmest man Andy ever met.

Steve had treated Andy like an old friend from the first day they met.

"Yeah, I did the corporate thing for a few years," he'd said. "I even owned a couple of suits. But it was just one characterless hotel after another, shaking hands with another guy whose name I'd have forgotten by the following day."

"I can't imagine you in a suit Steve. What made you change?" Andy asked, sipping *nam manao*... iced lemonade under the shade of the surf school's awning.

"I had this thing about security, savings, pensions... all that sensible stuff. I kept telling myself, 'I'll stick with it a few more years. I've got plenty of time to relax', I didn't think I'd know what to do with myself if I didn't go to work."

"So what happened?" Andy asked.

"They did." Steve laughed as a girl of about seven hurled herself into his lap but was then quickly retrieved by the elegant Thai woman who'd served them their drinks.

"Andy, meet Fah and Yoyo. My reason to give up the rat race."

Andy thought about his own father, Victor, and wondered if he'd ever hang up his suit and turn his back on his job. The thought was just too ridiculous to contemplate.

Victor Duncan had arrived in Hong Kong as a twenty-five year old, just one year after qualifying as a Chartered Accountant. It was standard career progression for a high flier with one of the world's largest firms. International experience, then back to the UK for fast track promotion to partnership.

In 1986, the gentlemen's club ethos of the UK Stock Exchange was bust apart and the market was opened to banks eager to take on the might of the Americans and the Japanese. Victor served his investment industry apprenticeship auditing a new firm created by one of Britain's largest banks. Convinced that the new rules were a licence to print money, they threw unlimited resources at the new venture. The result was unbridled chaos. Just as they started to realise that they'd bitten off more than they could chew, the Market Crash of 1987 struck. Instead of looking at super profits, the banks were nursing losses of hundreds of millions of pounds. Whilst one part of their business was evicting people for being a few thousand behind on their mortgage, their investment arms were trying to work out how they were going to recoup tens of millions from customers who should never have been allowed to trade in the first place. That issue paled into insignificance against the losses they incurred from stocks they held that became all but worthless overnight. The banks were so certain that they would make a fortune; all common sense went out the window. They dealt in anything, with anyone, without having much idea what they were doing. What drove them on was avarice and the terrible fear that if they didn't participate, their competitors would get the upper hand. It was the same herd mentality that sowed the seeds of the crisis of 2008 and beyond. Victor was horrified, appalled and totally fascinated. He decided to dedicate his career to bringing some semblance of order and discipline to the chaos. He started to specialise in investment firms and that led to his prestigious secondment to the firm's Hong Kong office.

Berwick Archer was then a brand new but infamously aggressive investment business. Victor was charged with auditing its Hong Kong subsidiary, it was to be his final assignment before returning to the UK. At eleven forty p.m. the night before the accounts were to be cleared, he was standing toe to toe with his client's Chief Financial Officer.

"We can't sign until you amend the accounts, we found an error in the pricing of one of your derivative contracts. You have to correct it," he told his client.

"Victor, it's late. Look I wanted to talk to you anyway; we need a guy like you here in Hong Kong. How about we just sign this off and then talk about a job for you here at Berwick Archer?"

"I'm flattered, but I couldn't discuss an offer like that until after the accounts are signed and that won't happen until you amend them."

"Jesus, you know your stuff and integrity too. We definitely need to talk about a job. OK, we'll make your adjustment."

Victor had never seriously contemplated staying in Hong Kong; the lure of a partnership in a global accounting business had been immense. But he also had to consider Emma Mortimer, the young student he'd been with every spare hour for the previous eight months. When the job offer was repeated the following day, he signed the contract and started to look for an apartment big enough for a newly married couple. Twelve months later, Mrs Emma Duncan gave birth to Andrew Cameron Stuart Duncan, their first and only child, in the Hong Kong Sanatorium in Happy Valley.

Andy would look at pictures of his mother without a flicker of recognition, even though she didn't leave until the day after his sixth birthday. The psychologist said his sub-conscious buried those memories too deep for him to access. It may also have been because his father only kept the oldest photos, destroying the ones that were taken after she formed a close and enduring relationship with Bombay Sapphire gin and a Frenchman called Yves. Victor felt no resentment, he'd neglected her, working six twelve-hour days a week and being too tired on Sunday to do much more than recuperate. Expatriate life sounds idyllic, with generous expense allowances, cooks, maids and nannies. The reality for a young, vibrant, intelligent woman, whose husband is never around, is more stark. Pushing a baby stroller around the footpath at the top of the Peak and swapping stories about lazy nannies and careless cleaners, with other mums who are far from home, is no substitute for a career in medicine. Victor sacrificed his return to the UK for Emma and she dropped her ambitions to be a doctor when their son was born. A marriage that started with such a huge compromise probably had only one way to go.

Victor liked to tell stories. While most of his son's friends were hearing about Hansel & Gretel or the Legend of Sleepy Hollow, Victor was sharing the tales of Ivan Boesky, Nick Leeson and Peter Young. Boesky was a master at manipulating the share price of quoted companies; it cost him two years in jail and a hundred million dollar fine. Leeson brought down the historic Barings Bank in London. An administration clerk, his employers gave him access to hundreds of millions of pounds to trade in securities neither he nor they really understood. He went to jail too, but it may have been some comfort that Ewan McGregor played him in the movie. Peter Young cost Deutsche Bank over three hundred million pounds, treating an investment fund as though it was his own cash. He dodged jail after asking the judge to call him Elizabeth and turning up to court in a stylish summer dress and high heels. The insanity plea may have been a ruse, but Young is probably the most famous man alive to decide to have a sex change then try to complete the procedure himself. It didn't go well. As Victor told his stories, Andy enjoyed picturing his father as the knight in shining armour, battling to keep the villains at bay.

When Andy Duncan received his degree from Imperial College on the stage of London's Albert Hall, Victor was bursting with pride. Dinner at the Savoy Grill was an awkward affair, conversation was hard to come by and neither man would admit to being relieved when Victor settled the bill and they could say goodnight. Andy had secured a generous allowance for a year of world travel with the single concession that first, he'd complete a three-month internship at Berwick Archer in Hong Kong.

**Spoof**

Sally Peng was a lesbian. At least that was a truth universally accepted by the male staff of Berwick Archer's Hong Kong office. Her hair was always tied back in a rather severe bun; she wore thick-framed spectacles and no make-up, and never joined the rest of the staff for a drink after work. Unlike most of the female staff she never slept with anyone in the investment department, conclusive proof she had to be "batting for the other side." As one of her colleagues whispered when he was sure she couldn't hear, "she doesn't actually wear dungarees, it just looks like she does."

There appeared to be no technical problem she couldn't fix and her bosses had long since stopped asking her how she kept the firm's computers running, they happily left her to it. Sally's mother still worked for the Chinese Space Programme in Beijing and her father was a professor of mathematics at the city's university. She left for Hong Kong after graduating top of her class; feeling like it was the only way of getting her parent's attention. Four years on, the strategy hadn't worked, so she threw herself into her job. Sally was very well paid, not because Berwick Archer truly recognised her importance, but because the firm had long since lost the plot on pay and bonuses. Handing out massive rewards was a macho thing, a way of reassuring the bosses as to their own success.

Sally knew the rumours as to her sexual preferences but cared little for what her colleagues thought of her personal life. She liked men, but not the kind of egotistical, testosterone driven idiots she believed populated the corridors of Berwick Archer. She was never interested in any of the employees of Berwick Archer until the day a young intern called Andy Duncan walked through the door. She'd always admired his father since, to her; Victor appeared to be the only man in the firm with an ounce of integrity. Sally was pleased to hear the handsome young man would only be with the firm for a three-month internship. He had a fleeting chance of getting out before being infected by the greed that consumed most of her colleagues.

After a few days of general clerical duties, Andy was given the task of producing Excel spreadsheets for the fund managers. Sally downloaded the necessary files from the main trading systems. Whilst they never talked about taking things further, the two established an easy rapport. Three weeks into the project, the fund managers were raving about the new information at their fingertips, Sally decided she might be about to break her rule about sleeping with a colleague and Andy cursed his luck that he was very attracted to someone everyone knew to be a lesbian.

"We need to buy another server, can you get Tait to sign the approval form for me? Sally asked.

Andy laughed. "Of course your majesty, anything else I can do for you?

"I'm sorry," she replied. "It's just that I can't bear the man. He's a pig and he treats women like dirt. I'd have to shower afterwards if I went to see him."

Andy paused to enjoy the image she'd placed in his mind. "I heard he was a legend, they say his team would walk through walls for him."

"Sure, and they're as bad as he is. Haven't you heard of 'The Bet?"

"Nope, can't say I have."

"Spend ten minutes with Tait and he'll tell you how they 'work hard but play hard.' That basically means eight hours in the office watching the screens and chatting to their mates, then out on the town chasing women, fuelled by San Miguel and cocaine as far as I can see. Twice a month he sticks his gold Amex card behind the bar and he calls it team bonding. Then they compete on who can get the new girl in the office into bed."

"I'm sensing that you're not a fan. So that's the Bet then?"

Sally seemed to shudder as she thought of it. "No, it's much worse than that. He waits until everyone's drunk then picks on one of the new girls. Says he'll bet her five hundred Hong Kong dollars he can make her nipples move in opposite directions without touching her."

"Awful." Andy was trying to look appalled at what he was hearing.

"Of course the girl accepts. She's drunk and he's the boss. Then he grabs her breasts, rolls his hands around on them and hands over the cash saying, "bugger, lost again.""

Andy had the terrible urge to giggle. "And they haven't sacked him for it?"

"I think they tried to back in London, but James Turner was coming out to head up the Hong Kong office and he saved Tait's skin. Brought him over as a senior fund manager."

"He's never tried anything with you right?"

"If he did I have a bet of my own. I reckon I could make his balls move in opposite directions using only my left foot."

Andy decided it was finally safe to laugh.

Brad Tait might have been asleep when Andy arrived on the investment floor. His chair was fully reclined, his shoeless feet were crossed on the leather surface of his desk and his eyes were closed. Only the phone at his ear gave any indication of activity.

Tait was six feet four, played Australian Rules football at university and was a keen and very capable surfer. Andy had heard him lament that his athletic physique forced him to have every item of clothing hand-stitched by a local tailor. Tait spent hours every day on his I-Phone, and told anyone who'd listen that keeping all those women at bay was a living hell, most suspected he just liked to use the phone's reverse camera feature. He could admire the thing he loved most in this world - himself. The phone call was clearly not a welcome one.

"So write me up, I don't give a fuck. I've got more important things to do than fill out forms for your pen-pushers." A quick glance around his desk gave no clue as to what those pressing duties might be. His trading screens were switched off and a small TV showed a cricket match where most of the players wore baggy green caps.

"So the auditors will send us a stiff letter, who gives a shit? They do it every year and the sky hasn't fallen in yet has it? It's your job to keep them off our backs. Now if you don't mind, I've got a few billion dollars of client's money to take care of."

Tait paused as he listened to the caller, shaking his head impatiently as though he'd heard it all before and it was no more interesting this time around.

"So talk to Turner, see where it will get you." He cut the connection, opened his eyes and sat up, taking in Andy's hesitant form standing a couple of feet from his desk.

"Andy... you must be adopted mate."

Andy couldn't think of anything to say, he'd forgotten why he'd come to see Tait in the first place. The Australian laughed at his obvious discomfort.

"You're an OK sort of bloke, but that father of yours is a prize-winning arsehole."

Andy suddenly realised who was on the other end of the phone line.

Tait was still in full flow. "Here we are, working our butts off day and night, making money for the firm and all he cares about is a fucking checklist and whether the auditors are going to give him a hard time." It vaguely crossed Andy's mind that the clock had barely struck six p.m. and everyone else had left for the pub, but he nodded in sympathy.

"Anyway, we're getting together at the Red Flag tonight. We work hard on my team and we play hard too." Andy suppressed a smirk as he thought of Sally's earlier comment. Tait continued. "Come and join us... a thank you for all the work you've done for us on the analytics." Tait slipped on his shoes, grabbed the gym bag slung over the back of his chair and headed for the door. He'd brought down the curtain on another of his favourite type of conversations, one where the other person isn't required to say a thing.

It's about a one kilometre walk from the IFC building to Lan Kwai Fong, the most popular post-work drinking destination on Hong Kong Island. Luckily for those who wish to avoid the crowds and the humidity, almost all of that can be done above street level and the majority can be achieved without leaving the air-conditioned sanctuary of the shopping malls that snake their way through the Central district. Andy was on his way to the Red Flag, as Tait suggested, but he took his time. After his trip to the investment floor, he went back to his desk to see if Sally could be persuaded to join him. Her screen was off and her bag was gone.

Andy sat for a while nursing a strong black coffee and thought about what he'd just witnessed. His father sat on the Executive Committee of the Asian business alongside regional Chief Executive James Turner and the accountant guy Sally worked for. Victor was one of the top three people in the business. He lived, at the company's expense; in a vast apartment on the Peak, Hong Kong's most exclusive district and flew first class whenever he travelled. He'd risen to the top of his trade and had everything you could want from a career… except respect. Tait languished well below him in the theoretical pecking order, but the Australian could talk to him like he was a minion. There was no doubt where the real power lay, in the hands of the investment staff. His father was there to keep the auditors and the authorities off their backs while they got on with the really important stuff… making money.

He always had an image of his father in his mind, of the powerful grandee who pulled the strings in a famous financial institution. All of a sudden the image became a little blurred around the edges.

In the days following Tait's get-togethers, the office came alive with war stories from the event. Andy Duncan was about to attend his first as guest of honour. Sally was nowhere to be seen and Andy was greeted with grunts of incredulity when he asked if she was expected to turn up. Nonetheless he spent most of the evening checking the door hoping she'd arrive. By the following day he'd have no recollection as to whether he consciously gave up on her, or the endless rounds of beer and tequila chased her from his mind.

As the evening drew to a close, Tait called for three magnums of champagne for a final toast to his team and the technological wizardry at their fingertips thanks to Andy's efforts.

Andy blushed as Tait proposed a toast to all his hard work then beckoned him over to the bar. Standing next to the Australian was a young woman in a sober, but elegant blue business suit. She wore a simple silk blouse and around her long, slender neck hung a small, elegant pendant. Andy had a fascination with faces. It's the same basic ingredients, two eyes, a nose and a mouth, the effect can be very pleasing, or it can have you screaming for your mother. Often he'd seen a girl and thought… if her eyes were not so wide apart, if her lips were not quite so thin, if her nose was a little smaller or her chin a little less prominent. Any one of those tiny imperfections could make a potentially pretty girl ordinary. Combine a few and the investment office boys would snigger, point and try to outdo each other with a cutting comment. "Well, she won't need to shell out for a Halloween mask," or "Everyone has the right to be ugly, but she abuses the privilege." Andy was looking at a woman with no identifiable flaws. Spend a while in Asia and it becomes surprisingly easy to distinguish Thais from Koreans from Japanese from Chinese. The product of a Thai/western union is known as a *hasip-hasip*… fifty–fifty child. There was no telling where this woman might have come from, only that she was mixed race and, thanks to her ancestors, was probably a ten–twenty–twenty–thirty–twenty, rather than a fifty–fifty. Andy thought mixed race kids were almost always good looking, and it might be a subtle message from God that the races should try to get on better together. Maybe he was up there on his throne, screaming down, "Procreate you bastards, you'll be better looking and you might stop killing each other."

The woman standing next to Brad Tait offered the perfect advert for relationships crossing racial boundaries. Her hair was a simple shoulder length bob and she appeared to be wearing no make-up whatsoever. Sometimes nature does such a good job, there's nothing more man can do. Andy was in no doubt she'd have the most dazzling smile, but he was not about to find out. She settled on that look only a truly exceptional woman can carry off. It's a slightly weary, seen-it-all-before look that says, "go on... impress me, I really doubt you can, but it might be amusing to watch you try."

Tait's voice broke through the reverie.

"Andy Duncan... meet Caroline Chan."

"Really... ummm... yeah like ummmm nice... ummmm nice to meet you." Andy blushed like a schoolboy and Chan regarded him as though she was inspecting an item of clothing offered by a shop assistant who'd failed to recognise either the taste or the purchasing power of their customer.

"Yes, of course," she said. "Your pet IT geek. Such a smooth operator."

Andy racked his brains for something smart to say, but the woman had already turned away and the men to her left parted like the Red Sea to admit her to their conversation.

"Ten thousand Hong Kong," announced Tait, waving the bill for the champagne in the air. "Let's Spoof for it." A murmur of excitement ran through the group and a few of the senior staff stepped forward, anxious to show they were up to the challenge.

"Andy, you're in." Tait beckoned the intern and grinned from ear to ear. Andy had a vague idea how the game worked but it never occurred to him he'd be expected to take part. Each player would place a maximum of three coins in the closed palm of their outstretched hand and take turns to guess the number of coins held by all the players combined. In each round, the player with the winning guess dropped out. The last man would pick up the bill for the champagne. Ten thousand Hong Kong Dollars represented more than a month of Andy's budget; he'd never be able to explain such a loss to his ever vigilant father. With eight players taking part, he just had to hope he got lucky.

As each round passed and another player punched the air in triumph and relief, the knot in Andy's stomach grew tighter. He could feel the acid in the back of his throat and the coins in his palm shone with sweat.

"I'm out," cried Aiden, the head dealer. He waddled drunkenly back to the corner table to make sure Carly, his prey for the night, hadn't sneaked away whilst his back was turned. Aiden had never successfully seduced a sober female, so he was relieved to see Carly tip back the last of yet another large vodka and tonic. There were only two players left. Tait would go first and Andy was one bad call away from a bill for nearly a thousand pounds.

"Spoof," Tait called, guessing the combined coin total to be zero. A clear signal he held no coins in his own hand. To win, Andy just needed to call the number of coins he was holding. That was three in the hand resting nervously on his knee, but no coins in the hand raised and trembling next to Tait's. His opponent had already made the winning call. The combined total was zero… Spoof. Andy barely made it to the toilets before he threw up.

It took him fifteen minutes to clean himself up and regain some composure. He'd ask Tait to cover the bill until morning and then beg his father for a loan. As he got back to the bar, only Tait and a couple of the other fund managers remained. The Australian had paid the bill and ostentatiously tore it in two as Andy approached.

"Don't worry mate," he said, "I've got your back. But you owe me one."

Andy staggered into the street and nearly fell into the path of a passing cab. Never again, he promised himself.

"So how was the party?" Sally Peng couldn't disguise the edge in her voice, but Andy was in no condition to recognise conversational subtleties. His head pounded and whilst he wanted to explain his disappointment that she'd not been there the night before, he decided a bacon sandwich and gallon of black coffee would be required first. He uttered only a few syllables.

"Breakfast first… want anything?" he ventured.

"Had mine two hours ago," she said, "you should check in on your new buddy Tait. He's an even bigger mess than you are." Andy could feel a wave of disappointment emanating from his colleague.

Andy had to cross the investment room to get to the kitchens where a full-time chef was on duty. A small price to pay, to encourage staff to stay at their desks as long as possible. When he saw Tait slumped in his chair, Andy asked if he wanted anything. Tait looked up.

"I'm gonna need a new fucking job mate. Can you help me with that?"

"What happened? You're leaving?"

"When the bosses find this one out, they're going to find a way of opening those fucking things," he said, gesturing at the huge picture windows and their view of the harbour hundreds of feet below. "I'm completely fucked."

"It's not HR again is it, Brad? No-one takes them seriously."

"No mate, it's not because I squeezed some bird's tits, it's because I reckon I just cost the firm twenty-three million US dollars."

"You did what?" Andy was lost for a more penetrating question.

"You heard of Carasol?" Tait's voice was a hoarse whisper as his hand came down hard on the desk in front of him. The vibration sent coffee from a huge yellow mug across a pile of papers, but the Australian didn't appear to notice.

"Sure, huge South American oil company. Last Saturday they pumped about five million barrels of crude oil into the Gulf of Mexico, the share price went down the drain." Andy was delighted to be able to show off his knowledge, forgetting the despair etched on Tait's face.

"Well the Emerging Fund had forty million dollars of their bonds and last week Carasol offered a switch into equity at a really good price. Two ordinary shares for every hundred dollars of debt."

"Yeah," said Andy, "but the offer period closed after the accident in the Gulf. Nobody took that offer."

"I did." Tait looked like a guilty schoolboy admitting he stole the church collection tin.

"But…" Andy wished he'd headed straight for the kitchen.

"I know, it's unbelievable. They used to talk about the dickheads who still applied for BP shares when the government sold its stake back in '87, even after the stock market crash. You could buy them from your friendly broker cheaper than you could buy them off the government but people still piled in. It was the stuff of legend, now I've pretty much done the same and I'm supposed to know what I'm doing."

"So what went wrong? Why did you do it?"

"The offer closed last Monday lunchtime and the admin staff reminded me on Thursday night. I was going to a three-day party at my pal's house on Lantau... he owns a model agency and the girls were... you know. I knew there was no way I'd be in on Monday morning. So I accepted the Carasol offer on Thursday night."

Andy's mind raced. He'd been at the firm for less than a month but he'd heard his father talk about the basics of the business for as long as he could remember. Even he knew what Tait had done was lazy, arrogant and, above all, reckless. He'd heard his father say it a dozen times.

"The problem with these guys is it all comes so easy to them, they think they can get away with anything, they think they're bomb proof - right up until a thousand pounds of Semtex explodes right under their hand-stitched leather chair. Then they expect me to pick up the pieces."

Tait punched the screen of his desktop in frustration.

"I barely looked at the portfolio yesterday and I've only just seen what it does to the holding. The shares are down over forty per-cent and I'm fucked."

An idea formed in Andy's mind. "How did you accept the offer?"

Tait looked confused, "Just clicked Yes on the screen, then the system does the rest."

Andy smiled. "So you never told anyone you accepted it."

"No, I don't talk to those arseholes in admin unless I really have to. I just hit Yes. It's all there for everyone to see, it even has a time stamp to show I made the decision three days before I had to."

Tait looked at the young intern as though he might deliver a solution. Maybe he could bail him out of the mess, but he didn't see how. This was a twenty-three million dollar hole and Tait was sitting right in the middle holding a gold plated shovel with the initials "BT" monogrammed on the handle.

"Well… good luck Brad. I'm really sorry, I'm sure they'll sort it out… everyone makes mistakes right?" Andy backed away, watching the fleetingly hopeful expression on Tait's face crumple and die. He looked like a man who'd made it to the lifeboat, only to be told it was full. What did he expect from a lowly intern anyway? Tait would need a time machine to get out of the mess he was in, something to take him back to Thursday night when he clicked Yes.

As Andy sat in the corner of the kitchen, waiting for his breakfast and thinking about what he'd just heard, he realised he might have the keys to that time machine. Obviously he couldn't go back in time, but there was definitely a way in which he could make it look like Tait had never made the mistake. Someone had to take the rap for such a massive error, but it didn't have to be Tait. The Australian would be destroyed if this came to light, his career would be over. If the blame fell on a junior staff member, they'd lose their job for sure but the firm would give them a pay-off to keep quiet and they'd start again somewhere else. His idea went against everything he'd been taught. His father spent years hammering on about honesty, integrity and honour. The need to own up when a mistake was made, justice would be swift but fair, a man should take his punishment and move on.

Victor told him how those principles served him well, they got him to the top of a cut-throat business, delivering financial security beyond his wildest dreams. That moral code made sure he could give his own son the best possible education and an opportunity to work in the same business. It was true his father had the job title, but he saw the way Tait spoke to him. He had a fair idea what his father earned every year and knew the Australian pocketed a multiple. His father looked worn and tired. Up until ten minutes earlier Tait always appeared to be having the time of his life. Sure, Victor was a lot older, but thinking back he always looked like he carried the weight of the world on his shoulders. Maybe it was the weight of a set of principles that went out of fashion years ago. Tait had none of the scruples that governed his father's life but it hadn't held him back. The Australian did not sit at the top table of the business, but he had status, money and the respect of men like James Turner. Andy couldn't help but think back to the night before in the Red Flag. The devotion shown by his team, they were obviously in awe of the flamboyant fund manager. Then there were women like Caroline Chan, who appeared to be equally beguiled by the Australian, drawn to the power he exercised. That was definitely a prize to be coveted.

Andy realised he might hold the key to Brad Tait's career in his hands. It would be quite something to see the look on his face if Andy could expunge the error that was about to cost the man his career. He'd be very grateful and one day Tait might repay the favour. One of the administration staff would have to take the fall, but they'd be back on their feet in no time.

The chef slid a paper plate across the counter, bone china had been sacrificed a few months earlier when London asked regional offices to cut costs. Suddenly Andy had more important things to worry about than a bacon sandwich. He grabbed his coffee and marched purposefully back towards his desk.

It was just before eleven the following morning, when the two administrators were escorted from the building, each carrying a black bin liner with the few personal possessions they kept in their desks. Brad Tait stared in disbelief at the printout Andy had handed him… a record of the decision he took regarding the Carasol stock conversion. The system now showed that he made his decision on the Monday ninety minutes before the deadline and that he rejected the proposal. In the comments box, was the reason Tait should have declined the deal in the first place. It said, "weekend collapse of ordinary share price."

Tait always thought the next stage in the process was automated, that the system executed his instruction. Andy had spent only a couple of days helping out in the administration department but he knew it was manual. The sheet was printed and a clerk communicated the decision to their bank. All it took to transfer the blame for the firm's biggest ever screw-up from Tait to a lowly clerk was to make it look as though his instruction had been processed incorrectly. A simple task as long as Andy could persuade someone with unfettered access to the company systems to make a few changes to the data. She wouldn't even have to know the purpose of the change or who'd be the ultimate beneficiary, she'd be doing a favour for a friend. Sally Peng often boasted to him she had a "backdoor" into the system, she could do anything she wanted and nobody would be any the wiser. She was flattered when he finally asked her to demonstrate what she meant and hadn't really focused on the changes he asked her to make. He made it sound like he was trying to correct his own mistake and that was a favour she was happy to do. After that Andy simply had to wait until all the administration staff went home and then locate the file for the Carasol offer. He removed the original printout showing Tait's decision and replaced it with the new version.

When a firm like Berwick Archer makes a twenty-three million pound mistake, no effort is spared to cover the tracks. A cheque is written from the company's accounts to cover the hole in the client's portfolio. Those deemed responsible are quickly replaced and those "in the know" are sworn to secrecy. The news that a clerical error had cost a firm such a colossal amount of money would be very bad for business.

Sally Peng had other things on her mind as she demonstrated her unparalleled mastery of the trading systems to Andy that morning. Later she was told a couple of people had been fired in the "back office" of the firm, no-one said why, so she had no reason to connect that with what she'd done for Andy. She was still hopeful the young intern might repay the favour with an offer of a drink after work or dinner. When Brad Tait announced two days later that Andy would join the investment team as a trainee fund manager, she went out of her way to say congratulations. Andy just nodded in her direction and returned to the conversation he was having with his new colleagues.

**The Apprentice**

Brad Tait was holding court, surrounded by his managers. The pretext was the introductory training session for the team's latest recruit.

"Andy, welcome to the investment team of one of the world's most prestigious firms. I trust you are already fully acquainted with our long and glorious history… given your dad's the Chief Warder around here." His loyal audience nodded their approval at the sly dig at Andy's father.

"Not really Brad. I guess it's really old."

Tait chuckled. "Absolutely mate, it dates right back to 1982. Our founding father was some bloke called Alan Hooker... genius by all accounts. Wanted to create a global firm to rival Schroders, Rothschild and Goldman. I'm guessing it was a bitter pill to swallow; when he realised no-one was going to take him that seriously if he put his surname over the door." The assembled crowd laughed even though they'd heard the line a hundred times before.

"So anyway," Tait continued. "Hooker needed a name that oozed respectability, reliability and financial rectitude. He fancied something Scottish but legend has it, he got bullied by some hairy bloke from Glasgow when he was at school, and he'd never forgiven them."

"So who are Berwick and Archer then," Andy asked.

"Seems our man Hooker liked his history books. Apparently, about seven hundred years ago, your King Edward I invaded Scotland and his archers did their practice near North Berwick. Hooker thought it was a joke, a name that suggests Scottish prudence but it's all about some English king they called the Hammer of the Scots. Sounds like our founder must have been a riot down the pub on a Friday night."

"So what happened to him? My dad's never mentioned the guy." Andy said.

"Yeah, they don't like to talk about him any more. He was trying to set up a deal in Asia apparently, when a bunch of guys offered him a couple of million for the firm. They're the main shareholders now."

"So why did he give up the great ambition so easily?"

"It's a sweet story really. The day he got the offer he met some girl in a go-go bar in Bangkok. She might have been the first girlfriend he ever had."

"So what's he doing now?"

"He and his missus run a go-go bar in a place called Pattaya in Thailand. They advertise it as a beach resort, but it's basically a ten square mile whorehouse."

Andy laughed, "Yeah, I've heard of it. Sin City they call it. That's a bit of a comedown from building your own investment firm.

"I guess so," Tait replied. "But at least Mr Hooker finally owned a business where he could put his name over the door."

Cue another round of dutiful giggles from Tait's loyal team.

"Right," Tait said. "Down to business. Most of us remember the good old days right?" The older members of the team all nodded. "Well to be honest it was before my time too, but it gives you an idea of what they used to get up to. Andy you'd never believe it. They used to buy stock and not decide which client paid for it until they knew whether it was going up or down. If it went really well they kept it for themselves. If one client was doing well and another was losing money, they just swapped something over at below market value and… job done. First client is no wiser and the second client is back in the black. If your mate at a broker's having a tough month, you gave him a few extra orders or upped his commission. Golf days and lap dancing would be your reward. Fucking brilliant. I wish I'd been in charge when you could do all that stuff."

The rest of the team nodded in unison and Andy tried to work out whether he should express his disgust at these deceptions or join the others in mourning a golden age now lost in the mists of time. He had to say something.

"It's all pretty tight now then? All that's been stamped out, I guess."

"Pretty much," said Tait. "Thanks to people like your old man." A murmur of disapproval spread amongst the assembled fund managers, it was as though Victor had just been identified as the Child Snatcher. "We can still have some fun though, all depends on size. It helps if you have a big one." The others loyally tittered at the cheap innuendo and Andy managed an awkward smile, he still had no idea where this was going. Tait pulled up a screen showing a list of six stocks. From the page heading it was clear the Research team had marked them as stocks expected to underperform. Tait waved his arms dramatically and made a poor attempt at a theatrical voice.

"You my friend," he pointed at Andy. "You're an intelligent sort, you can help me with something we call…" he paused and looked around the group, "… magic." The team had little choice but to play along and gave a short round of applause.

"Pick a stock, any stock." Andy pointed at MRP, the third in the list.

"No mate, no point in selling that. We own it."

"We shouldn't sell one we own?" Andy sounded confused.

"Eventually, but not this time. Sell it and it's game over. We've locked in the profit or loss. Sell something you haven't got and the fun's only just started. You're making a bet that you can buy it back at a lower price later."

Andy shrugged and pointed at the next stock on the list, Asean Cement. Without hesitating, Tait placed an order to sell thirty million dollars worth of the stock that Andy had picked completely at random. "Now watch and learn," Tait said with a smirk.

It took over half an hour. The team started to talk about football and the latest recruit to the firm's research department.

"Great tits," Aiden remarked. Then they saw confirmation that the sale was complete. Tait pulled up the screen tracking Asean Cement's market price. It was already lower than the price at which he sold it and as the ticker changed each time, it dropped another cent or two. Tait smiled triumphantly.

"Enough tuition for one day. I reckon it will be off about sixty cents within a couple of hours, then we can buy it back. Got that?" The question was directed at Aiden who just nodded. Tait threw his arm around Andy's shoulder and guided him towards the coffee machine.

"That's the power we have Andy. We put an order like that in the market and it moves the price. We sell something we don't have, people get nervous, the price falls and we close the position at a nice profit. Easy."

"It's not illegal?"

"No chance, we're taking a risk. If the price doesn't fall our funds take a hit so there's nothing they can get upset about."

"So it doesn't always work?"

"Only most of the time and, when it doesn't, it's not our money anyway."

As the two men selected their coffees, the door to the lift lobby flew open and a small, round, red-faced man appeared and began to cough as though his lungs were in a final swansong. Andy had seen him several times at the entrance to the building, invariably shrouded in cigarette smoke as he worked his way through another pack of Marlboro Lights. Alex Cruickshank was Berwick Archer's top salesman in Asia, having moved from London three years earlier. He started his career selling investment products to Financial Advisors, who in turn dealt with the general public. After ten years driving around the southwest of England banging on the doors of anyone who might buy his wares, he was rewarded with a move to London. In no time, he was dealing with the country's largest institutional investors, from banks and pension schemes to local government bodies and charities. James Turner liked his style and Cruickshank's reward was a transfer to Asia. His job was to find the clients who put up the money that Tait and his team invested. The salesman had opted for traditional old-school City of London uniform and in all probability his tailor had dressed several generations of the Cruickshank family without ever changing style. The suit had broad chalk stripes, the shirt; also striped, was double-cuffed with heavy, crested cuff-links and collar stiffeners. A floral tie with a contrasting pocket-handkerchief completed the ensemble. There were many expressions to describe the effect. Understated elegance was not one of them.

Tait shook his head. "Jesus, I told Alex never to use the stairs, it'll kill him one day."

"Eighteen floors? Doesn't he know there's a lift?" Andy asked.

Tait laughed. "He works on seventeen, that's one flight of stairs. Alex needs a lie down after he's tied his shoelaces in the morning."

Cruickshank's role required him to entertain and that, he claimed, was the reason he carried what he described as a few extra pounds. In truth he fought an endless and unsuccessful battle with his weight. His desk was stocked with boxes of miracle pills and food supplements, and he was an authority on the many diets that claimed to guarantee dramatic weight loss without the need to abstain from any of his favourite food groups, such as red wine and cheese. He was the kind of man who'd see a sprig of parsley on top of a huge mound of mashed potato and call it salad.

"Alex, can I get you anything?" Tait pointed to the coffee machine. "Oxygen maybe?"

"Fuck off Tait," the salesman wheezed as he replied. "Just thought I'd drop by and check how much money you guys have pissed away this month. Got a few client meetings coming up and I need to know how much flak I'll be taking."

"It'll be a breeze mate, we've had a great month. They'll love you."

"Great, still the meetings aren't till next week, try not to screw it up between now and then." Only then did he acknowledge Andy's presence, "Who's your friend?"

Andy was still trying to work out whether the men despised each other or if it was just banter. He settled on the latter as Tait replied.

"Meet Andy Duncan, new recruit to the investment team." Cruickshank offered a chubby, slightly damp hand.

"Delighted. Son of the blessed Victor I assume. Best of luck, you'll need it with this bunch of clowns. Anything you need to know about the sales side, always happy to chat over a glass or two."

Andy felt like he ought to ask something, just to show an interest and offer some acknowledgement that he knew what Cruickshank did at the firm.

"Well Alex, I hear you worked with advisors before you switched to institutions. What's the change in approach when you're targeting such a different audience?"

Tait and Cruickshank exchanged glances; Andy was pleased with his insightful question and certain that the salesman was about to reveal some profound secrets of his art. Cruickshank paused before he replied. "Well basically, advisors like to go to girlie bars and football matches, we tend to take the institutional guys to the opera." Tait chuckled as he joined in, "Well they are more sophisticated investors." Cruickshank continued, "I guess, but I reckon they'd prefer to do the girlie bars too, it's just their employers tend to frown on that sort of thing." He paused and then looked Andy up and down. "Still you'll be a great asset to the sales and marketing effort."

"I will?" Andy asked with a little too much pride in his voice.

"Sure, they all love golf and I'm buggered if I can do eighteen holes these days. Someone told me you can play a bit." With that he was gone.

Tait punched Andy gently on the arm.

"There, you've learnt how to sell stocks short and you got a detailed insight into our sales and marketing process. Not bad for starters."

Andy was still letting his first morning sink in as he walked past Sally Peng for the second time that day. Trying to decide whether he was fascinated or horrified by what he'd learnt, Andy didn't mean to ignore her. It just looked like he had.

# CHAPTER THREE

## A chance in a lifetime

Song appeared to be completely absorbed by what was on the screen of his computer, he didn't even acknowledge Boonamee's arrival. It was less than a minute before he spoke, but to Boonamee it felt like an age. Their business was usually concluded by telephone, it was highly unusual to be summoned to see the great man in person. Unusual was rarely a good thing.

"Prem, I have been presented with the most incredible investment opportunity."

"I'm pleased for you *Kuhn* Song. When I next visit the temple, I will pray for its success."

"I have every reason to believe its success is already assured but let me tell you a little about it." Song gestured to Boonamee that he should sit before he continued. "Edward Jenner runs Hunter Stanhope, I'm looking at the website now. They are clearly a company of considerable substance and have a number of famous people as clients."

Song turned the screen so that Boonamee could see. The home page was well designed, proudly displaying partnerships with the World Bank, UNICEF and the European Union. A sidebar included a host of testimonials from contented clients and in the top left-hand corner of the page was the beaming face of Edward Jenner himself. The man exuded confidence, competence and prosperity.

"*Kuhn* Song, they are clearly a very successful company."

"Indeed they are and they have offered to take me on as a client, what do you think?"

"It is not for me to say *Kuhn* Song, but if this company has been recommended to you, I am sure they will provide you with excellent service."

"No they were not recommended. Mr Jenner called me himself and explained the excellent rates of return he could achieve if I were to give him my money."

"So you don't know anyone who does business with this firm?"

"Mr Jenner explained that they have only just started operating in Thailand, and I would have the opportunity to be one of the first of our countrymen to invest."

"But *Kuhn* Song, how do you know that they will do as they promise?"

Song gestured at the screen. "Look at the website. It shows the returns they can make. I could borrow money from my bank and they would still make sure I turned a profit. Their clients are delighted and look at all the famous names they do business with. They also say that they have access to all the new stock issues. There is a wonderful letter from one of their clients who invested in Microsoft right at the beginning, all on Jenner's advice. That man now owns a mile of Californian beachfront and a private helicopter. I'm not a greedy man, but who would not be tempted by such a prospect?"

Boonamee could not meet the gaze of his employer; he clasped his hands in front of him and tried to think of something positive to say.

"I will... pray for your good fortune."

"Prem, you don't look convinced, are you jealous perhaps?"

"It's not that… it's..."

"What? Tell me what's on your mind."

"*Kuhn* Song, I know nothing of investments, I'm sure you know exactly what you are doing."

"But?"

Boonamee wanted to answer honestly but feared it would result in a massive loss of face for one of them.

"Prem, if you have any concerns about this, I want you to tell me now."

"*Kuhn* Song, you say you have never met this man. It is simply that my father taught me to trust only those I know or those people my closest friends trust." Boonamee paused, waiting for a reaction.

"That is indeed excellent advice. What other thoughts do you have?"

Boonamee was emboldened by the response and decided he had nothing to lose. "*Kuhn* Song, the website is impressive but such things are straightforward to produce. If you could really borrow money and still make a profit, why would they not do that themselves instead of sharing their good fortune with strangers? Unless you have checked the claims they make and looked this man Jenner in the eye and spoken to his clients, it could all be… made up."

"You really think this is possible? It could all be a confidence trick?"

"Yes, *Kuhn* Song, and if you will forgive me, it is not the Thai way to make such investments. When we have money we buy things you can touch. Land and property and gold, not pieces of paper that say we own a little piece of a foreign company..." Boonamee could have continued but lost his nerve, he was lecturing the man who gave him his livelihood. Suddenly, he wanted to take it all back.

The tension was broken when Song's assistant entered the room accompanied by a *farang* in a crumpled linen suit. He was tall but maybe thirty kilos overweight. His shirt was untucked on one side and, on the other, his gut was so prominent, it had folded his belt over the top of his trousers. The man hadn't shaved for several days and possibly hadn't washed that recently either. Boonamee was certain he'd never met the man before but there was something familiar about his face.

"Prem meet Edward Jenner."

Boonamee didn't know how to react. He'd just accused Song of being a fool for investing money with a stranger and now the man was there in the room.

"You are of course correct, Prem. Jenner is a crook and a fraudster. He used to earn an honest living. The photograph on the website was taken when he worked for one of New York's best known firms. Now he and his associates telephone gullible, greedy *farang* and offer them the opportunity of a lifetime. It is really quite staggering how many of them are happy to hand over the money. It's a very famous scam; they call it a Boiler Room. Someone even made a Hollywood movie about it, but there is still no shortage of willing victims."

Song only paused to point to a chair where Jenner should sit, then continued.

"They start by offering to buy some well-known shares, then once a quarter, they run a special offer. The client is asked to hand over as much as they can find to invest in a share where Jenner has the inside track. It's a fiction of course, but the money usually rolls in from the greedy and the gullible. Every so often the company name gets changed, a new website appears and the cycle start again. Some of the clients get a little upset when they realise they own nothing. It keeps the trail nice and cool."

"And you would invest with them?" Boonamee was incredulous.

Song laughed. "Prem, as you so astutely observed, no Thai would be so stupid, but I'm delighted to say that a remarkable number of *farang* are more than happy to sign up. Mr Jenner here is our latest employee. For the moment he and his associates are based in Chiang Mai, but for obvious reasons we have to keep moving them around. I wanted you to meet him, just in case you and Kong have to help them with security from time to time. "

"And that's why you asked me to come here today?" Boonamee asked.

"And to give you a modest bonus." Song tossed him a thick envelope. There were plenty of notes inside; Boonamee just hoped they were thousands. Then Song continued, "I'll be calling you in a few weeks, we have another job for you up north."

Jenner seemed to be oblivious to the exchange between the two Thais, it was clear that he didn't speak their language. Song switched to English, "Mr Jenner, I've been telling my colleague here about your activities in Chiang Mai. Do you have anything to say?"

"Yeah… have you got any scotch?"

## CHAPTER FOUR

**White ghosts**

For Andy Duncan, three years had passed in a flash. From newest recruit he'd become Tait's deputy and Sally Peng was still the wizard who kept the Asian systems of Berwick Archer running. Their exchanges were friendly and polite, but the rapport from his first few weeks at the firm had long gone and Sally wished she never let her guard down. She always scoffed at girlfriends who said men were all the same. Nonetheless she suspected that for those who worked in the investment industry and got the merest taste of the rewards on offer, it might just be true.

Andy tossed the portfolio report aside and shook his head in disbelief. "For fuck's sake Simon, I told you to sell that position days ago. It was a dog when you bought it and now it's a sick dog."

Simon Tudor, Berwick Archer's most junior investment manager, apologised, unable to make eye contact with his boss.

"Sorry Andy, I was sure it was going to turn."

"And it did… like milk. Dump it."

Andy turned away, appalled at the naiveté of the eager young man standing opposite him. Simon had been in the job just four months, and it might have been a mistake to let him make his own investment decisions; but that was how you learnt. Anyway it wasn't Andy's money, it didn't even belong to the company, it was a small portfolio for a sleepy little charity, based near Basingstoke in Hampshire. They cleared landmines in Myanmar and were too clueless about things financial to spot the cock-ups anyway. So… no harm done.

Andy turned to see if Brad Tait was watching him from his desk by the window and as the older man nodded his acknowledgement, Andy rolled his eyes and shrugged. The trading loss was no big deal; there were two reasons for giving Simon Tudor a public dressing down. He went to Eton, then King's College Cambridge. The guy was so posh, there was every chance his ancestors were the Tudors who ran the country back in the sixteenth century. Andy went to the best public school his father could afford, and Imperial College, London, but there was still something in the British psyche that said money was only really safe in the hands of families who'd had it for generations. Simon Tudor would probably end up as Chairman of the board at some stage, whilst Andy would get a black bin liner to clear his desk when things got tough. That's how the system worked, so it was better to push the little toff around a bit while he had the chance.

The other reason was to impress Tait. The Australian had given Andy his big opportunity and this was a way of showing his confidence wasn't misplaced. Tait smiled and nodded, the closest Andy would get to a pat on the back.

Andy quickly checked his screens, and settled back in the huge leather swivel chair with a sense of satisfaction. His Bloomberg terminal was a sea of green, indicating that every stock he owned for clients or was thinking of buying, was trading higher than at the start of the day. He was making money and he hadn't bought or sold a single share. There was a list of messages in his inbox and he scanned them quickly to find the urgent ones. It took fifteen minutes to organise a game of golf for the weekend, set Dave at KPMG straight about Chelsea's chances of getting three points at United on Saturday and trade a few insults with Paul on the dealing desk before agreeing where they'd be drinking that night. Then he could relax and take in a view he was sure he'd never get used to.

The International Finance Centre was a suitably prestigious address for the Hong Kong offices of Berwick Archer. Around two-thirds of the total space was set aside for a sumptuous reception area and the meeting and dining rooms where clients were reassured their money was safe with the principal Asian office of one of London's fastest growing investment businesses.

Andy's seniority was recognised with a window seat, trumped only by the corner space occupied by Brad Tait, the department head. Directly opposite the IFC was the nearly matching International Commerce Centre. Perched waterfront on the Kowloon side of the channel; the ICC was the other half of the gateway to Hong Kong. From his swivel chair, Andy could watch the endless flow of cargo ships that had been the basis for the wealth of what was once a British colony. Panic merchants suggested in the 1990s that once Hong Kong became a Special Administrative Region of China, the Red Guard would march down Queens Road and the region's unique brand of capitalism would come to a shuddering halt. China was on the verge of an even more dramatic transition and, following the handover, the new rulers of Hong Kong would embrace the entrepreneurial spirit of its new possession and crank it up a bit.

The weather was clear by Hong Kong standards, but a grey blanket of pollution hung constantly over the harbour front. Out of the corner of his eye, Andy spotted a Sky Shuttle helicopter take off and swing slowly out over the water. Twice each hour, from nine in the morning until eleven at night, they carried the high rolling gamblers and wealthy tourists from the island to Macau. The old Portuguese colony had long since overtaken Las Vegas as the biggest gambling resort on the planet. Andy had made the trip a couple of times, once to entertain clients at the Formula One Grand Prix, but he never got a taste for the gambling. He'd buy a handful of chips and play a few rounds of *Sic-Bo*, the casino version of Thailand's popular *Hi-Lo* game, but a couple of hundred U.S. dollars of stake money was his limit. Friends teased him that his job was no different than playing roulette or blackjack but they missed a crucial distinction.

Andy's best friend at school was Hugh Allinson but they'd seen little of each other since he moved to Hong Kong. Six months earlier, they visited a London casino and Hugh launched into a favourite rant.

"Come on Andy, what you do is just the same. Stake some money on red or your lucky number and hope it turns up," was the jibe.

"It couldn't be more different, Hugh. I'm nothing like those guys," replied Andy, confidently manipulating a small stack of chips though his fingers.

"Bollocks, it's all chance, you've just conned people into thinking investing is respectable."

Andy laughed. "I didn't say it's not basically the same. I said I'm nothing like the idiot who turns up with a big pile of cash and then has to borrow the cab fare to get home. I'm not playing with my own money. I get paid whatever the outcome. If my client does well, I do really well. If markets tumble, they pay me anyway.

I can take the gambling comparison, but don't mark me down as a mug punter. We own the fucking casino."

His friend had looked away in genuine disgust. The Allinson family ran their textile business for over two hundred years until the bank refused to renew the company's credit lines. Three hundred staff lost their jobs. Allinson Clothing was bust, deemed an unacceptable credit risk to a bank whose investment arm lost a fortune in the crash back in 2008.

Andy hadn't thought of that exchange with his old school friend for a while, but the sight of the Macau helicopter brought it flooding back. Just like its passengers, he was a gambler for sure, but it was someone else's money and someone else's risk. Unless he did something monumentally stupid, the salary cheques would continue to drop into his bank account every month. Once a year there'd be a bonus, the size of which his old friend Hugh could only dream about. In a bad year it was generous, in a good year, obscene. The UK Lottery uses the slogan, "It Could be You" to get punters to part with their cash. Andy knew it could be him and it was. Every year he felt like he'd won the lottery the day his bonus cheque cleared.

From his vantage point in the IFC building, Andy could see one of Hong Kong's most famous landmarks. His eighteenth birthday treat had been a visit to his father's favourite haunt. Victor believed that champagne in the Captain's Bar of the island's iconic Mandarin Hotel was Andy's first alcoholic drink. Luckily the staff failed to recognise that he'd downed four pints of lager from their trademark metal tankards only two nights before, when celebrating with friends.

Victor loved the place. Legend has it that the financial future of the island has been determined in that bar for decades.

"The Mandarin used to be right on the waterfront." Victor had told his son.

"Seriously?"

"There's always been an insatiable appetite for building land, so they just reclaimed the harbour. I guess it must be at least a ten-minute walk to the ferry now."

"It's all changed then Dad."

"God yes. When I got here the locals were subservient. At least, they only referred to us as *gweilo*... white ghosts, behind our backs. Back then if a white face appeared in a meeting room, the conversation instantly switched to English. Now you just get a polite nod and they carry on in Mandarin or Cantonese. They even gave themselves an English first name so we wouldn't get confused by a couple of syllables of Chinese. It's amazing how it's changed."

"For the better?" Andy asked.

"Under British rule, Hong Kong was one the most vibrant cities in the world, the Chinese took over and fitted a turbo charger."

Victor tried to inject some admiration into his voice, but it sounded like a man lamenting the passing of a bygone age.

One of the perks of Andy's location in the office was that every time Vanessa Merchant went for a coffee, she had to walk past his desk.

"Drinking later, Andy?"

"Sure Vanessa, see you about six."

"Can't wait." She sounded like she meant it. Andy was used to the attention from his female colleagues. Even a modest English public school rarely fails to instil a degree of poise and confidence in its students. He was fit and athletic looking, even though his sporting regime stretched to little more than a weekly round of golf and a seat in front of Asian TV's endless stream of English football. Blond hair and blue eyes were a popular combination with the ladies and Andy never tired of telling the story that the faint scar bisecting his left eyebrow was the result of a high speed tumble on a rally cross bike. There was little kudos in admitting he'd stumbled against the dining room table when he was four.

Andy Duncan wore his success as conspicuously as the brand names on his shirts and ties. He commanded the respect of his colleagues and the attention of some of the most desirable women in the office, but he'd be the first to acknowledge the thing many of his conquests admired most, was his status as the second most important fund manager in the department. Colleagues would agree that he was a pretty cool guy and Andy did all he could to maintain the image.

He had his share of insecurities. Nobody could say whether his childhood asthma was brought on by anxiety or cat fur, but the problem never left him. He still carried the small blue inhaler and once or twice a day would find a quiet corner to deal with the tightening in his chest that said an attack was on its way. Showing any form of weakness was taboo in the investment room and Andy did all he could to hide this minor frailty from his colleagues.

Andy watched Vanessa glide down the corridor towards the lifts and wondered if he might be in luck. It was only three weeks since she joined the firm and Brad Tait's introduction was still fresh in his mind.

"Andy meet Vanessa. She's just joined Charles Maybury's Research team. We managed to lure her over from Nikko; she speaks some Japanese and is a mathematical genius by all accounts. She's a terrific hire."

Vanessa blushed at the compliment and extended a perfectly manicured hand, attached to an equally perfect arm, body and head. As she made eye contact with Andy, she quickly removed her glasses and tucked a stray strand of golden blonde hair behind her ear. Like all of Charles' team she was, by any measure, extremely hot. There was no prize for the self-styled wit who, predictably, dubbed them Charlie's Angels. The Head of Research was a brilliant investor and a grade one dirty old man.

Andy nodded, smiled politely and enjoyed the first of many occasions when he'd just watch in fascination as she passed his desk.

"That's quite a C.V. she's got Brad. Charlie needs a Japanese speaker?"

"No mate, he said he hired her because she has an ass like a peach and a mouth that could suck start a jumbo jet, but HR gets pissed off if you introduce people round the office like that."

Both men giggled like schoolboys, exchanged matey backslaps and headed back to their desks.

Andy was a very contented man. He just picked stocks, chatted to the occasional client and marvelled anyone would pay him so much for doing so little. He looked again at Simon Tudor, twenty-two and barely out of college, an apprentice at the investment game. Andy could hardly acknowledge he'd been in the same position only three years before. He saw himself as an old hand, an experienced professional. He watched movies where young soldiers were catapulted to senior positions in the heat of battle and saw a direct parallel with his own experience. Andy had just celebrated his twenty-fourth birthday and he thought he knew it all. The cash the company deposited in his bank account every month gave him every reason to believe they shared his opinion

**Turner**

"Jesus, Turner must be spitting blood at this one," Tait said as he dropped an all-staff announcement on Andy's desk.

"What's the problem? It's from the Board, so James must be OK with it," Andy replied, still acutely aware that the politics of the firm was a closed book to him.

"James would never agree to this, they're bringing in one of those strategic consultancies and he's got absolutely no time for them. It's Timothy Clarke the Group CEO in London, he's James's boss and he wouldn't wipe his own butt without commissioning an independent study."

"What's the point in having a boss who needs someone else to tell him what to do?"

Tait laughed. "No mate, you don't hire these guys to tell you stuff you don't already know. You get them to write a report recommending what you knew you were going to do anyway."

"What's the point of that?" Andy replied.

"So you have someone to blame when it all goes tits up. You can't sack the CEO if some fancy advisors charged you five million to check it all out before you started."

"Nice work if you can get it."

"James wouldn't give them the time of day, but Clarke's spent millions on reports that just tell him what he wants to hear. It's a source of a little bit of tension so I hear."

"Sounds like five million straight down the drain."

"It's part of the scam my friend. Pay fifty grand for a study and it can't be up to much. Pay a few million and it must be good."

James Turner, Chief Executive of Berwick Archer's Asian business, had a reputation as an aggressive, occasionally ruthless investor who'd made his mark back in the 80s. The City was a gentleman's club and Turner gained admission simply by being extremely good at what he did.

Early in his career, Turner picked up the nickname, the Bull. He liked to think his colleagues had spotted a strength and tenacity and matched that to his star sign, Taurus. The reality was more prosaic. His face was a little too long; his ears were perched a little too high on his head. The overall effect gave his head a distinct bovine quality.

"It's all bullshit of course," Tait had told Andy, "but they say the Met police in London are still after Turner."

"You're kidding me."

"Story goes he told this guy to turn down his music player on the underground. The guy told him to 'fuck off', so Turner took him apart there and then."

"I've got a bit of sympathy with that to be honest," Andy replied. "Is it true?"

"No idea, but he's got a hell of a temper. If I were you, I'd try not to piss him off. They're taking bets over on the dealing desk as to what will send him over the edge next."

"So what are the bets?"

"Usual stuff, a cock-up in the office, someone talking too loud on their mobile phone when he's had a bad day, queue jumpers, bad drivers, take your pick."

"So where's your money?"

Tait laughed, "I reckon Heathrow Terminal Five. He'll be stuck behind some woman who's chatting to her friend right up to the x-ray machine. She'll be arguing with the staff about having to put her I-Pad and phone in a separate tray. She's never heard of the rule about liquid and the little plastic bag and then she'll take three attempts to get through the scanner before they find all her coins, jewellery, belts and God knows what. James is late for his plane and that'll be it. They'll be counting the bodies for days."

56

"And that's why they call him the Bull?"

"Yeah, I guess. But it didn't help that he once shagged one of Charlie's Angels. Gorgeous girl she was, Spanish... I think her name was Manuela."

"What's that got to do with it?"

"She told her girlfriends that she'd only want to see the Bull again if she was carrying a red cape and a sword."

Turner was certainly an angry man. Had he been born ten years earlier, he'd never have got past a clerical role amongst the firm's backroom staff. He celebrated his twenty-eighth birthday on October 26, 1987 when the UK government changed the way the City worked. They called it Big Bang and ordinary folk like James Turner suddenly had the opportunity to work at the sharp end of the investment industry. His bosses were happy to reap the rewards that came with his relentless skill and expertise, but there were parties to which he'd never be invited and clubs on St James's in London where membership would never be offered. As Turner celebrated his fifty-fourth birthday and his thirtieth year with the firm, he could look back on a career of distinction. He ran the firm's Asian business and was extremely well paid for doing it. There was only one thing that rankled.

The top floor of Berwick Archer's offices in London housed the office they called the Par Five. To gain access you had to speak to the secretary who guarded the door, the only way you could do that was to speak to her secretary. Once inside you'd be struck by the oak panelled walls, the huge table large enough to accommodate a meeting of the entire sixteen-man board and an array of art that would not have disgraced the Tate Gallery. The room got the nickname due to its sheer size and because the walk from the door to the desk at the end often felt like it took forever. The occupant was Timothy Clarke, the man who got the nod six years before when the board selected a new Chief Executive. James Turner was summoned to the office by his new boss to explain he was being shipped out to Hong Kong. He had high hopes of getting the top job himself, but lost out to Clarke, a dullard who'd done the Eton and Cambridge thing and was considered to be "a safe pair of hands." Clarke was barely able to conceal his glee as he banished his rival to the opposite side of the globe. Pointing to a wonderful nineteenth century landscape that adorned the wall of the office and had recently been insured for sixteen million pounds, Clarke smirked at his rival and delivered the line he'd probably been practicing for weeks.

"Looks like that's the only Turner you'll be seeing in this office. Best of luck with the chinks."

Turner grimaced, shook the hand of his new CEO and vowed he'd wipe that smug grin off the man's face. It might just take a little time.

Six years had passed since James Turner and Brad Tait arrived in Hong Kong. It had become the most profitable business in the company's global operations and the new Head of Asia began to realise the grin on Clarke's face was growing wider. London staff enjoyed bigger bonuses than ever before on the back of the growth of the Asian business. Clarke was lauded for his strategic genius in sending Turner to Hong Kong and there was talk of a knighthood for the safe pair of hands who'd done nothing more than be in the right place at the right time and then send his biggest rival as far across the globe as he could manage.

James Turner would have to swallow his pride and keep cashing the cheques, unless he could think of another way of getting even with the man who occupied the office that should rightly have been his back in London.

# CHAPTER FIVE

**Cargo item 97**

The man in the exquisitely tailored suit had no need to raise his voice to gain their attention. Silence fell as soon as he opened the door.
"How many do we have tonight?"
The question echoed round the high ceilings of the disused aircraft hangar and Paran stepped forward to present the manifest for the cargoes soon to be dispatched. Twenty years in the parachute regiment bred habits that were hard to break, and it was all Paran could do to stop himself saluting the much younger man. In that line of business, age was no guide to seniority. The "suit" had the natural confidence of someone used to being obeyed, more important, he paid the wages. Paran clipped his heels together and briefly consulted the single sheet of paper lying on the table in front of them.
"One hundred and twenty boss, the transport should be here any minute."
"Excellent. Show me the merchandise." Prem Boonamee straightened his tie, smoothed down the back of his jacket and dropped casually into the only chair in the building.
Paran flipped open his laptop and practiced fingers tapped furiously at the keyboard. A series of records appeared on the screen. Each item of cargo had a photograph, alongside the source, cost of acquisition and commissions paid to introducing agents. There'd be four transports that night with about thirty items in each. The screen showed the price paid by the customer and the profit on each transaction. The two men examined the screen and each made a mental calculation of his share of the action.
"What are the destinations?"
Paran shifted the mouse deftly and with another couple of clicks, the information appeared.
"OK boss, Cargo One is going to Chantaburi. The ship leaves port at eight in the morning and we need to be there by six. That won't be a problem. This is the merchandise."

The ex-para scrolled quickly through what was heading for the ship. Boonamee nodded his approval.

"Next?"

"Two and Three are going north, the first will go to the factory over the border, the second will go to the despatch centre."

Boonamee gave the photos a cursory glance. Together with the accompanying descriptions, it appeared that the goods were according to the client's specifications.

"And Cargo Four?"

There were three other men standing near the table, each dressed in nondescript black, including a loose fitting top to conceal the firm's standard issue Sig Sauer handgun. As Paran called up the fourth cargo, they each edged closer to the table hoping to catch a glimpse of what they all knew would be the most interesting batch of merchandise.

"Karapong's found a taker for most of them and we have a location for direct delivery about five miles outside Pattaya. The rest are going to Mr Shin near the beach by Naklua, so we can do it in one hit." Paran paused, unsure whether to risk a little levity. "Shin likes the freshest produce."

The men laughed in unison. Based on the photographs on the screen, Mr Shin would be delighted with the delivery.

The assembled group all nodded appreciatively as they watched each of the photographs of Cargo Four appear on the screen. As always the Chinese customer had been taken care of very well indeed. He paid the highest price because he was very specific as to his requirements and he'd be receiving exactly what he requested.

Nok and Kanni, managed to scrape together eighty baht. It bought some barbecued pork, a small bowl of soup, a little fruit and some water. This had become quite an adventure, the sisters had never been far from their own village before and everyone they met was incredibly friendly. Han was tall, strong and handsome and Nok struggled to hide her disappointment when he explained he had a wife and a young son at home. Sunnee and Yan were sisters too, but much older than Nok and Kanni, maybe as old as their own mother. They'd been kind when Kanni felt sick earlier in the journey and it was a small favour to share a little of the food the two girls had bought.

The driver said he was ready to go and the passengers eagerly got back on board. They were all heading to a better life, with prospects they could only dream of back in their villages.

Han had been shown the uniform he would wear as a despatcher at Suvarnabhumi airport. Fifteen thousand baht a month was a pittance by western standards, barely two nights accommodation in a four star Bangkok hotel, but double what Han could earn in his village. Sunnee and Yan had not been promised nearly as much but they knew they were not qualified to do anything other than clean. The alternative was a nine hour day in the fields of a local farm, with two hundred baht… four pounds as their reward. Working at the airport, they could share a room and maybe save a little of their pay so one day they'd be able to go home. Nok and Kanni had seen the pictures of the restaurant where they would work. They were told they might have to do a little kitchen duty at the start, but they were both smart and pretty. In no time they'd get jobs in the main restaurant and maybe even learn a little English. They were sure that soon they'd be sending money home to their mother. Initially the girls were concerned that, at just fourteen, Kanni might be too young to work at the airport, but they were assured the position was already approved.

As the bus pulled away from the petrol station, the driver picked up his mobile and made a brief call. They were due to arrive in less than an hour. The team should be ready to greet the new arrivals. There was rarely any trouble. Even when they took the identity cards from each passenger they rarely suspected anything was amiss. Trouble only ever kicked off when they reached the final destination, but there'd be armed guards to take care of that.

Han would almost certainly be in Chantaburi before he realised Cargo One was not heading for Suvarnabhumi. They'd need the armed men to make sure he, and the rest of the consignment, boarded the fishing boat but the crew was experienced in working with forced labour. In twenty-four hours they'd be in the Indian Ocean and Han could do as he was told, or take an enforced swim to shore. It was unlikely that a man brought up on the border of Thailand and Laos could cover three or four hundred miles of open water to safety.

Sunnee and Yan would be a little trickier as they were heading for different locations, but middle-aged women were not likely to give anyone any trouble. Sunnee was due to join Cargo Two and by the following day, she'd be allocated a place on the production line of the largest amphetamine factory across the Burmese border. Her sister would be in the despatch centre learning how to pack the small round tablets into the cylindrical containers used for their transportation to a network of dealers in Thailand and across the world.

Nok and Kanni were unlikely to realise they were to be separated until a few miles outside Pattaya. Nok, the older sister, had been chosen to work in a karaoke bar owned by one of Karapong's family. She was not expected to sing, she was required to entertain the many men who came to the bar from when it opened at ten a.m. to when it closed at two the following morning.

Kanni would arrive at Shin's house half an hour later. Nobody knew of any enterprise of the Chinese that employed girls. In the local community he ran a respectable construction business that had been in his family for years. Shin lived alone in a large rambling house on the edge of the city. Every few months, around half a dozen very young girls were shipped in. None of them were ever seen again.

As the first bus arrived, Paran gently nudged Boonamee's arm. The younger man had been dozing in his chair. As he sat up, Boonamee caught sight of a picture of cargo item number 97. The assembled group agreed she was by far and away the pick of the crop. The picture was of Nok and as Boonamee stared, a shiver ran down his spine. For a second, he thought it was Pom and, in that brief moment, he felt the knife in his heart and the voice screamed in his head… so much blood.

# CHAPTER SIX

## Living above the office

The plane landed in Bangkok at eleven twenty-five in the morning and shortly after midday, Tait and Andy were drinking ice-cold water in the back of a Lincoln town car headed for the State Tower on Silom Road. The meeting with James Turner lasted no more than eight minutes, but in the seven days that followed, Andy's life was picked up and tossed in the air.

"We need a presence on the ground," Turner explained. "There's a good chance of some government money to manage and we have clients queuing round the block already. They've seen what we do in Hong Kong and they want a piece of the action." His fingers drummed on the desk, he wasn't used to explaining his decisions to junior staff, but this was an exceptional case.

"Can't we manage the money from Hong Kong?" Andy asked.

"Thais are the worst racists in Asia, sending money out of the country is treason. If we have an office in Bangkok, with a few token locals on the staff, the money will flow. Tait's heading up the office and you get to be the number two." Turner looked at his watch and Andy took the hint. He picked up the new contract and headed for the door. He'd been made an offer he couldn't refuse.

Tait and Andy were used to thinking of themselves as being indispensible in Hong Kong but Turner had decided the interests of the firm were better served by them being in Bangkok. The firm allocated seven billion dollars of existing portfolios to the new office and they were confident more would follow. Suites were booked in the Lebua hotel at the top of the State Tower and as Andy nursed a chilled Singha on the observation deck, he was certain he'd been there before.

"Hangover II," said Tait.

"Huh?"

"The movie… this is where they filmed that bar scene. Best view in Bangkok, they reckon."

Andy had grudgingly watched the movie at a friend's apartment one night and he finally made the connection. Tait explained that the film was a cinematic masterpiece. Andy thought it was trite racist horseshit. The annual family holiday to Phuket left him with a lasting affection for all things Thai and he resented the lazy characterisation of the movie. Thais were portrayed as sexually ambivalent, thieving imbeciles, ultimately outwitted and defeated by their American counterparts. It occurred to Andy that it might be Hollywood payback for the fact that, in the real world, the USA generally got its butt kicked when it ventured into Southeast Asia.

Tait called for another round of beers and, as the waitress arrived with the tray, a middle-aged Thai appeared at their table.

"Gentlemen, my name is Tanawat Chanpol." The name suggested Thai, but the accent would not have disgraced a 1940s BBC radio announcer. Andy had to shield his eyes from the sun to see the owner of the voice. It was thirty-four degrees in the shade and humidity felt like it was off the scale, but the man still wore a jacket of immaculately tailored linen. His tie was neatly pinned with an ornate gold badge that probably indicated membership of an exclusive club, and the Rolex on his wrist suggested the owner wouldn't have to worry unduly when the annual subscriptions fell due. Chanpol gave the famous Thai smile his best shot, but only the lower half of his face joined in. His forehead appeared to be locked in a permanent knot, indicating either disapproval at his mouth's insincere attempt at jollity, or complete disdain for the men in front of him. Chanpol's gleaming white teeth were a monument to modern dentistry and mercifully drew one's attention from eyes that were glacially cold. Andy had the impression the new arrival strained every sinew in his body to appear friendly and welcoming, but the stress might kill him if he had to do it for too long.

Tait immediately jumped to his feet and made a clumsy attempt at the traditional Thai greeting, the *wai*. He brought his hands together loosely then nearly dislodged his sunglasses as he dipped his head. Chanpol could barely disguise his amusement.

"At your service gentlemen," said the Thai, extending a hand and allowing the formalities of introduction to revert to a safer, western form.

Tait was obviously expecting the man.

"Andy, like I said on the plane, Mr Chanpol's done all the heavy lifting for us. He set up the company, found us the offices and made sure we're in good shape to get this thing off the ground."

The Thai shrugged modestly and offered his hand to Andy, who briefly wiped his own on his leg before reciprocating. The move had the desired effect of ensuring a firm handshake, free of perspiration and condensation from the beer glass, but left an unfortunate dark stain on the young fund manager's grey linen trousers.

It was a short ride in the elevator to the brand new offices of Berwick Archer, just a few floors below the hotel bar. Tait was supposedly up to speed with the project, but even he looked surprised as Chanpol keyed in the access code and opened the door to their new offices. The reception area was small but extravagantly furnished, the firm's logo hung proudly over a mahogany desk and the men were greeted by a perfectly executed *wai* from one of the most exquisite looking women Andy had ever seen.

Chanpol waved a hand nonchalantly in her direction as he led the men towards the door to the inner offices.

"Tanni... your receptionist."

The door opened before they got to it and another exceptionally appealing Thai greeted them.

"This is Sam, secretary, office manager and the person who will call me if there is anything we have overlooked." The expression on his face indicated he thought that extremely unlikely.

"Mr Turner was insistent that you should have no concerns other than clients and their money. We will take care of everything else."

Sam treated the men to a dazzling smile and a brief but respectful *wai* before beckoning them into the open-plan office space beyond the main doors. She was dressed head to foot in what looked like genuine Armani, and there was the faintest trace of what Andy guessed to be expensive scent.

On the plane, they'd talked about it taking several weeks before they'd be operational, but this was like walking into an established business that had been up and running for years. Andy and Tait each had an office, two familiar faces from the Hong Kong administration team were already hard at work and when Andy switched on his PC, it was identical to the desktop he'd used for three years back in Hong Kong. As he looked across the office, a familiar figure crossed the floor. She turned and managed a weak smile before picking up a small piece of luggage and disappearing through the door. Andy started to head after her but was intercepted by Tait.

"See that? Sally the dyke's been here to set up the systems. There's nothing for us to do. We're up and running."

As Chanpol came over to bid his farewell, Andy promised himself he'd call Sally to thank her for her hard work. By the time he'd remember again, it would all be too late. He made a note to pop in and say hello next time he was in Hong Kong.

Tait took the larger of the two offices, but both men enjoyed an extraordinary view over the Thai capital and the Chao Praya river, a vital waterway which, in the rainy season, becomes a fearsome threat when the water level rises. As Andy looked out over his new home city, the river was in benign mood, almost calm for the tourist boats and merchant vessels plying their trade. He vaguely recalled a boyhood dragon boat ride with his father. The tide was high, and the boatman tried to cut across the wake of a huge cargo transporter. The long thin prow lifted from the water and as it slammed back onto the surface, Andy was sure he'd be tossed into the filthy river. A shiver ran down his spine as the memory came back to him. That was so long ago. Today the river was millpond still and his Bloomberg screen showed that markets were up across Asia. An e-mail popped into his inbox, sent from the office across the way,

"Beers at six? Brad."

## A fellow professional

Three months passed in a blur. Markets were kind and investment performance was good. Andy saw little sign of the queue of new clients that Turner promised and a couple of meetings organised with government officials were yet to yield a single baht in new money. Nonetheless, a flying visit from the Bull ended with a warm handshake and an assurance that Hong Kong and London were delighted with the new office.

Chanpol returned only once to check that everything was working as it should be, and Sam had handed each man the key to his own apartment in the residential part of the State Tower. They still lived over the shop, but neither man had any complaints. The workload was light and everything in Thailand moved much more slowly. In the Hong Kong office, Andy had spent many a Saturday checking mails, catching up on Facebook and playing chess on the net with a broker from JP Morgan. Being in the office every hour they could, was just another way of telling the world how important and indispensible they were. In Bangkok, Tait was the boss and clocked on and off whenever he pleased. Saturday was always spent on the fairways of Laem Chabang Golf Club, courtesy of Berwick Archer's corporate membership.

Keeping pace with his boss in the clubs and bars of Bangkok was far more demanding than Andy's daytime duties. In eight weeks, the two men tried virtually every go-go bar in Nana Plaza and Soi Cowboy and shared breakfast with more than their fair share of those bar's female employees. For two good-looking, professional, highly paid young men there was a peculiar etiquette to be observed. It was unthinkable that either would pay for a working girl. That was for the sad old sex tourists who flocked to Bangkok's infamous entertainment centres. Tait and Andy enjoyed the atmosphere of the go-go bars and tipped lavishly, ensuring a constant flock of young dancers eager to make their acquaintance, but they would never pay the bar-fine, fifteen pounds or so, required to secure a girl's release for the rest of the evening. Instead, as the night turned to morning, they would head to the clubs. Often it would be one of the dancers they'd met earlier, who'd failed to secure a customer. In the morning the men would give their girl a generous tip to cover the taxi home and some shopping on the way. Net expenditure would be slightly more than if they'd paid the bar-fine but then they'd have to admit to paying for sex.

Alex Cruickshank had spent three weeks at the new office. His brief was to plan the first year's sales and marketing activity and deliver a truly memorable launch party, where all of the firm's Asian clients and business partners were invited. The party was a great success and Andy was pleasantly surprised to see the guest list included a number of extremely attractive young women. A vast quantity of champagne was consumed and several of the more eminent guests were seen leaving with young ladies who could easily have been their daughters. At a quarter past midnight, Andy and Tait stumbled into a taxi with May and Lucy and it was just before one a.m. when they opened another bottle of Krug on the balcony of the Australian's apartment. At midday, Andy served scrambled eggs to Lucy in the spare bedroom, the other pair were nowhere to be seen. May was still around... a single stiletto shoe lay on the carpet by the glass coffee table, and her red silk dress was draped carelessly over one leather armchair.

"Can I see you again?" Andy was used to the girl making the suggestion. This was unfamiliar territory and he did not expect the reply.

"Sure, just call the agency and tell them if it's on the company or you're paying direct."

Andy stabbed himself in the cheek with an egg-covered fork as the words sank in.

"You're a... professional?"

"Paid by the hour darling... but you're such a sweetie I took you off the clock when you went to make breakfast. I thought you knew, Brad certainly does, he's a regular."

"I have to pay you?" Andy sounded like a young boy caught with his fingers in the candy jar and the storeowner was demanding cash.

"No, last night was on the company, but there are always more girls than required, so you and Brad got the leftovers." Lucy gave the sweet little pout that had been so captivating the night before and then pulled back the duvet.

"One more time?"

Andy had vowed he'd never sleep with a hooker, but now he'd done it and nobody died.

"Sure, what the hell," he said and climbed back into bed.

"Where is he Sam? He's not been in all day." Andy was desperately trying to stay calm, recalling the fifteen minutes of cultural training they'd received back in Hong Kong. Confrontation is rarely a good tactic when dealing with Thais.

Tait's secretary and office manager did not even lift her immaculately made-up face before she answered.

"He'll be here by six. You have drinks with Pan Asia Securities then dinner with a potential client."

"We need to talk first. I've just seen the performance numbers and they suck. The Bull's going to be all over us by the end of the week and we need to have answers."

"He'll be here by six." Sam turned and walked into Tait's office, making it clear she had nothing more to say on the subject. Andy returned to his own desk feeling helpless, he stared at the sea of red ink on the report in front of him. Markets had risen again since the previous month end, but all portfolios run out of the Bangkok office had lost money, in spite of the market rise. Each fund had failed to achieve the target agreed with the client and, as far as he could see, their competitor's products were all doing way better than the Berwick Archer equivalents. Stocks they sold had subsequently risen in price and virtually everything they bought was floundering. Andy suddenly realised that in three years this was the first time his funds had fallen back. He always liked that military analogy, seeing himself as a young man with a lot of responsibility because of a series of battlefield promotions. Now the comparison was coming back to haunt him. This must be what the German army felt like in 1942. They conquered half of Europe in a trice and the opposition melted away in front of them, then the Russian winter set in and the opposition started fighting back. He suddenly realised he didn't have the vaguest idea what to do next and the only man who could help him was missing again.

Tait's behaviour was as erratic as his attendance in the previous month. The two men still enjoyed a couple of nights on the town each week and they always spent Saturday afternoon at the golf club. The Australian frequently left a message saying he'd work from home and when he arrived in the office he'd be detached and weary. Their last trip to Laem Chabang was a disaster. Tait's golf game was in tatters and Andy won with consummate ease. The Englishman was relieved when they reached the eighteenth hole, as his partner had been morose and uncommunicative throughout the round. Andy hit a perfect drive that bisected the fairway to the right of a huge bunker. Tait topped his tee shot into the stream that ran across the front of the tee. Declining to hit a second, he threw his club to the ground and as his caddie stooped to pick it up, he took the driver's seat in the buggy and floored the accelerator. For the first ten seconds it looked as though he would negotiate the bridge across the stream without difficulty. But the last thirty yards were particularly steep and overnight rain had left the cart path rutted and muddy. Andy assumed that his colleague must have touched the brake because the cart slewed to the left and smashed into the frame of the bridge at top speed. Tait was thrown from his seat like a rag doll but was evidently unhurt as he landed on the grass.

"Fuck it," Tait screamed, picking himself up and marching towards the clubhouse.

"Brad... you OK?" That was about all Andy could manage. "Your clubs mate... what about your clubs?"

The Australian paused and looked back at his brand new Titleists and the leather bag that bore his name, stitched carefully along one side; courtesy of a grateful broker. He clearly had second thoughts as he strode purposefully back towards the cart and retrieved his bag. Tait unzipped a side pocket and retrieved his car keys, then appeared to lift the bag onto his shoulder to carry it back to the clubhouse. Andy was about to offer to place it on his own cart when he saw Tait lift the bag a little higher, then hurl it into the stream. Without even a look in Andy's direction, Tait turned on his heel and marched up the fairway to the clubhouse.

Andy spent an hour with the club's director and wondered how to classify a replacement golf buggy on his expense claim. The appearance of his Berwick Archer Amex card took some of the heat out of the discussion, but it was made clear the firm's corporate membership would not be renewed. Tait had left by the time Andy changed and, as he waited for a cab to take him back to Bangkok, he doubted his boss would be joining him for drinks that night as planned.

At eight that evening Andy arrived at the Sports Bar in Soi Five as arranged. It was another forty-five minutes before Tait surfaced, looking heavy-eyed and listless. He perked up a little on the back of a couple of very cold Singha beers but picked unenthusiastically at the selection of appetisers Andy ordered to tide them over until dinner. Tait made it clear he had no interest in discussing the day's events and constantly eyed the door as though he expected someone to appear at any moment. Andy spotted a movement out of the corner of his eye as Tait almost leapt from his chair. The woman was tall, blonde and dressed to impress, the Australian was clearly extremely pleased to see her. Andy was vaguely annoyed he hadn't been consulted about her joining them, but couldn't help an admiring glance. Stilettos helped, but she was only a couple of inches shorter than Tait and, it occurred to Andy, her legs appeared to end on a level with Tait's midriff. No Thai would show that much thigh or cleavage in public, even a dancing girl, and Andy was guessing Eastern European or Russian. There were plenty of gorgeous women in the bar but all eyes were on the new arrival, proving once again the old adage that the "grass is always greener." A few of the male customers clocked the looks of pure poison from their Thai girlfriends and returned their attention to their drinks, their food or an unfinished pool game, but the new arrival was oblivious to it all.

"Brad, my darling." There was a definite hint of a Russian accent as the woman leant in and kissed the Australian passionately. "I hope to see you later."

Tait looked like he'd never been happier and mumbled something incomprehensible as she took each of his hands in hers, then ran a finger slowly across his cheek and then down his chest towards his crotch. Inside one minute she was gone and Tait disappeared in the direction of the men's room.

Andy took around thirty seconds to work out what had happened. His conclusion was confirmed when Tait re-emerged from the bathroom a few moments later. There was lightness to his step, a febrile energy in his eyes and a wide contented grin on his face. He rubbed his nose feverishly and shook his head, as though something had flown into each nostril and he was trying to dislodge it. There was also the merest trace of white powder above his lip.

"Jesus Christ Brad, do you have to be so obvious? You might as well have taken out an advert in the Bangkok Post mate. That shit's supposed to happen in dark corners."

Tait looked at him as though he was a silly child.

"It's all part of the buzz my friend. All part of the buzz."

Andy hadn't seen his boss since that Saturday evening and a series of texts and phone messages remained unanswered. Sam said she thought Tait would be in before six and there was so much to discuss. The office was performing badly in investment terms and the Bull would be on their case in no time. They had an important dinner that evening with a prospective client and there was no telling the condition Tait would be in. What else could go wrong?

"India will be here at nine tomorrow." Sam stood at the door to his office. Andy couldn't make sense of what he was hearing, all those problems and an entire sub-continent was scheduled to turn up the following day?

"Who or what the hell are you talking about Sam?"

"The new intern, didn't Brad mention it?"

"When would he mention it? He's never here."

"India Clarke, she is here for a month, you're going to teach her to be a fund manager. Should be enough time, shouldn't it?"

Andy ignored the jibe, the name was familiar but he'd never heard it in the context of an internship.

"Who in God's name is India Clarke?"

"Her father is Timothy Clarke, the CEO in London," she replied.

Andy had been certain things could not get any worse, until that very moment. His mouth opened and closed as though he was gasping for air but did not have the energy to make a real go of it. That's when he noticed Brad Tait scurry into his office, slam the door shut and then lower the blinds so no-one could see what he was doing.

Tait emerged from his office five minutes later, looking smart and bright as a button. Only the slightest shake of his head and a hand drawn quickly across his nose might have betrayed the source of his good humour.

"Brad, where the fuck have you been? We're up to our armpits in shit." Andy didn't know whether to be angry or desperately grateful he was no longer in this alone. He pulled the inhaler from his pocket and took a double hit of the medication.

"Relax mate. I've seen the performance numbers… they're a blip. We can blame half of it on the shit research we get from Charlie's Angels back in Hong Kong and it's only a month's worth of figures. This guy we're meeting tonight has all but signed the forms to give us thirty million US Dollars, so Turner's going to love us for winning a big client. The guy's got more connections than Kevin Bacon, so it's the first of many. Don't get so fucking panicky… relax, OK."

Andy felt the tension in his body ebb. It all sounded fine when Brad put it like that, he was the senior guy, he'd been around. Maybe it wasn't all as bad as he feared. Then a thought struck him.

"What about India Clarke. We've got the boss's daughter here for a month. How's that supposed to work, she must be a spy for her father."

"For Christ's sake Andy, calm down. I met the girl in London last year, she's fine. We've had a few chats on Facebook and she's really cool. India thinks her old man's a dickhead too. She's on a world tour at his expense and she's stopping off here on her way to the Full Moon Parties down on Koh Phangan."

It really did sound like Tait had it all covered and Andy finally started to relax.

"Anyway, we're late. We've got drinks with Pan Asia and you are in for a treat mate. We're meeting my favourite broker."

Caroline Chan was already perched elegantly on a stool when they arrived at the rooftop bar of the Lebua. She'd worn the same pendant the night Andy first met her at the Red Flag in Hong Kong and he was slightly embarrassed he remembered it so clearly. Once again she was in business attire, but this time, an ivory silk dress with buttons that ran from neckline to hem. On such a beautiful woman, it was impossible not to imagine undoing each one slowly and watching the dress slide from her shoulders. Once again she looked at Andy and smiled as though she knew exactly what he was thinking.

"You can call me Caro." She offered a hand and Andy resisted the urge to kneel like an Elizabethan courtier and touch his lips devotedly to her exquisite fingers. That was when he noticed her perfume and couldn't help himself from inhaling deeply.

"Notorious," she said with a mischievous smile.

"Huh?"

"My perfume. It's called Notorious." Caro clearly enjoyed his obvious discomfort.

"I'm Andy," he replied, unable to think of anything else to say.

"I'm told I underestimated the geek. Brad says you're the little gem he and the Bull have been searching for."

She and Tait exchanged glances like proud young parents who'd realised their offspring was merely slow to develop and not retarded as they feared. Tait nodded in confirmation.

"Andy's a star, just what we needed."

There was little opportunity for Andy to impress Caro further. She and Tait briefly discussed three stocks she thought he should buy for the Emerging Fund and then she was gone, bidding him farewell with a smile and an enchanting little wave with the tips of her fingers. The two men drained their glasses and headed for the street, they had twenty minutes to get across town to their next appointment.

Andy was still thinking of Caroline Chan as Tait paid the taxi driver and then explained to the restaurant's maître d' that Mr Worrapon was expecting them. Two waitresses appeared as if by magic and the fund managers were whisked up the stairs to a private room, where a tall, muscular Thai handed each of them a crystal flute of champagne. They were on refills before the door opened and the man they were waiting for appeared. Thais are rarely physically imposing, to westerners at least, but their dinner companion gave the impression he was surrounded by a force field of electrical energy. As Andy shook his hand, he was vaguely surprised that he'd not been sent flying across the room on the wrong end of a few thousand volts of sheer charisma. Worrapon's clothes appeared to have been tailored to every single centimetre of his body. There were few other signs of his wealth. Checking the type of watch a man wore is an old-fashioned method of assessing the means of a new acquaintance. The practice was made obsolete by factories that knock out counterfeit Rolexes, that sell for thirty pounds but are indistinguishable, for most people, from the real thing.

    Before they left Hong Kong, Tait and Andy vowed to immerse themselves in Thai culture, so they could hit the ground running in their new home. In practice they'd not got much further than watching the Ong Bak movie trilogy on DVD. Tony Jaa plays the humble villager schooled by an eminent monk in the martial art of Muay Thai. Having achieved mastery of this lethal sport, he then vows he'll never use it to hurt a single soul. When a gangster steals the relic the villagers believe protects their harvest, he embarks on an orgy of unrestrained violence to get it back. It's a family film, men watch it for the amazing fight scenes, women watch it and wonder what it would take for their menfolk to get a physique like Tony Jaa. Like the main character in the movie, Ben Worrapon appeared to be a nice enough guy, but you wouldn't want to make him angry. He certainly had the sort of presence that enabled one to pick him out in a room full of suits as a man of means and power. And he was on the verge of signing up as Berwick Archer's first Thai client.

    Two hours later the three men were in the back of the largest Mercedes Andy had ever seen and Worrapon confirmed that thirty million US dollars would be transferred to the client account when his office opened in the morning. At no stage had the men discussed investment matters, their new client assured them he just wanted a segregated clone of the existing Emerging Fund and he saw it as a long term investment, he had no intention of badgering them about short term fluctuations in the value of the portfolio. Worrapon was a client made in heaven.

    Andy had passed the office block several times since his arrival in Bangkok but never been inside before. The Mercedes slowed to a crawl as it entered the underground car park and the driver carefully negotiated the tight corner at the bottom of the slope. As they followed the arrows, Andy wondered where they'd find a space for the oversized car. As they came to another turn he gasped as the car carried on, heading straight for what appeared to be a concrete wall. The driver pressed a dark green button on a small gadget in his right hand; the wall disappeared in front of their eyes. The car entered a separate chamber and as a uniformed flunky appeared to their right, the driver pulled over to let the passengers out.

Andy and Tait both tried to look as though this was the kind of thing they did every day as the flunky pushed the only button in the lift they entered and they were whisked silently upwards. Both men had visited the finest gentlemen's clubs in London and Hong Kong but this was on another plane. In minutes they were seated in a sumptuous alcove of the club, sipping the finest single malt whisky served from a bottle already waiting for them on the table. Andy knew many clubs encourage members to keep their own personal collections of fine wine and spirits.

"It's a fabulous place, Mr Worrapon," Tait said.

"Thank you Brad, I'm glad it pleases you."

"I'm guessing the whisky is from your own private collection," Tait added, anxious to show he knew how the system worked. His attention was diverted slightly by the waitress who delivered a selection of hors d'oeuvres. Everything they saw in the club was impeccable and clearly the same effort went into selecting the staff.

"Yes of course and this is my private alcove." There wasn't a trace of conceit in the remark, but the two fund managers started to calculate what such a facility might cost. A club where members each had a private area, that was off the scale.

Tait smiled at Worrapon and then looked at the waitress standing quietly at the side of the table.

"She's mine too Brad, but you can borrow her for a while if you wish."

Two hours passed and Tait had still not returned. Andy initially panicked at the thought of being left alone with their new client but Worrapon turned out to be the perfect drinking buddy. His knowledge of English football was encyclopaedic, his passion was golf and he appeared to be genuinely interested in Andy's life as an expat in Hong Kong and his early days making his way as a fund manager.

It felt like chatting to an old friend right up until Worrapan switched the subject matter back to investment and explained his younger brother was Head of Corporate Finance with the largest independent investment bank in Southeast Asia. His department had dealt with around thirty per cent of the new stock issues by the region's public companies in the previous four years.

"I like you Andy," Worrapan said. "You remind me of me, when I was in my early twenties."

"Thanks, Mr Worra... I mean Ben." Andy was getting anxious about the turn the conversation had taken and looked round for any sign of a returning Tait.

"Andy, my brother handles dozens of new issues, he knows who is going to be taken over... normally before the board of the company that's doing the buying."

Andy nodded nervously. His father had talked him through every scam ever conceived by the investment industry; the best known was insider trading, and it was illegal. Markets are supposed to work on the basis that all participants have broadly the same information and profits are made by those who interpret the data more effectively. Nobody really believes it, but to maintain the fantasy, regulators come down very hard on those who are found to be dealing with the benefit of privileged information. Andy feared Worrapon was about to suggest making use of his brother's position to do just that, and he was correct.

"Information like that could give your portfolios a bit of extra zing. Obviously we can throw a few bad ones in to make sure no-one gets suspicious, but you'll only need five or six a year and you'll be kicking the competition all over Bangkok. What do you say?"

Andy squirmed in his seat, desperate for Tait to return, for the fire alarm to ring, or for a vengeful bolt of lightning to strike from the heavens. Anything so he didn't have to answer the question he'd been asked, any response could jeopardise the relationship with their new client, or utterly destroy his career.

"What have I missed?" Tait returned looking as though he spent all his life dreaming impossible dreams but they all just came true.

"Nothing Brad, idle chat," Worrapon said. "Now if you'll excuse me, I have an early start. Andy, you will call me if you come up with an answer won't you?"

Andy nodded and shook the man's hand.

"What answer did he want?" Tait asked him as they headed back to the State Tower in a taxi.

Andy could not trust himself to look at his boss. He desperately wanted to tell Tait what Worrapon had suggested but feared the consequences. They'd had a lot to drink, maybe he'd misunderstood, the new office just couldn't afford to alienate the only substantial prospect they'd unearthed since opening. Andy had declined the offer anyway; maybe it was best just to pretend the conversation had never taken place.

"Oh… he wanted to know if an Australian had ever won the US Masters. I said I wasn't sure but I thought it unlikely." "Fuck off…" said Tait and proceeded to list every Aussie golfer he could think of regardless of whether they ever competed at Augusta.

Andy replayed Worrapon's offer in his head over and over in the days after their meeting. A week passed and, whilst their newest client visited the office once and they'd spotted him in the bar of the Lebua, there was no further mention of using the inside information his brother could provide. Maybe it was time to relax a little and put it all down to drunken exuberance.

India Clarke arrived as planned and she turned out exactly as Tait promised. She arrived around ten and left about five each day, making sure she sent a few e-mails to her father from her address on the company systems. Andy had seen Timothy Clarke and the only possible conclusion, was that India must take after her mother. Clarke was a squat, ugly little bastard whose dental work dated back to before they perfected the art. She was tall and lissom with shoulder-length blonde hair and one of those cute little upturned noses that shouldn't be pretty but are. Who wants to see up someone's nostrils for God's sake? It must satisfy some primal urge. Tait suggested she might be a party animal but there was no sign of it in the few days she'd been in Bangkok. The previous night they took the staff for a drink and a meal after work and India arrived wearing the demure pink shirt and knee length black skirt she had on all day in the office. She might have flirted with Tait a little but appeared to be sipping Coca-Cola all evening. When Andy left around nine, for his date with an air stewardess he met on his last trip from Hong Kong, India was stone cold sober.

As Andy Duncan looked out into the main office the following morning, India Clarke was staring at her screen with what appeared to be a look of unbridled horror. Sam was also at her desk, equally absorbed by whatever was on her computer, her shoulders quaking with uncharacteristic mirth. Billy and Yasmin, the two administration imports from Hong Kong shook their heads in apparent disbelief.

Andy's computer pinged to indicate receipt of a new message and he moved his mouse to clear the screensaver. The message was from an address he did not recognise but the title was catchy enough. "Berwick Archer in Sex and Cocaine Scandal." The link was to a blog of which he was vaguely aware, the author had gained a reputation for supporting the Occupy anti-capitalist movement and almost any new pieces of sleaze about financial firms appeared there first. One more click took Andy to a YouTube video, the first few frames showed a large meeting room, not unlike the one he and Tait used for client presentations on the opposite side of the floor. The images looked like they were from a standard office teleconferencing facility. The table was a familiar shape and the notepads set carefully in front of each chair looked very much like the one at Andy's elbow, but from a distance it could still be one of a thousand offices anywhere in the world. Nonetheless, Andy was in no doubt he was looking at the main meeting room at Berwick Archer's Bangkok office. It wasn't the furniture or the seating plan, but the girl lying on the table wearing a pink blouse unbuttoned to her waist, and a demure black skirt hitched up over her hips. Even from a distance the cute little upturned nose was unmistakeable. It was harder to identify the man, at least until he turned and looked towards the camera. The video was of Brad Tait and wrapped round his back were the long slender legs of India Clarke, daughter of the Group's Chief

Executive. The film even showed the time in the bottom right-hand corner; a quarter-to-midnight the previous evening.

Whoever got hold of the footage worked pretty hard to get it out and on the net in the hours since it was taken. They obviously knew their stuff too. As a static camera, there was no zoom facility but as the film came to an end, it flipped back for a brief replay of the final ecstatic moments. The tape then cut and clearly the film-maker had used technology to slow the frames in replay, and zoom in on a section of the table close to the two stars of the show. Next to India's thigh was a torn plastic bag and four white lines on the table, one stood out more clearly than the rest. Tait stood and stretched then reached down to zip up his trousers as India Clarke pulled her skirt over her legs. The couple smiled at each other then Tait bent down until his head obscured the four lines on the table. When he stood upright, the fourth line was as faint as the others and Tait shook his head and briskly rubbed his nose.

Sam and India had disappeared when Andy finally emerged from his office. Tait was nowhere to be seen and everyone else studiously avoided eye contact and appeared to be utterly engrossed with their work. Sam returned a few minutes later and with a mixture of irritation and relief, Andy realised she'd taken charge.

"Andy, I've spoken to James Turner in Hong Kong, he is on the way to the airport and should be in the office here by six. India is on her way to Suvarnabhumi and should be back in London this evening. Brad has been told to stay away and you are not to speak to anyone about this, Group PR in Hong Kong will deal with the fallout."

What followed was the longest day of Andy Duncan's short career. He sat in his office and watched the screens, not daring to place a trade in case he had to speak to someone and ignoring the flood of e-mails hitting his account. The Bull arrived, as promised, at five thirty and Sam beckoned Andy into the meeting room now familiar to the six hundred thousand people who viewed the YouTube video before it was taken down.

Turner looked pale and drawn as Andy entered the room, but in seconds was every inch the man in charge.

"It's a total fuck up Andy. Someone hacked our systems, they managed to switch on our video conferencing facility without our knowledge and they could tape everything that happened in that room. Chanpol's team has done a thorough review and they are certain it's an inside job. Whoever it was clearly hoped they'd get details of our best investment ideas and they ended up with that horny Aussie bastard doing the CEO's daughter."

Andy thought he saw a flicker of amusement on Turner's face as he said that, but it quickly returned to stone.

"Any idea who did it?" Andy couldn't think of anything else to say.

"Well that little dyke in Hong Kong office is out on her ear, we'll make sure she never gets another job past refilling the paper tray in an office photocopier. She was either in on it, or she looked the other way when it happened. We'll find out one way or another, in the meantime we've kicked her out."

"What happens next?" Andy barely registered that it was Sally Peng Turner was talking about.

"Tait's gone too, he's an embarrassment to the firm. It will take months to smooth this one over."

"So... who's going to run this place?" Andy started to feel tightness in his throat and a wave of nausea worked its way up from the depths of his gut. His inhaler was in the inside pocket of his jacket, but to grab it at that moment would send all the wrong messages.

"Congratulations Andy, you're the boss now. Don't worry about the clients or the press, Alex Cruickshank and I will handle that. Just take care of the portfolios. We've got every confidence in you."

# CHAPTER SEVEN

## Lifting the lid

"Surely that's what we have Kong for, he's the muscle." Boonamee tried to keep the desperation out of his voice.

"Prem, you have to do this sort of thing, if you want to keep moving forward in the business. There are others out there who'd kill for an assignment like this. I made the recommendation to the Boss myself and he's keen for you to do it. This shows he has confidence in you… we both have." It was the first time Song had indicated there might be anyone higher up the chain of command than him.

"By sending me into the jungle with a bunch of peasants and a train of pack mules? What's the big deal about that?"

"You could be running this part of the business soon, it's our most profitable operation and those involved get the rewards that go with it. You can't do that unless you see what happens on the ground. Take it or leave it. If you don't want it, I'll tell the Boss and you can take the consequences."

Song sounded more than a little exasperated and if there was one word Boonamee had learnt to fear more than any other it was "consequences." Since he started working for Song, he'd learnt consequences were never a good thing.

"OK I'm sorry, I hadn't seen it like that. All part of learning the ropes, I thought you were just short-handed and I was making up the numbers. You can tell the Boss, I'm honoured."

"Good boy." Song sounded like a man whose dog had returned with the stick he'd thrown. "It's an opportunity to understand how the supply chain works and to meet the men who work in the field. It will be as dull as hell, just a couple of days in the jungle, but Nung will be pleased with your dedication to the cause."

Boonamee regretted his initial petulance; Song was clearly looking out for him. More importantly, he'd opened up about the wider organisation, having previously given the impression he was the top man. Song is the Thai word for the number two and that should have been a clue. Now Boonamee was aware his boss was deputy to another, unsurprisingly code-named Nung… Thai for the number one.

Once Boonamee resigned himself to the task, he decided he might as well enjoy himself. Weeks before, he spotted a clothing store off Khao San Road and it appeared to be exactly the place to go to kit himself out for a jungle adventure. Much of what was on offer looked second hand but it was all in good condition. The assistant… "My name is Suk", was sweet, charming, extremely gay and more than happy to help the handsome customer make a selection. Suk insisted on taking measurements of Boonamee's chest, waist, hips and inside leg, despite the fact his customer was adamant he knew exactly what sizes he needed.
"You must go to the gym, you couldn't possibly keep yourself so fit unless you worked out?" Suk said.
Boonamee smiled, gave a modest shrug and turned back to a pile of t-shirts that had caught his eye. Suk took the opportunity to check his own reflection in the mirror next to the fitting room door. His hair was short, shaved at the sides and back, but he still used handfuls of gel to keep what was there under control. Like many women in Thailand, his eyebrows were shaved and replaced with a carefully etched tattoo. His pencil-thin moustache was either courtesy of the same tattooist or the result of meticulous daily shaving. A little eyeliner helped to accentuate what was certainly his best feature. His eyes were almost western; they were so big and round. The only other help he sought from make-up was a little lip-gloss and the ubiquitous powder Thais use to whiten their skin. Suk chose his clothes from stock but his shorts and shirt both appeared to be several sizes too small. Hoping to give the appearance of someone who was comfortable trekking through a sweaty jungle, Suk just looked like he'd be keen to offer a warm welcome to a man who had.
Camouflage trousers with a couple of matching shirts were selected with minimal debate, the two men then discussed at length which of two short-sleeved jerkins were more appropriate. Suk was adamant the green one was more stylish and practical, with a host of pockets for money, lip balm and sunscreen. Items you'd not be seen dead without in the jungle. Boonamee was

drawn to a khaki top, certain he'd seen Stallone wear one like it in the Rambo movies. After much debate, both tops went into the bag. There were still boots to buy and Boonamee had been eyeing a pair Suk told him were standard issue for the parachute regiment. It took an age to lace the boots and Suk knelt before his customer to secure the fastenings just below Boonamee's knee. They were the perfect finishing touch to the ensemble and Suk clasped his hands together and sighed. Boonamee nodded his approval and slid a wad of baht notes across the counter as Suk handed over two large shopping bags and the receipt. As he clasped Boonamee's hand, Suk slipped an address card into his palm.

"If there is anything else I can do... and I mean anything. This is my number."

Boonamee parked his four-by-four, as instructed, in a petrol station forecourt near a small village four miles from the Cambodian border. There was a brief rap on the car window and he found himself looking at a wizened, brown face only partially concealed by a wide, round-brimmed hat. Boonamee's stomach lurched, for a second he was certain he was looking into the eyes of the man he so recently dropped into the Chao Praya river in Bangkok. It didn't occur to him before, but the unlucky farmer came from a village not far from where he sat. The man crooked his finger and then pointed to a battered pickup truck being filled with LPG. Boonamee stepped out of the car and threw a small rucksack over his shoulder. It had a change of underwear, a spare shirt and his phone. Whether he'd get a signal where they were going remained to be seen. The man who tapped on his window looked him up and down for a couple of seconds, taking in Boonamee's paramilitary outfit. Then he shrugged in a clear physical version of one of the expressions you hear more than any other in Thailand... "Up to you..." It clearly wouldn't have been his choice of wardrobe for the challenge ahead, but this guy was the boss. As long as they all got paid, the new arrival could wear a taffeta ball gown as far as he was concerned.

They drove for only ten minutes and parked just off the road by what turned out to be a narrow track through the jungle.

Forty minutes after they set off down the muddy path, Boonamee's companion informed him they'd crossed the border. Almost another hour had passed before they arrived at a clearing where a teenage boy waited at the wheel of an ancient pickup truck. It was another ride of around twenty minutes to the village, where the only sign of any activity was a group of six men puffing their way through pungent, hand-rolled cigarettes. Occasionally they nodded in the direction of eight mules, tethered to a stake driven into the ground next to a wooden water butt. Each animal carried a pannier with a large leather sack on either side. Boonamee looked around, he'd envisaged dozens of mules and a small army of men to deliver enough *yaba* methamphetamine tablets to make it all worthwhile. The men turned in unison to see the new arrival from the capital. They all gave him the same look he received when he first stepped out of the four-by-four. Then, like the driver, they gave the "up to you" shrug. Boonamee jumped as he heard a sharp cry from his left, only to turn and see a couple of tiny children chasing a puppy into the trees. Neither could have been more than four or five years old, wearing t-shirts that were filthy and torn and shorts that looked like hand-me-downs from an older sibling. Neither wore shoes and it was only possible to guess whether they were male or female by their haircuts. The two children stopped to look at the stranger in their midst and the puppy reappeared from behind the tree stump where it had found sanctuary. The taller child, probably a girl, pointed at Boonamee and said something to the boy, then both children laughed before resuming their pursuit of the small dog.

  The men had also lost interest in him and chatted amongst themselves. Their uniform was familiar to Boonamee but a far cry from what he anticipated. After Song's motivational speech he expected to be leading a crack group of highly trained smugglers. The men wore pyjama type pants and tops, with the same flattened, conical hats as the driver who picked him up at the petrol station. It's the outfit of choice for the thousands of rice farmers who live and work in the area. Boonamee started to feel very self-conscious about his choice of garb, but as the men nodded in his direction and started to untie the mules, he decided that to change at this late stage would be an admission of an error of judgement, resulting in a catastrophic loss of face. He decided to tough it out.

Song was right, this was all useful stuff, learning how their supply chain really worked, he just wished the senior man's invitation had come with some indication as to the required dress code. Boonamee expected to see young, athletic, well-armed men as escort. These guys were middle-aged, far from fit and carried only machetes and a couple of ancient looking rifles. Boonamee already had a whole list of suggestions he could make to Song as to how the process could be improved. Maybe he'd get to meet the mysterious Nung to present his recommendations personally.

The tallest and oldest of the six men introduced himself as Jar and then gestured for the entire group to move towards a path leading from the edge of the village. Boonamee fell in behind him and easily kept pace with the convoy. The remaining men followed behind with the mules and progress slowed as the track became narrower and more awkward to navigate. Boonamee discovered the hard way that if he followed too close, a branch Jar pushed back would recoil and strike him in the face as it was let go. If he dropped back too far, it was harder to follow the man's tracks and remarkably easy to stumble on a root, twist an ankle on the uneven ground or lose one's footing in the soft, wet mud at the side of the path. The boots looked great in the shop; suddenly they were pinching around his toes and rubbing what felt like large swathes of skin from his heels and ankles. He desperately wanted to ask how long they would walk before a break, but as Jar looked back occasionally, Boonamee got the distinct impression that was exactly what the older man hoped. Sweat soaked his clothes and every inch of his flesh felt like it was providing a feast for the mosquitos swarming through the humid air. He gritted his teeth and pressed on.

Three hours passed before Jar indicated they should stop for some water and a little food.

"Welcome back to Thailand." Jar gave a humourless and largely toothless grin. Each man tugged at the length of cloth at their waists and then began to unwrap the small parcel secured against their stomachs. Jar looked quizzically at Boonamee and when he realised the younger man had brought no provisions, he offered some of his own. Boonamee smiled weakly, in no doubt who'd won the unspoken contest for who was the group's Alpha male. Jar hadn't even broken sweat.

It was fifteen minutes before Jar gave the signal for the men to continue. The break let Boonamee's feet recover a little, but as they started to walk again, he could feel the blisters that had formed under the tough leather of the boots. Every step was an ordeal and he prayed for it to end. The trek was to come to a conclusion much quicker than he expected and in a way he could never have foreseen.

Jar paused in a clearing, waiting for the mules to catch up when fourteen heavily armed soldiers appeared from the jungle. From their midst emerged an older man, wearing a slightly more elaborate uniform and carrying what looked like a well-used riding crop. His bulky frame was still mainly muscle but a slight sag at the jawline suggested a man whose body was heading into decline. There was a hint of a swagger in the way he crossed the clearing, the drug smugglers were far too intimidated to recognise it had been carefully cultivated to disguise a limp. Colonel Rakat had spent twenty-nine years in the parachute regiment and only switched to a desk job when his final jump had gone horribly wrong. He rarely did any fieldwork any more but this was an assignment he'd been determined to lead.

Each of the soldiers held a modern automatic rifle trained on Boonamee's six men, three of whom had already fallen to their knees in supplication.

"Tie the mules to the tree and round the men up next to the path," Rakat ordered.

Boonamee's couriers had already dropped what weapons they carried and stumbled to the edge of the clearing without any further encouragement from the soldiers. Rakat turned to Boonamee.

"Welcome, we've been expecting you." He eyed his captive's now muddy army surplus uniform and smiled. "We didn't expect to find a fully fledged colonel with this bunch of misfits."

It was what Boonamee had dreaded; an informer from their own ranks was always their biggest risk. In Bangkok, they paid the police to make sure it never came to anything. Now, he was looking at the insignia of the Thai Parachute Regiment and no-one ever said anything about the need to keep them sweet, even if such a thing was possible.

"You knew we were coming?" he asked meekly.

"Of course, the only surprise was that you took so long. I guess a city boy might find the going fairly tough." The old soldier was clearly enjoying the exchange.

"So what happens now?" Boonamee was pretty sure he knew the answer. The penalty for drug smuggling was death, normally after a lengthy stay in one of Thailand's squalid prisons. Had he been face to face with a police officer, he was sure Song could get him out but looking at a soldier he felt no such confidence.

"We wait." Rakat looked at a hand-held device much like Boonamee's own Samsung tablet.

"Wait for what?"

"The TV crew. You'll love the reporter. She's doing a documentary for the BBC in England. Pretty little thing, but as dumb as your father's buffalo. You should check her out on YouTube. She likes to think of herself as an investigative reporter, how do they say? Lifting the lid... yes that's it, lifting the lid on what a barbaric bunch we are here in Thailand."

Boonamee could barely believe his ears. His agonising trek through the jungle had put him firmly in the hands of the Thai army, now his shame would be presented for all to see on TV.

Rakat smiled as he checked the screen of his tablet.

"They are almost here, we're ready to roll. Are the men all set?"

He was answered with a curt nod from the young soldier who appeared to be his deputy.

"Run."

The order was directed at the six men from Boonamee's convoy but they just looked confused. As Boonamee stepped forward the senior officer grabbed his arm and shot him an exasperated look.

"Not you."

The soldiers raised their guns. "Run... now." This time the instruction was shouted and the paratroopers took a threatening step forward. Jar made a break for the only track that headed away from the clearing and when the soldiers made no attempt to stop him, the others started to flee too. The guards watched the six men go, but as the last one disappeared into the jungle, there was a volley of automatic fire from the direction in which they were running.

Boonamee stared at Rakat in horror, certain he was next.

"Well we couldn't very well shoot them in the back, now could we? Not with a BBC film crew a few hundred metres away."

Rakat smiled an awful crooked smile, then turned to his deputy.

"Make sure each body has a gun next to it, you've got about a minute and a half."

Rakat turned his attention back to Boonamee.

"The film crew will be here in a few minutes. I want you to stand very still and look as though you might be on the side of law and order. If you do anything to attract their attention, I will personally shoot you in the head, the second they leave."

Boonamee nodded dumbly, he was grateful for the instruction as to how he should behave, as his head was in turmoil and he really had no ideas of his own.

Within a few seconds two more soldiers appeared from a corner of the clearing. Trailing in their wake was a young and undeniably pretty *farang* woman flanked by her crew. Like Boonamee, it looked as if she'd spent a great deal of time choosing her outfit for the day's adventure. She'd gone for a similar combination of olive green and khaki, topped off with one of those wide brimmed, flat topped Boonie hats popularised by the US Army… or at least by the guys who made movies about the Vietnam War. Boonamee realised that he recognised her from a couple of YouTube videos where she claimed to expose the plight of the poor and vulnerable across the globe. Thailand was one of her regular locations and he always assumed it was because there were plenty of five star resorts for her to stay in while she made her documentaries. Her style was simply to wander round a foreign country with a permanently dropped jaw, pointing in awe at the savagery and barbarism of the little brown people she came across. Boonamee noticed the chinstrap on her Boonie hat was tightly tied, possibly the director had insisted on that to keep her jaw a little more under control.

As she surveyed the scene in the jungle clearing, the reporter was almost hopping from foot to foot with joy. Her latest assignment was to "lift the lid" on the Thai drugs trade. They'd already filmed a ton of stuff in Bangkok and Khon Kaen. Viewers would be convinced it was impossible to walk fifty yards in either city without being accosted by a bleary eyed teenager selling heroin or *yaba* and that every street corner had a couple of crack whores offering their bodies in return for enough cash for their next fix. The presenter would claim she had painstakingly traced the supply lines back to their source and was now being rewarded for her diligence by being right there as the Thai army intercepted a vast shipment of narcotics. The producer and director were still arguing about whether they could claim it was their "investigation" that led to the discovery of the "huge" train of pack mules now under army control.

Rakat stepped forward and proudly offered to answer any questions the BBC might have. His English was flawless and the reporter was clearly entranced as he explained that a vicious firefight had taken place only moments before they arrived. Excerpts from the interview would be broadcast across the world the following day, but for the full version, eager viewers had to wait for the documentary to appear.

"They are highly trained fighters from across the border," the colonel explained, as the reporter looked on in trademark open-mouthed astonishment.

"We believe many of them used to be part of the military of our neighbouring countries. They now make a living by smuggling drugs into Thailand. Regrettably a number of them have made their escape through the jungle, but their commander detailed six heavily armed men to attack my soldiers. We had no choice but to engage them in combat, mercifully none of my unit were injured. The six criminals were shot dead."

The camera crew was led to where the bodies of the men lay thirty yards from the clearing. They'd been turned to face down, so it was impossible to guess how old they might be. Next to each man lay a modern automatic rifle, carefully placed by one of the Thai soldiers now standing guard to make sure the crew could not get too close. Once they had enough footage, the TV crew were led back to the clearing where the mules were still tethered to a tree.

Rakat smiled again for the camera. "We are still rounding up the animals that ran away when we arrived, some are already on their way to a shelter in Udon Thani."

The reporter began a breathless report to camera, whilst fondling the ears of the cutest looking mule, so the colonel returned to the other side of the clearing. Boonamee stood stock-still but, remembering Rakat's instructions, did his utmost to inject an even greater degree of rigidity into his frame. Just to be on the safe side.

"We are so fortunate to have the BBC to reveal the sordid goings on in our country, don't you think?"

The young Thai nodded helplessly, as Rakat continued.

"I think this documentary will be a massive hit. Everyone involved will want a credit, but I doubt the viewers will ever know the truth. Produced and Directed by the BBC, storyline conceived and delivered by the Army of the Kingdom of Thailand."

He chuckled and then saluted to the departing camera crew and their pretty but monumentally gullible reporter.

"Did you see the look on her face, when I said we sent some of the pack mules to an animal sanctuary, I think there were tears in her eyes. I hadn't even planned to say that bit. Damn it, I should have asked for her number."

Rakat turned to his men.

"Load the bags with the merchandise into the jeeps and let's get out of here." Although the order was addressed to nobody in particular the paratroopers responded immediately.

"What about the mules, sir?"

"Shoot them," he replied before turning back to Boonamee.

"You really have no idea what is going to happen next do you?"

Boonamee closed his eyes and shook his head. It was all he could do to maintain control of his bladder. It occurred to him to call out when the camera crew were there, but the colonel could easily have decided to kill them too. Trying to run was pointless, he had no idea where he was and the episode with the six couriers showed the Army had more men waiting in the jungle. Boonamee simply decided all he could do was pray and, by this stage, he decided the best outcome was probably that when the end came it might be quick. Rakat spoke again.

"That's the problem with all this secrecy stuff, you never know who knows what. I assumed Song gave you a full briefing, then you turn up, dressed like a pantomime general..." His voice trailed off and he shook his head in disbelief.

Boonamee heard the man say "Song" and felt like he'd been punched. The soldier spoke about him like they were old friends.

"So, I'll assume Song has told you nothing," Rakat continued. "We'll take the bags obviously, they have to be checked in as evidence, then the forensic team will confirm they are the real thing. One of my men will drop you back at your car; he has an envelope with your hotel booking for this evening. He'll call you tomorrow when the merchandise has been verified and documented. It may take an extra day so you might have to stay over."

Boonamee's jaw dropped in a passable impression of the BBC reporter who left them a little earlier. The pieces started to fit together in his head. Song knew the cargo would be intercepted; it was him who told the soldier where to find them.

"Song set this up?" he asked.

"Of course, how else do you think we found your little troop of peasants?"

"But the tablets are real, why would Song hand over all that stuff?"

"He said you had a lot to learn... think about it. The Army only has a token presence on the border, if we couldn't point to the odd success, some deputy stands up in Parliament saying more effort should be made to combat the smugglers. The Americans might even insist on putting some observers in place to see where we were going wrong. In no time the place is running with guys determined to close the border. This way, we get the credit for stemming the tide of drugs and Song only has to put up with a minor disruption in his supply lines. Everyone's happy."

Boonamee was stunned; a wave of conflicting emotions ran through his body. Song said he'd meet the men involved in the smuggling operation. Boonamee thought he meant Jar and his ramshackle collection of farmers. He actually meant Rakat and his unit of the parachute regiment. There was relief that he was clearly not about to be shot and thrown into the undergrowth, indeed his captors were about to hand over a hotel reservation for the night. Boonamee couldn't help but admire the simplicity of the plan, the soldier would be greeted as a hero, yet he was an integral part of Song's team. At the same time there was a rising tide of anger that Song had put him through the ordeal. He could just as easily have explained how the product was imported and allowed Boonamee to go along with the knowledge of what would happen. He was in no doubt Song would claim it was part of a test, their way of letting him prove his mettle, earning his spurs with Nung, the real boss in the organisation. Some of that, Boonamee thought, might be true, but he knew the real reason Song had set it all up in this way. It was because he really enjoyed the power he could exercise over the people who looked to him for their living. Boonamee was still incredulous that Song was willing to sacrifice even this modest shipment.

"So Song is happy to hand over all this *yaba*, just to keep the heat off?"

The officer looked quizzical and appeared to be slightly disappointed by Boonamee's naiveté.

"Don't be ridiculous. Song would sell his own grandmother for a convoy a fraction of this size. He's not going to let it rot in a police store somewhere. The cargo will be tested and certified as genuine. Then we swap the goods for sugar pills. That's why we need you to stick around for a day or so. You can come and collect them and drive them to Bangkok." He handed an envelope to Boonamee. "These are the instructions for my payment. Tell Song to be quick about it. It took him four days last time and I'm an impatient man."

Boonamee was stunned. "I just drive the merchandise to Bangkok?"

"Of course, that's how it always gets there. Nobody uses pack mules any more," Rakat paused and laughed. "Unless we want some good headlines about how the Army is cracking down on drug smugglers all along the border."

# CHAPTER EIGHT

## The turnaround

Andy Duncan hadn't had a drink in four weeks. Working fourteen-hour days, he'd rarely left the State Tower since the YouTube scandal broke. As instructed, he focused only on the investment portfolios, trawling through each account, painstakingly analysing where they were underperforming. It took him no time at all to spot the main issues. Tait had always been responsible for strategy and for defining the overall construction of the pots of money they managed, Andy picked the individual stocks they bought and sold. It quickly became apparent that Tait lost the plot several weeks before the fateful encounter with India Clarke. Research received from Charlie's team in Hong Kong was positive about China but negative about the Eurozone, it made the case for energy companies and spotted the imminent correction in banking stocks following their rally in the spring. Tait received a directive, from Turner himself, that he should switch the portfolio weights to include more equities relative to bonds and to reduce the level of liquidity across the board. Tait implemented none of it, his only interaction with Hong Kong being a series of e-mails telling the Portfolio Review team to back off. That group was tasked with identifying accounts that diverged from the "house view", and the Bangkok office must have flashed red on their radar screen. Andy checked Tait's calendar for the two weeks before he disappeared. It was empty apart from a couple of conference calls with James Turner. An e-mail from Turner said he was coming to Bangkok because they had to talk and he was due to arrive two days after the video clip aired on YouTube. It was obvious that Hong Kong was well aware that Tait was out of control and Turner was coming in for a showdown. The Australian probably knew his time was up and decided to go out in style. Andy called Tait's mobile several times but was transferred to voicemail. Sam said Tait's apartment in the State Tower was empty. A few of his clothes were still in the bedroom, but he'd clearly packed as one might for a very long holiday. Andy decided Tait was history and it was down to him to fix the investment problems.

Two weeks into the task, Sam told him the welcome news that Hong Kong was about to despatch a junior fund manager to help him out. Andy hadn't been too impressed when he discovered the new man was Simon Tudor, the trainee assigned to him before he left for Bangkok. Once Tudor arrived, Andy was happy to have the extra pair of hands as he ploughed through more and more analysis and tried to keep track of the flood of research coming from Hong Kong.

In the days after Tait's departure, the share price of Berwick Archer fell sharply. It was anticipated that such a sordid scandal would result in many of its ultra-conservative clients taking their accounts elsewhere. Sex and drugs were for pop stars and overpaid footballers, not the senior employees of a reputable financial institution. The tabloid press had a field day, all their dreams came true when they discovered the girl on the table was the daughter of the Group Chief Executive. The Sun newspaper detailed a small team to analyse every single tweet she ever made and to forensically dissect her Facebook account. India was a friendly girl and allowed public access to her Timeline. There were a few pictures of her in a bikini looking as though she'd had a liquid lunch and a couple of photos from a girl's night out where she appeared to be a little under-dressed. Otherwise there was nothing incriminating. The team did, however, find a Facebook friend whose brother had been charged with marijuana possession and a post, which India "liked", containing a very poor joke about a sheep and a Welshman. That was enough for Britain's premier tabloid to run a two-page spread labelling India a drug raddled racist. Mainly it was an excuse, once again, to reproduce a series of stills from the YouTube video, suitably pixelated to protect younger readers. Lawyers for the Clarke family wrote to the paper to point out the video contained no evidence that India had taken drugs. It was a rookie error. The paper simply turned it into a story about how the lawyers of the rich and famous had tried to silence the free press but failed.

For two full weeks, little else appeared to happen in the world as the Berwick Archer sex scandal featured over and over again on the internet and in the tabloids. The firm's press department went onto a war footing and London's top PR agencies fought it out to advise the beleaguered firm. James Turner took to the road with Alex Cruickshank; personally visiting each of the firm's major clients to assure them a one-off embarrassment had been dealt with promptly and effectively. Timothy Clarke was advised to take a back seat through the crisis as his personal brand was now slightly tarnished. After all, he brought up "the little whore who screwed her boss in front of over a half a million YouTube viewers."

Twenty-two days after the video appeared for the first time, James Turner punched the air in triumph. He knew the story had run its course. This was partly because Berwick Archer had commissioned a hugely expensive and extremely effective PR campaign to neutralise the scandal. More importantly, a recent winner of Britain's favourite talent show drank herself to death in a stylish, but sparsely furnished, apartment in London's Docklands. The press was suddenly bored with Tait and Clarke. The host of a weekly news quiz on the BBC consigned the story to history with a single line, "People shagging in Thailand? It's hardly the scoop of the century is it?" The audience tittered politely and sat back to listen to the panel dissect the case of Suzee Collins who achieved her lifetime dream two years earlier aged only nineteen. She was the nation's darling when she won the final round of "Star Track", and fame and fortune were just around the corner. Two years on and nobody could remember the name of that annoying single she released, the CD was still in pre-production and Suzee appeared to have celebrated her twenty-first birthday alone apart from two, litre bottles of vodka and a cellophane bag of ecstasy tablets.

James Turner knew the press hyenas had another corpse to pick over, literally this time, and he could go back to managing money. As he looked out over Hong Kong harbour, he realised he could just about put a face to the name of the young singer. His niece in London had been quite keen on her for a while. The girl unwittingly ended the media storm that had gone on for much longer than he expected and given herself a small piece of the immortality she craved. "Thank you, Suzee," he said, raising his coffee cup in a toast.

"Andy, it's looking good. I reckon we've turned it round."
Andy gave his young assistant a withering stare.

"I mean… umm, well you... you've turned it round. I helped though right?"

Simon Tudor was desperate for a pat on the back, some indication from his boss that he played his part and it was recognised.

"Of course Simon, you've done a great job. I had you down as a bit of a dickhead back in Hong Kong but you've done really well."

Andy smiled graciously and Tudor's face lit up with pride. The two men were looking at the latest performance report for the Bangkok accounts. They all made money in the month, most were still behind their benchmark but the gap was closing fast. Tudor also pointed out that two of Berwick Archer's main competitors had problems of their own. Harrington Sharp had lost an entire investment team to Blackrock, the biggest investment business in the world, whilst Reid Partners had clearly made some dreadful investment calls. Their performance had collapsed and there were rumours of an imminent defection by some of their largest clients.

Simon Tudor looked at Andy as though he'd follow him to the end of the universe if required.

"So what's next boss?"

Andy had a more modest objective in mind.

"Simon, we're going to get as drunk as two men have ever been and you're paying."

The waitress was at least thirty feet away, but she made a point of keeping tabs on the two free-spending *farang* sitting in the corner of the rooftop bar. Andy raised his index finger and mouthed the words 'one more.'

She didn't need to hear him to know he wanted another bottle of Louis Roederer Cristal champagne. At ten thousand baht a bottle, a healthy tip was likely to be on offer if she took care of them properly. She'd seen Andy before, but he'd always been with the Australian who thought he was the sexiest man alive. Neither had been in for a few weeks and while, in spite of big tips, she never cared for the other man, she was attracted by Andy's blond hair and liked the way he treated the staff with respect. They chatted a couple of times; he introduced himself and explained how he got the little scar on his face. She told him she had a similar accident and blushed at the suggestion she show him her scar. Staff were not supposed to consort with guests but she'd definitely find a way if Andy suggested they meet outside work. She rushed to the bar to get the second bottle of champagne.

Andy noticed the waitress was paying him extra special attention and took a little longer than usual to taste check the new bottle. He was about to ask her if she liked champagne and whether she might want to sample some on her next day off, when a familiar voice cut in.

"Cristal… my favourite," Caroline Chan removed the huge sunglasses that obscured most of her face and treated Andy to her brightest smile. He'd never seen Chan in the same outfit twice, they'd met only a few times socially but she'd visited the office for several meetings with Tait. On each occasion, she looked like she'd stepped straight off a catwalk, having been dressed for a sixty second appearance in front of an army of eager cameraman and a critical panel of judges.

As Andy stood to greet her, he inadvertently nudged the waitress into a passing colleague and Chan swept forward to plant a professional but affectionate kiss on each of his cheeks. She dropped into the spare chair and despatched the young server to bring another glass.

"Andy, it must have been hell, but I hear you've turned it all around. You really are the star they thought you were."

Andy was still standing and feeling somewhat overwhelmed, as usual, with the arrival of the human whirlwind that was Caroline Chan. Embarrassed by his failure to offer her a chair, he wanted to apologise to the waitress who'd been so brusquely dismissed while simultaneously trying to find the words to introduce Simon Tudor, who responded as most men did on a first acquaintance with Ms Chan. Tudor self-consciously flicked at his hair to make sure it was in place and checked his palms were dry in case she deemed him worthy of an introductory handshake. Unable to handle the combination of social challenges, Andy sat down, flashed what he hoped was a winning smile and shrugged.

"Well it took a little time but I think I'm on top of it now."

The next ninety minutes passed in something of a daze for Andy. He barely acknowledged the waitress when she returned with a glass for Chan, or when she delivered a third bottle of Cristal. He vaguely remembered introducing Simon Tudor, who was granted a full second and a half of Chan's undivided attention before she turned again to Andy and insisted he tell her more about how he single-handedly led Berwick Archer's Bangkok office from the brink of oblivion. Tudor finally gave up on being part of the conversation and explained there was somewhere he needed to be. Andy smiled and nodded, Chan simply raised her hand in what might have been a wave, but looked like that gesture you might use to indicate to a street vendor his wares are of absolutely no interest whatsoever.

"So can you solve the mystery for me?" Andy asked.

"Mystery?" Chan looked intrigued.

"Brad called you his favourite broker but there's no record of the business you did together."

Chan smiled ruefully.

"He never gave me a single order."

Andy was shocked.

"You're kidding. I thought I'd found another one of his schemes. I reckoned you got the business but that maybe it was through something offshore so it never showed up in the reports. You were always giving him ideas, I can't believe he never used them."

"Oh, I'm guessing he used them, but he never placed the business through us. He never gave us a single deal."

"But you met him socially and were in the office several times for meetings. Why did you do that if there was no business in it for you?"

"Andy, I've only been doing this for a couple of years. Berwick Archer was identified as an important target for my firm. We knew if we got on your list, it would be worth a fortune to us, and give us credibility with other firms. I wasn't going to admit to my bosses I couldn't get your business, so I just kept plugging away."

For the first time since they met, Chan looked vulnerable. The young ambitious woman was struggling to make it in an environment totally dominated by men. It was a momentary lapse. In seconds the mask returned and she was every inch the capable professional broker she'd been before.

"Did Tait say why he never gave you any business?"

"Of course, he said there was only one thing that stopped him placing a huge amount of business with my firm." She trailed a finger through the condensation gathered at the base of her champagne glass and appeared to be drawing abstract patterns on the table-top.

"So why wouldn't he deal with you?" Andy felt the urge to cover her hand with his own.

"Because I wouldn't sleep with him."

Andy half expected that was what she'd say, but hoped for a proper, professional reason that didn't give him another motive to despise his erstwhile boss.

"I'm sorry Caro, that's awful. I thought you liked him, to be honest I thought that maybe…" Andy had started a sentence he didn't know how to finish and decided to abandon it. Chan started to laugh.

"It's a pity but that's often the way. If a woman is getting sales in this business, people generally assume she's shagging her clients."

"No… no… I'm really sorry, that's not what I meant at all. I heard some of your ideas… they were very good. I thought you guys got on well, so it was natural to think that maybe…" He abandoned that sentence too.

"Brad Tait is a pig. I spent time with him because my bosses told me to." She noticed the look on Andy's face and realised what he must be thinking. "Oh Andy, you don't have to worry. After my lamentable failure with Tait, they've moved me sideways and… down. They're still targeting your firm but they've given the account to someone else. I'm off the case."

Andy Duncan had been the first to arrive in the office every morning for over a month. Either Sam or Simon Tudor was next, around seven-thirty, the new boy having been detailed to bring coffee and muffins. Andy checked his watch and smiled at the thought of his double strength latte going cold on his desk. He stretched the full length of his bed and pulled the light duvet up to his chin. He wasn't cold, he just felt very warm and snug and the action reminded him of when he was a kid and how safe and contented he felt when tucked up in a warm bed whilst the English weather did its worst outside. The rain hammering on a dormitory window had been replaced by the sound of the shower in the next room.

Andy closed his eyes and tried to replay the previous evening in his mind. After the revelations about Tait and Caroline's demotion, they agreed not to talk about their respective employers again. Chan spoke briefly but with little warmth about her family. Like Andy, her parents split when she was young and she learned to call boarding school her home. Even in the holidays she was often farmed out to stay with school friends as her mother was travelling or simply too busy to take care of her. The school automatically pencilled in her name whenever a trip was organised, knowing her mother would always write out a cheque rather than welcome her daughter home for the holidays. She wasn't the only girl in the same predicament and with a couple of friends she quickly became an expert skier and a very proficient sailor courtesy of the school's out of term activities. Caroline was always top of her class but that didn't stop her mother paying for private tuition that laid the foundation for fluency in English, French, Mandarin and Cantonese. It was essentially a very expensive form of babysitting, but Chan was ultimately grateful for the skills she acquired. She explained how she'd picked up only a few words of Thai, but chatted confidently in the language when a local joined them briefly from another table. It was after two a.m. when Andy paid their bar bill and suggested coffee in his apartment a few floors below.

The shower had been switched off while Andy was enjoying his reverie. There was a gentle cough from the end of the bed and he opened his eyes.

Caroline wore only a towel, without the stilettos she suddenly looked tiny and, without the business suit, much younger and a little less confident. Her hair was tied up the night before, now it was loose and fell in a perfect shiny black curtain to a few inches below her shoulders. Andy felt his chest tighten, she might tell him it was all a mistake, they'd been drunk and it shouldn't have happened. She might throw on her clothes and back out of the door with an unconvincing promise to call him later. He suddenly realised what she said next was very important to him indeed and that frightened him just a little.

"I've got a meeting…" she said, toying with her necklace and avoiding direct eye contact.

"Right, yeah, that's fine… of course no problem…" He would have to work on being nonchalant.

"It's at two o'clock."

"Huh?"

"My meeting is at two. I have to go by eleven… midday at the very latest." Caroline gave him a mischievous smile. "That's if you have time for me."

"Oh yes, I have time," he said, as she dropped the towel to the floor. "I have all the time in the world."

**Falling**

It's a macho cliché when a man says he can't even remember most of the women he's slept with, Andy really couldn't. It wasn't the sheer number, although he was sure his tally compared favourably with most young men of his age. Had he been asked the question a few months earlier he might have made a half decent shot at naming them all. Like when someone asks you to name the fifty states of the USA, the first thirty or so are easy and it only gets really tricky when you get down to that bunch of little ones on the east coast. Andy would have hated to admit it, but the reason he couldn't remember was that every day he spent with Caroline Chan, the other women with whom he'd shared even a few months of his life receded a little further in his mind. She never made that meeting the day after their first night together and Andy called in sick well before midday.

The investment issues Andy inherited from Brad Tait appeared to be under control. A video-conference with the team in Hong Kong ended with a public "attaboy" from James Turner, acknowledging that Bangkok office had turned the corner and the sales and marketing team could start another push for new Thai based clients. Simon Tudor proved to be a surprisingly able deputy and, like Andy himself a few years earlier, was extremely grateful for the trust his new boss had placed in him. Andy regularly left the office just after six and on three out of five weekdays, he joined Caroline for dinner and they'd end the evening at his apartment in the State Tower. Her mother was ill and every fortnight, she flew back to Hong Kong to check on her. On alternate weekends they'd either spend a lazy couple of days in the Thai capital, or head for Koh Kood, Koh Samet or Hua Hin. His new girlfriend was no stranger to luxury travel but even she was impressed when Andy found the Koh Kood resort which ships its visitors in from Bangkok in its own private plane. But Andy was determined not to take his eye off the ball. He saw what happened to Tait and made a personal vow not to go the same way. The Australian had started to believe his own publicity and that was certainly the beginning of his downfall.

Once a week he called his father. It was the dutiful thing to do, an infallible method of keeping himself grounded and the best way of keeping in touch with what was happening in Hong Kong. Caroline was with her mother for the weekend and, as Andy finished their daily Skype call, he reached for his landline. His father had no time for the new fangled technology of the internet.

"Dad, it's me. How's it going?"

"Not so bad son. James is singing your praises over here. You dug us out of quite a hole."

"I guess so Dad, but it wasn't so tough. Brad lost it big time and I just needed to tidy up the portfolios a bit. Hardly rocket science."

Amongst Victor Duncan's favourite mantras was "there's no need to bang your own drum." If you had something worth boasting about, much better you keep your mouth shut and someone else will eventually do it for you. Andy was desperate to explain what a brilliant job he'd done spotting Tait's mistakes but he knew it wouldn't go down well. Waiting for the bucket of cold water that would eventually come from the other end of the phone, it came quicker than he expected.

"Well don't let it go to your head that's all. You know what it's like in your end of the business, you're only as good as yesterday's performance numbers." There it was, Victor never missed a chance to tell his son that, as a fund manager, he walked a very dangerous tightrope.

"So how are you doing Dad, everything OK?"

"Of course son, maybe we can check our diaries and catch a weekend down in Phuket. We haven't spent any time together for ages."

Victor sounded weary and Andy was anxious to end the call. Every time, one of them raised the possibility they might get together for a weekend just like the old days. Neither would acknowledge they never spent much time together when they went to Phuket before and neither ever suggested a firm date. Andy put the phone down thinking his father sounded a little older and a lot more weary than the last time they talked.

Andy hoped his reunion with Caroline would give the new week some of the buzz his weekend had lacked, but Caroline was distracted. He guessed her mother had taken a turn for the worse.

"Is she OK?" he asked.

"No not really. Physically she's fine. It's her mind that's going. She gets half way through a sentence then she looks at me and realises she thought she was talking to my sister or her friend that lives down the hallway. I'm not sure I can leave her in that apartment for much longer."

Caroline looked like she was struggling to maintain her composure and Andy reached out and took her hand.

"Anything I can do?"

"No, honestly, it's fine. You're being great already; some guys would get all itchy about me going to see her so much. You're really supportive."

"If there's anything you need, just tell me. You know I'll be there for you."

Caroline looked like she might cry.

"There's nothing. It's not so tough really; you know we've never been that close so I'm only there out of some bizarre concept of duty. They hammer that into little Asian girls you know. You have to take care of your mother, even if she's a self-centred callous bitch."

The outburst seemed to be cathartic and Caroline laughed and pushed her plate away. Her hand ran up the length of his thigh and the look of daughterly concern had gone.

"Let's go to bed."
Andy called for the check and asked the maître d' to phone for a taxi.

It was after three a.m. when Andy awoke and realised he was alone in bed. He grabbed the light silk kimono Caroline bought for him in Hong Kong and went in search of his girlfriend. She sat at the desk by the window, entranced by the endless stream of traffic on the Chao Praya river. Her laptop was open but she'd lost interest in whatever was on the screen.

"Caro," he said as softly as he could, but the girl looked like she'd been slapped. With one hand she slammed the laptop shut and with the other scooped a printed document from the table and dropped it into her briefcase. By the time she turned to look at Andy, Caroline was a picture of composure.

"Sorry darling, I couldn't sleep. Just checking the sales reports. I know we said work was off-limits when we're together but I needed something dull to make me drop off."

He led her back to bed and within minutes she was sleeping at his side. Andy closed his eyes but there was something about her body language in the other room. She was worried about whatever had been on her screen and he was anxious to find out what it was. Andy waited until Caroline was in the shower the following morning before he went to check her laptop. The machine came to life as he opened it up, but the cursor hovered stubbornly over a flashing box that demanded a password. There was no way he could risk a guess, her laptop could easily lock as a consequence and it would be obvious what he'd tried to do. As he turned back to the bedroom, he could hear her phone announce an incoming text. Picking up the handset. He could see the message was from Daniel, her boss at Pan Asia Securities. It was short and to the point.

"Caro, your sales numbers suck. Don't forget we have lunch at 1, need to hear how you're gonna turn it round."

Andy remembered the printed report she dropped into her briefcase the night before. He moved quietly past the bathroom door to make sure the shower was still running, then returned to the desk and fished the document out of her bag. It was the monthly financial report for her firm, a yellow post-it marked a page about three-quarters of the way through. Pan Asia clearly ranked their sales staff according to the volume of deals they secured with fund managers like Berwick Archer. Out of a dozen staff, Caro ranked a distant twelve with zero point four per cent of the total business generated by the sales team. Daniel was being kind when he said her numbers sucked. They were so much worse than that. Andy barely had time to return the report to her briefcase and make sure the phone and laptop were where she left them, when Caroline emerged from the bathroom.

"Busy today?" he asked.

"Sure, always busy. Markets are good and clients are forming an orderly queue round the block."

Andy knew from her sales report that Caroline had secured only two trades that week. It wouldn't be too hard to keep her clients in an orderly queue.

"You doing anything for lunch?" He was sure her shoulders slumped a little as he asked the question and she looked away.

"Oh yes, I think I have lunch with Dan. Just the usual sales strategy stuff, nothing important." By the time their eyes met, the mask was back in place and she looked every inch the confident, successful broker.

"Tonight?" Andy asked hopefully.

"You couldn't keep me away."

The morning passed slowly. Andy couldn't keep his mind off what Caroline must be going through ahead of her lunch. There was every chance she'd arrive that night, having been told to clear her desk at Pan Asia. It was so unfair. She'd been given a terrible list of clients to deal with and all because she failed to get any business out of Brad Tait. There was no doubt she was a talented broker, but he'd seen the list of small institutions she had to cultivate. It was a miracle she got any business out of them at all. Now she was caught in a vicious circle, she'd never be given a better client list unless she landed a few big deals but she'd never land any deals without a better client list. Berwick Archer was partly to blame because Tait withheld the business he should have given her. Andy knew he could put it all right, with a click of a mouse, but their relationship thrived on the basis they'd keep business out of it. His father would have been horrified to hear he was dating a broker, he'd have hit him with the endless list of the conflicts that inevitably arise when a fund manager is sharing a bed with someone who might want to sell him something. Well it wouldn't be a problem for much longer if he did nothing, Andy was certain that unless Caroline could turn it round this morning, she'd be unemployed by nightfall.

They agreed right from the start it was OK to discuss investment matters but there should never be any question of them entering into any trades. There could never be so much as a suggestion their personal relationship might have influenced their work. Only once had he done anything on her prompt and that was completely above board. They were both busy at their laptops in Andy's living room and she only asked for his opinion.

"Andy what do you know about these complex ownership structures they're using in Africa. A and B shares, where only certain people can invest in each."

Andy puffed out his chest; he'd completed a study on it for the firm back in Hong Kong.

"It's a bit of a dodge really. There's loads of Asian money piling into Africa so they nicked it from what the Koreans and Japanese have been doing for years. They split the capital in two, westerners can buy the B shares, but all the ownership rights sit with the A share holders so the B shares always sell at a big discount. The good governance lobby is furious about it. Why do you want to know?"

"Oh it's a project at Pan Asia. We want to get into the governance game so we're trying to put a bit of pressure on East Africa Resources to buy back all the B shares and issue only A shares. We need someone who has some leverage."

"We bought four and a half per cent of the A shares through a Chinese registered sub-fund. I could write them a letter if you want, I doubt they'd respond but it's a bit of pressure. No skin off my nose, it makes a lot of sense to me."

"But the price of the B shares will rise won't it? And that's not good for your shares."

"It's peanuts for the fund and it makes sense for the company, much better in the long run. I'd be happy to do it."

107

There was a small amount of press coverage and Berwick Archer was lauded for taking a stance not necessarily in its own direct best interests, but which was certainly for the benefit of East Africa Resources and its other shareholders. A London based investment firm said how Andy himself should be applauded for standing up for what was right and not focusing on short-term returns. Caroline got the credit from Pan Asia, but clearly the feel good factor had long since evaporated.

Andy touched the screen in front of him and it came to life showing the composition of Berwick Archer's Emerging Fund, the flagship product of the Bangkok office. At just over five billion US dollars it was the largest single account run by the Asian business. The research staff in Hong Kong and the Portfolio Control team subjected it to almost daily review, ever since the "Tait Debacle," and James Turner himself went through the holdings every week. Andy called up the latest strategy document released by Charlie's team in Hong Kong. It advocated a switch from retail stocks into infrastructure and listed the recommended buys and sells. Andy chose the stocks he wanted to deal and input the trades to the order model on his computer. The cursor whirled for a couple of seconds and a new portfolio presented itself, showing how the Emerging Fund would look if he were to make the trades. Andy liked what he saw, a portfolio with slightly lower risk but a higher dividend yield. It also showed a greater convergence with the models prepared in Hong Kong. The boys back at base would be delighted with him. With another click of the mouse he placed orders to sell two hundred million dollars worth of stock and to reinvest the proceeds in the construction companies Berwick Archer believed were about to take off all across the developing economies of Asia. It took all of eleven minutes but was pretty much all he had to do for the day. As he picked up his bag to head for the gym he made one call.

"Simon, I need you to talk to the dealers for me."

"Sure Andy, what do you need?"

"I just placed orders for Dao Kin Construction, Samaran Corp and TRP Holdings. They are on the back of some research I got from Pan Asia. Tell the dealers to give them half the trades."

"No problem, will do."

"And Simon… tell them to go through Caroline Chan, she gave me the ideas."

"Done."

"I'm grateful, I really am, but we made a deal, we promised to keep business out of our relationship." Caroline tried to look angry but the relief was clear on her face. Andy desperately wanted to tell her he knew the mess she was in and he genuinely felt his company owed her the business for the way Tait behaved, but then he'd have to admit to checking her phone and looking in her briefcase.

"Caro, I promise it was legitimate. We were switching into construction stocks and I overheard you talking about Samaran and TRP the other day. You were on the phone and you were really positive about them. So you may not have meant to, but you gave me the idea. Fair's fair. The more I look at them, the happier I am with the trades."

It was true he heard her talk about the companies but he was watching football on the TV in his apartment at the time and had no clear recollection of what she said. He was desperate to justify what he'd done and that did the trick. He pressed on with the case for his defence.

"It's out of my hands now. You're on the approved list, so you'll get a decent flow of deals from the fund without me specifying you as the broker."

She smiled and took his hand. "Andy I really am grateful, I just don't want you to deal with my company because we are together. OK?"

"Promise." he said, proffering a crooked little finger. Caroline linked her finger with his and they both tugged gently, before she kissed him softly on the lips.

"So are you impressed with Samaran and TRP?" she asked.

"Sure, they've both grown really fast in Thailand but now they're really well positioned in China too. And they're both backed by that Howard Hughes type character. I guess that's the secret of their success outside Thailand, he's half Thai half Chinese right?"

"Narong Sunarawani, he's quite a guy."
"You know him?"
"Of course."

Andy was astonished, the businessman had a reputation for staying well out of the limelight, delegating the running of his businesses to others who were more comfortable in the glare of an inquisitive business press and the insatiable Thai paparazzi.

"My mother knows him really well. I don't think they've spoken for a while but he still sends me gifts at Christmas and birthdays. I have lunch with him from time to time. Got one coming up I think."

'That's quite a coup. There isn't anyone in the Thai business community who wouldn't want that sort of access, he's a legend."

Caroline picked up her phone and started to flick the screen with an immaculately manicured finger.

"There," she said triumphantly. "Lunch next Friday… join us. He's always telling me I need to find a good man, he'd love to meet you."

# CHAPTER NINE

## Vortex

Sam paced the floor of Chanpol's office. She was seething with frustration.

"I am a graduate of Chulalongkorn University, I have degrees in Finance and Business Administration and you want me to make tea and organise golf games for *farang* who make a fortune playing with other people's money."

"This is our most important project by far and sacrifices have to be made."

"And I have to make those sacrifices?" Her irritation was clear and Chanpol shot her a warning look. She'd been with him since he started out but that did not give her licence to forget who was the boss.

Chanpol's expertise was in setting up complex legal structures, principally designed to get around Thailand's draconian laws on foreign property ownership. Cynics claim the laws provide a cornerstone for wealth creation for Thailand's poorest families.

At the heart of the process is a steady flow of foreign men who come to Thailand looking for love. This is of course a commodity that can, they believe, be purchased at any one of the thousands of go-go bars and nightclubs to be found in cities like Bangkok, Chiang Mai and Pattaya.

"It's like the Gold Rush in nineteenth century America," he'd told Sam. "Thousands of desperate men swept in, searching for a few nuggets of pure gold. A few were rewarded beyond their wildest dreams but most returned home destitute or died in the attempt. The only people who really succeeded were the men who sold maps, donkeys, tents and shovels."

"And sex tourists are the same?" she asked, clearly unconvinced by the argument thus far.

"Millions of men look for the girl of their dreams in a Thai bar, a few live happily ever after with their devoted partner. Most spend what little money they have on a series of women and their extended families. Some will end up on the mortuary slab, their file will say suicide, the local newspapers will gleefully report another "Pattaya Plunge" and the western media will peddle endless rumours about the avaricious ex-wife who is now living with the man they all thought was her uncle. The winners, this time, are the bar and restaurant owners and the hoteliers who provide the stage on which the actors are brought together."

Throw a stick across the street in Pattaya and you will hit at least a couple of guys who have fallen for the most well-worn sales pitch in the world.

"I not want to work bar, but have to take care mama. No choice."

The girl will flutter her eyelashes and deliver that slow, seductive smile that melts your heart at a hundred paces. The man will remember the nights they've spent together and his blood will curdle at the thought of this sweet young thing in the arms of another man.

"I could send you money."

"But I have mama, papa, brother and baby sister. Have to take care."

"I send you twenty five thousand baht."

"Every month?"

"Sure."

"Thank you *teelak*, you have good heart."

A girl only needs two or three guys like this and she's on easy street for as long as her looks hold out. Her family will be thrilled and her Thai boyfriend will give up his job with a motorbike taxi so he can spend more time with his girlfriend's money. The problem with this approach is it works only as long as the bank transfers keep coming. In spite of the horror stories told by many westerners, Thais are genuinely warm, hospitable and generous. When they have money, they will spend it, lend it and share it. Tomorrow will somehow take care of itself. The girl who snares a western "sponsor" or two will generally make sure her friends and family are well looked after and if the cash stops coming there is nowhere to go except back to the bars. Smart girls go for the bigger prize. The law that forbids foreigners from owning freehold land sets up the perfect opportunity for an enterprising lady to relieve her western boyfriend of some serious cash.

A youthful Tanawat Chanpol made his living advising the ladies of Pattaya and Bangkok, on how to complete the purchase of businesses and residential property so the involvement of their western beau could cease on the day the last cash payment hit their accounts. It was a short step from there to establishing an intricate network of holding companies, which allowed wealthy foreigners to own bars, hotels and night-clubs. Anyone who took the time to trace the labyrinthine corporate trail would believe ownership was in the hands of Thais at every level. Chanpol had perfected a structure based on a concept he called leakage. At every step in the corporate chain a little more of the profit was syphoned off and returned to the foreigners who financed the enterprise, less a healthy fee reflecting the tireless efforts Chanpol put in on his clients' behalf. At the end of the line was a series of unsuspecting Thais who were happy to sign a few documents and lend their postal address in return for a nominal fee. Sam had devised the complex financial model that controlled how money flowed through Chanpol's corporate chain, and ensured everyone got their rightful share of the dough. It was her contacts that brought Chanpol his other business interests. She spearheaded the move into what they called logistics. Import and export was by far the most lucrative, but the Berwick Archer contract was too good to turn down. They were told to make it happen, no expense spared. Chanpol was pretty sure Sam's involvement would be over in a couple of months, in the meantime he had to press on without her. The corporate chain Chanpol created was working better than they could ever have anticipated. New businesses could be added, but he and his associates no longer bothered with small bars or individual properties. They were making so much money it really wasn't worth the effort. A tsunami of cash was flowing in from Russia and Eastern Europe and that had brought Chanpol to Walking Street in Pattaya.

It was three days until the opening of the biggest go-go bar and night-club complex in Thailand. A Ukrainian syndicate financed the project and the sheer scale of the enterprise set a host of challenges, even for tried and tested structures that had worked for years. Chanpol came in person to deliver a lengthy document detailing how the profits would be routed back to the Ukrainian and his partners. The man was sipping champagne when he arrived.

"*Kuhn* Tanawat, you are most welcome. Champagne?" Yuri Bezhepov did not wait for an answer before he filled a crystal flute and handed it to the lawyer. Chanpol's client was an unlikely nightclub owner. Well past his sixtieth birthday, his full head of white hair was brushed straight back from his forehead. At little more than five feet seven, he was never going to intimidate anyone physically. Instead he went for the trendy professor look, with half-moon spectacles, over which he peered a little condescendingly at his visitor.

"You start the party a little early *Kuhn* Yuri. I thought you were not opening until Saturday."

"I celebrate every day my friend. Life is good and about to get so much better. You have done an excellent job with the club and my associates are very impressed with your plans for routing our profits offshore."

Chanpol bowed very slightly in what he hoped was a gesture of modest gratitude. The two men raised their glasses and the lawyer touched his to his lips, without taking a sip. He hated the taste of alcohol and despised anyone who drank to excess. To lose control was a cardinal sin in his opinion.

"I'm intrigued by one thing," he said. "The club… Vortex, what made you think of such a name?"

Bezhepov leant forward and beamed at his guest. He was only too happy to explain.

"Many years ago I worked as a scientist for the Soviet government. I was one of the country's leading experts in fluid dynamics and I became fascinated by the vortex. There are so many examples in nature and they are both beautiful and powerful. Everyone has seen a tornado or dust devil on TV, the carnage they can cause is well known. My fascination was born when I observed what happens with a vortex in the ocean."

The Ukrainian was warming to his subject and Chanpol was well practiced in appearing to be utterly fascinated whenever a client spoke. He simply mimed another sip of his champagne and settled back to what he feared might be a very long story indeed.

"Have you ever seen a vortex up close *Kuhn* Tanawat?"

"Errrr, no… I think not," replied the lawyer.

Bezhepov slapped the table in unbridled glee.

"I am certain you have, even today. The water disappearing from your bath-tub is acting under the power of a vortex, albeit a very weak one. Unless you are say… a spider." He paused to make a slow rotating gesture with his finger and as his hand lowered, Chanpol could imagine a spider flailing for its life as it disappeared down the drain. Bezhepov continued.

"In the ocean this same action can result in a ship being dragged to the bottom. They are beautiful things to be observed from a distance, but as you come closer they have the power to drag you in. Slowly at first, then more rapidly as you get to the spinning core, then… it's too late. You are at the bottom of the ocean."

The Ukrainian raised his hands as though waiting to take the applause of his audience. "Did you know, many people believe this is the source of the power of the legendary Bermuda Triangle, that is claimed to have dragged so many helpless souls to their demise?"

"No *Kuhn* Yuri, I was not aware of that. And you think this is a good name for a go-go bar?"

Bezhepov finished his champagne in a single gulp and wiped his lips with a linen cloth the waitress had placed next to the bottle.

"It is just my little joke. I see it as a metaphor for what happens in business and in this business in particular."

"How so?" Chanpol was suddenly intrigued by his client's analogy.

"Tourists come here from all over the world. They read the books, they join the web forums, they see their friends who have been bled dry by a scheming Thai woman. They are determined they are not going to be so foolish, so they observe from a safe distance. Then one night they have a beer too many, they meet a girl who is "different." In a few months they are wondering where their life savings have gone. Then it is their story on the forum and their friends are asking how they could be so foolish and the cycle begins again. That is the power of the vortex."

Chanpol chuckled. "Oh of course… *farang*. They keep their brains in their trousers. They are no match for our women."

"The women too," Bezhepov continued. "They too are subject to its power. Your society gives them a choice, ten hours a day in the fields for a couple of hundred baht or an hour a day, writhing underneath a sweating *farang* in exchange for a reasonable income. They tell themselves they will work as a waitress, they won't go with customers, when they have saved a few baht they will go home and train as a hairdresser. Then they see the go-go dancer with the I-phone and her friend with a new motorbike and they want some of that too. In a few months, she's another scheming, grasping whore who will do anything for a few baht. It's the vortex at work again. The effect is hypnotic, you just have to take a look and before you know it, you are in its grip. Nobody is immune."

"*Kuhn* Yuri, you can expect no more from *farang* and Isaan whores. It is fortunate for us they are so susceptible to your vortex, this is how we make our money."

Chanpol had started to enjoy the Ukrainian's analogy and reminded himself of some of his own acquaintances who were dragged down by either need or greed. He'd been lucky enough to relieve some of them of their assets as they descended.

"And you?" The Ukrainian's question sounded like an accusation.

"Me what?"

"Do you think you are immune?"

"From your vortex?" Chanpol laughed. "It is for *farang* and Isaan buffalo who know no better than to pull in the direction they are told. It is not for people like us. Yuri, you will need another analogy for the people who hold the strings in business. There you can have that one… we are puppeteers, are we not?"

"For a little while maybe," replied the Ukrainian as he considered the lawyer's idea. Then his eyes narrowed and he tapped the air with his index finger. "I think we all have our own personal vortex. The sad old *farang* and the scheming bargirl are like the spider in the bath-tub. The ride is short and unpleasant and the end is quick. For men like you and me, it is more like the great tidal vortices of the ocean. With a little more will, we could navigate around them, but their beauty and power draw us in. We think we can withstand them, but it is not possible. The journey will take longer and will undoubtedly be more invigorating but the end is still the same. The bottom of the ocean."

Chanpol's laugh was a little more nervous than before.

"And you *Kuhn* Yuri, you are subject to this lethal vortex too?"

"Of course, as are you. I am guessing your material wealth is far greater than you ever dreamed when you were a young man."

"For sure, I had no idea how much money I could make in business."

"But you did not stop when you had achieved those dreams… and you never will. That is the vortex. The more you have, the more you want. As you become richer, it merely gives you access to people who are wealthier still and they will have something you want. It is a road that can have no end, because you will never be satisfied. It will destroy you first."

Chanpol's customary composure was about to desert him. It was a favourite pastime of his to reflect on his immense good fortune. The relative poverty of the vast majority of his countrymen was the perfect sauce on an already delicious dish. Having everything you could want was a lot more fun when there were so many people out there with virtually nothing. Bezhepov painted a much less appealing picture. Everyone was damned, but for some the ride took a little longer and was a shade more picturesque. Chanpol suddenly felt like a man about to die in a plane crash, trying to take comfort that, unlike those in the back, he had a seat in First Class.

"And you *Kuhn* Yuri, are you still observing from a safe distance or are you in the grip of the vortex?"

The Ukrainian threw his head back and laughed. Turning to a young waitress standing discreetly out of sight, he clicked his fingers and motioned a hand towards the champagne bottle. She scurried towards the bar to find another.

"My dear friend, I too am on the road to destruction like everyone else. I recognised that a very long time ago."

"And how do you cope with that?"

"I am resigned to my fate. I just intend to enjoy the ride."

# CHAPTER TEN

## The dutiful daughter

"It's nothing really, it's just been one of those days."

Andy watched helplessly as Caroline scurried into the bathroom and closed the door. Things were going so well. Ever since he arranged for the three stock purchases to be made through her at Pan Asia Securities, she'd been on top of the world. Her bosses were apparently delighted and had allocated her some new clients. He saw the list and they were decent institutions likely to give her some good business. As he told her at the time, there was no need for him to give her more trades directly. She was on the approved list for Berwick Archer and as long as she kept in touch with research and new ideas she'd get a good flow of business automatically. The past week was hectic and Andy himself had been out of town. The quarterly portfolio review was scheduled in Hong Kong and he'd flown out the previous Sunday night. They had a lazy and romantic weekend before he headed for the airport. Caroline was full of life saying how she felt she'd really found her feet with Pan Asia at last.

James Turner's parting words were still ringing in Andy's ears when he arrived home in Bangkok that night.

"It's a blip, Andy. I'm sure it is. Your performance has been excellent since Tait left and it will come right. Just for the moment, we've got your portfolios on the watch list. We can't afford to slip behind the competition, so you need turn this round. I'm sure you will, we're all right behind you."

It was a gentle reminder that, as his father always told him, a fund manager is only as good as his last set of performance numbers. His were mediocre to say the least. Turner's promise that they were right behind him should have been comforting, but he couldn't help but recall the comment attributed to a famous British football manager. His team hit a bad run and he was asked about the news his Chairman was right behind him. He replied, "I'd rather have the bastard in front of me, where I can keep an eye on him." The club started its search for a new manager shortly afterwards.

Andy was looking forward to seeing Caroline again. He had no intention of telling her about his own problems, but needed an injection of that joie de vivre that was so evident when he left on Sunday. It was only nine p.m. when he opened the door to his apartment and found the lights out in the hall and the living room. "Marvellous," he muttered to himself, "she knew I was coming back and she's out on the lash." He picked up his mobile to see if there were any messages and, if not, to send a terse reminder that he was back.

"In here," Caroline's voice called from the bedroom. Andy's spirits rose. She'd obviously planned a special homecoming.

If there was a party, he quickly decided, she'd started without him and it had been planned without a lot of thought. Caroline was in bed, but wearing his cotton bathrobe rather than a silk teddy as he hoped. There was wine, but she'd drunk nearly two thirds of the bottle and a cigarette was stubbed out in the bottom of the single glass by the side of the bed. Lying on the carpet was a discarded microwave pizza box. Caroline only went for what she called comfort food when she was really down and he'd never seen her smoke. As he approached the bed, he could see her eyes were red and teary.

"My God what happened?"

"Nothing it's just been a bad day."

"Tell me."

Caroline was initially reluctant to explain what had happened. Then he held her as she explained how her mother called and delivered a virtuoso performance to make her feel guilty. She didn't want to go into detail but it was clear the usual maternal levers had been applied to make Caroline feel like the selfish daughter who abandoned the woman who brought her into the world. They cuddled, he made her laugh with a few stories about his own father and things started to feel better again. He kissed her and she responded eagerly, then her robe fell open and his hand reached inside. They'd been lovers for months but Andy still lost himself every time he touched her. It took him a few minutes to realise she was going through the motions. Her body was available to him but her mind was clearly somewhere else completely. That was when he pulled away and asked what was wrong and she fled to the bathroom.

It felt like an age before she returned and as she crept back into bed the phone rang. Andy picked up the receiver, saying only a brief "hello", before the caller launched into a lengthy discourse. After a full minute, he covered the mouthpiece and turned to Caroline.

"It's your mother, she says she's sorry she hasn't spoken to you for a while, but she spent the weekend in Bali with a friend. She wants to know when you are coming to see her." Andy dropped the phone on the bed and made his own retreat to the sanctuary of the bathroom.

"Andy, I'm so sorry, I didn't want to lie but it was the first thing that came into my head."

"I'm listening, why would you make up a cock and bull story about your mother?" Andy could barely contain his fury at the deception. It never occurred to him that Caroline would lie to him, but now she'd been caught out and he had no idea why she'd make up a story as to why she was upset. It had to be a man, what else would she find so difficult to talk about?

"I thought you wouldn't be home for a while. I didn't think you'd find me like that. I was going to clear up and put on something sexy, make sure I was in the mood... you know."

Andy shook his head. "Yeah great that would have completed the deception. I'd never have known you were hiding something from me. It's a real shame I spoiled that one."

"No, no that came out all wrong. I just didn't want to burden you with it, that's all." Caroline looked like she was going to cry again.

"With what?" Andy gripped the edge of the duvet, knowing that if he didn't do something with his hands he might place them round his girlfriend's perfect throat. "Is it a man?"

Caroline looked genuinely shocked. "No, no, absolutely not."

"Then what? What's so terrible you can't talk to me about it?"

Their eyes met briefly and then she shook her head and turned away.

"For fuck's sake." Andy was almost out of the room before Caro called him back.

"Andy, wait, I'll tell you. I'm just so ashamed."

"Just tell me."

"It's work, I can't hack it. They've given me until the end of the month to turn things round or I'm out. I didn't want to tell you. It's all so easy for you, you're a natural at this game and I'm really struggling. I thought if I told you, you wouldn't respect me."

A wave of relief flowed through Andy, closely followed by a large shot of guilt. Like most men, the thing he feared above all else was infidelity. As soon as he started to think his girlfriend might have been unfaithful, he felt like his whole world was falling apart. Any problem seemed insignificant by comparison. He'd not told Caroline about his own issues at work and now she was telling him she felt inadequate by comparison. How could he criticise her for not opening up, when he failed to do it himself? Andy's earlier anger evaporated and all he wanted to do was to get to the heart of what was troubling his girlfriend and make it go away.

"Caro, sweetheart, how can you have problems at work. You were the star performer last month. You showed me the reports, I heard Daniel sing your praises only two weeks ago. They love you."

Caroline shrugged, "That's ancient history, they wiped the slate clean. I had a great month and all it's done is raise their expectations."

"You can't be serious, you're their third biggest producer with the stuff you get from us and your new clients.   That's serious money."

"They're taking that for granted now. They reckon they'd get that business with or without me. I've got a couple of clients where I'm way below target and they say I'm not coming up with investment ideas either. They hired a guy to assess our performance and he keeps talking about added value. He says I'm not delivering."

When Andy first met Caroline she was the epitome of poise and confidence, she had everything any young ambitious woman could want. Suddenly she looked helpless and vulnerable, trying desperately to make her way in a man's world with everything stacked against her.

"So what's this guy like, the one who's on your case?"

"He's a total creep. I reckon he really gets off on the power they've given him. I wouldn't let him babysit my daughter... if I had one that is."

Another knot formed in Andy's gut. "Has he hit on you?"

"No... no... well not really. He said we should have lunch... but I'll just fob him off. That's not a problem."

Andy disagreed. "I'll kill him, what's his name?"

"Andy, leave it. He's on a power kick and in the end he's right. I can't do this, it's better I do something else." Caroline looked completely resigned to her fate, as though getting the secret off her chest somehow made everything alright.

"Caro, you can't let a little shit like that beat you. It's not going to happen. If you decide to walk away that's fine, I'll support you every step of the way but you can't let someone like that drive you out."

Andy's fists were clenched and it was fortunate for Caroline's office nemesis that he wasn't in the room. He'd be a dead man.

"Andy, there's nothing you can do. I wish I'd told you before. I can't believe how understanding you've been. You're an amazing man." She leaned forward and kissed him softly on the lips.

"Just tell me about your clients, what's the problem?"

"I came up with a great idea about three months ago and bought some stock for two really important clients. The idea turned out to be a little less great than I'd thought. Now I couldn't give it away. Even if I could get back what I paid for it, the clients would be back in good shape, but it's not going to happen."

"How much cash are we talking about?"

"About five million US dollars, all told. I know, it's peanuts but it's the private accounts of a couple of the boss's friends. It sticks out like a sore thumb."

"OK, and what about the other issue. They want ideas right?"

Caro nodded. "It's the whole 'value added' thing. Everything I've recommended for the last six months has gone down as soon as we buy it. They make jokes about it in the office. Someone said we could make a fortune if we did the exact opposite of everything I suggest. Most of the ideas have turned out fine within a couple of weeks but they focus on the short-term dip."

Andy smiled and took his girlfriend's hands in his. "We can fix this, you just have to do exactly what I say."

It was almost inevitable that Andy Duncan would receive a phone call from his father the following morning. He almost confessed to the felony before his father said a single word, he was so certain the older man would already be aware of his plan.

"Andy. It's me son. How are you?"

"Fine Dad, anything wrong?"

"What should be wrong? Just calling to remind you of your aunt's birthday. You know what she's like if she doesn't hear from you. Send her a card or something won't you?"

"Yeah Dad.., for sure. I'll get onto it now.

Andy's heart was still pounding long after the call ended and he dwelt on how he was about to do a couple of deals that were in nobody's interests but Caroline's. When Andy told Simon to put the last set of trades through her firm, it was a victimless crime. Another broker lost out on a bit of commission but they'd never know.

The solution to Caro's latest problem was a much more dangerous proposition. It involved using his client's money to rescue her ailing portfolios. The Berwick Archer Emerging Fund would buy out the stock for which she paid five million dollars, even though it might be all but worthless. Andy would then take a deal he planned and share a little of the profit with her clients. He managed billions of dollars in client assets and nobody would be any the wiser. For his own accounts it was the equivalent of the loss experienced when a maid empties the loose change from the pockets of a wealthy guest in a five star hotel. For Caro it would be a major lifeline that could put her career back on track and get that little weasel at Pan Asia off her case.

Andy picked up the phone to Simon Tudor.

"Si, I've decided to punt a bit of the Emerging Fund, some really small holdings. I'll see how they go and if it works out I'll do a bit more later in the week."

"Of course Andy, what do you want me to do?"

Andy hesitated; once he gave the instruction there'd be no going back. "Caroline at Pan Asia gave me a couple of ideas over the phone just now. I'll stick them in an e-mail. Put them through at the prices I give you. There's no market in the stock and I don't want to place it with the dealers because as soon as someone sees us sniffing around, the price will move against us. I reckon she's doing us a favour here." Andy realised he was saying too much, he didn't need to justify his actions to a junior. "Just do it, OK?"

"No problem, it's done."

As he cut the call, Andy realised he'd been holding his breath and his chest was getting tight. He emptied the contents of his briefcase on the desk to find his inhaler. He'd read every book of substance about securities fraud and this barely registered compared to the ones that made the news. Famous Wall Street names swindled their clients out of billions and some became so famous that, like Charles Ponzi, the scam went down in history with their name attached. If a Ponzi fraud rated ten on the scale of wrongdoing, what Andy Duncan had just done was barely a two. What he was about to do next, however, easily hit five. Caro was all set to complete her part of the plan at eight-thirty that morning. Andy waited until just before lunch to do his. For nearly four hours he trawled through e-mails and played endless games of on-line chess to take his mind off what he was about to do. At twelve twenty-five he picked up the phone to Simon Tudor again.

"Si, I've got some more deals for the Emerging Fund. There are four stocks with a hundred million US in each. We can fund half of it from cash but you'll need to sell that government stock we talked about last week. I'm loading the orders onto the system now. OK?"

"Got it Andy." The young assistant was delighted to be moving some proper money around. The deals with Pan Asia that Andy instructed earlier were done and forgotten.

Again, Andy cut the call and pulled up details of the four large industrial companies, headquartered in Bangkok, Vientiane, Kuala Lumpur and Seoul. A plan to do the deals had been agreed with Charlie's Angels the previous week in Hong Kong. They decided to hold off until after the weekend as there was some unexpected volatility in the market and they wanted that to settle down. The four deals were exactly in line with investment strategy and everyone involved was certain they'd pay off well for the clients. What had not been planned was that Andy Duncan would reveal the names of two of the companies to his tearful girlfriend the night before. She had the opportunity to buy five million dollars worth of both stocks for her clients before Berwick Archer placed an order. By the end of the day, everyone would know the Berwick Emerging Fund owned a large stake in each of the four companies. The price would rise substantially on the back of the boost from Andy's original purchases. Caroline Chan's clients would make a sizeable profit and her reputation for recommending stocks that immediately tumbled in value would be history. The Emerging Fund would only suffer a loss if Caro's purchase caused the market price of the stock to increase. Even if it did, it would be pennies in the context of the deals he placed. Only the unsuspecting investors who sold their stock to Pan Asia would suffer a loss. They'd never know the cards had been stacked against them.

An intense feeling of nausea dogged him for the rest of the day and only as he got back to his apartment did his guts start to settle. Once again the lights were out in the hall and the living room, once again he heard the voice from the bedroom. "I'm in here." Caro lay on the bed but the cotton bathrobe was nowhere to be seen, she wore only a simple string of pearls he'd bought for her as a birthday present. Champagne was on ice on the bedside table, two glasses were filled to half way. Caroline knelt in front of her boyfriend and started to work on his trouser belt. As soon as he was naked from the waist down she took some of the champagne into her mouth but didn't swallow. In seconds the last thing he'd be thinking of was business but, at that moment, he came to terms with what he'd done.

He'd always been aware he was responsible for vast amounts of money, but it all felt so abstract before. He could see the Emerging Fund was valued at over five billion US dollars but it was just a number on a screen. After all, you couldn't even picture what that amount of money would look like in cash. It always felt that it was like playing a huge game of Monopoly, until today. What he'd done was exactly the sort of thing his father was employed to deter and detect, it undermined the basis on which everyone dealt in the market, it was a shameless abuse of his position. On the other hand, it was the first time he felt like he'd done anything real, anything that made a genuine impact on what was happening around him, the first time he'd exercised any real power. Then he realised the feeling of nausea was long gone, there was a new sensation in his gut and it felt good, really good.

## A one season wonder

"Andy, I thought you understood the pressures here. The guys in London allocated three hundred million from their pension clients to the Emerging Fund, in anticipation of that recovery we talked about. You're off another fifty points since then. I've got Clarke himself screaming down the phone at me. And you know what he thinks of the Bangkok office, every time he hears the name he thinks of his daughter with her legs in the air." James Turner was in full flow, which paradoxically was a relief. Andy had no idea what he'd say when the senior man stopped talking. It was so easy at the start, the profits just flowed and there was always someone above him to take the flak when the bosses got upset. Now he was on his own and feeling very lonely indeed.

"How the fuck did I ever get into this mess in the first place?" Andy startled himself, for a moment he thought he might have said the words out loud, but as he regained a tiny part of his composure, he realised the Bull was still raging and didn't sound like he was about to stop any time soon.

Turner once confided that, had he discovered his passion; skiing, before he started making money in the City of London, he'd be a ski bum not an investor. Andy Duncan was one of dozens of employees who experienced the Bull's rants and wished he'd hit the slopes for the first time when he was a toddler. It would have saved them so much grief.

The essence of James Turner's message was, "your performance sucks, you will sort it out or we will find someone who can." Like many people at the very top of the investment industry, Turner believed he should never use only a dozen or so words, when he had the time to deliver a fully-fledged sermon. There'd be anecdotes from his own years as a junior fund manager, how he turned around a hopeless position with a combination of courage, guile, intuition and sheer bloody willpower. He cajoled, he encouraged, he threatened and then he took the subject of his ire under his wing and did the old thing about how he mustn't let the firm down, he mustn't let Turner down, he mustn't let his colleagues down but most of all he mustn't let himself down. Andy had seen it before but mercifully, until now, he'd never been subjected to the full Turner treatment himself, and he reckoned there was still some way to go. The Bull was telling some story of a client who was about to fire the firm just after the crash of 1987 and how he, Turner, had saved the day. Somehow he sounded like he was talking about the D-Day landings, relating how he took Omaha Beach single-handed while the rest of his battalion was still working out how to get off the landing craft. Andy decided it was safe to tune out for a bit and try to determine exactly how he got into this mess. It was hard not to think back to the dinner with his father at the Savoy. All he wanted was a cash advance to enable him to travel the world, in return he agreed to spend three months as an intern at Berwick Archer. In retrospect, it suddenly felt like some sort of Faustian pact. It was clearly not his father's intention to lure him into being a fund manager, he wanted his son to have a "proper" job with substance, maybe like his own. His father's words came back to him.

"Andy, I want you to see what the business world is like. Three months with a good name on your c.v. will be really powerful. One of the big accounting firms will snap you up with your degree and experience like that. It's a great qualification, and you won't have to specialise for another few years."

At the time, Andy just nodded, thinking it a price worth paying for a year travelling the world at his father's expense. Victor wasn't finished.

"There are plenty of young men at Berwick Archer who don't have the sort of grounding an accounting qualification will give you. Some of them make a lot of money for a few years but it normally catches up with them after a while. Then they have nothing to fall back on. You can't get yourself into that trap. It's not your thing anyway, they're generally loud, brash and obsessed with money."

Andy realised his father probably had a picture of Brad Tait in his head when he used those words.

"They think they know it all, but it's not as easy as it looks. Anyone can make money when the market is rising; it's when you get a bit of volatility that it sorts the wheat from the chaff. Then you realise for half these guys it's been more luck than judgment. Three months later they're selling Skodas from a garage forecourt in Romford."

Maybe that was it; maybe Andy's run was luck not judgement. He and Tait used to while away endless hours in the bars of Bangkok showing off their encyclopaedic but generally pointless knowledge of English football. Inane riddles were circulated by e-mail and the men tortured themselves trying to work out which club names start and end with the same letter or the only club with a name that starts with three consonants. A whole evening was lost when Andy discovered there was only one English club name containing none of the letters of the word "mackerel". There was a brief debate about the type of person who thinks up questions like that, then working out the answer became a battle to the death. Tait flatly refused to give up until he got it. The fact that he only screamed "Swindon Town", seconds after he disappeared to the toilet with his phone was the subject of a further lengthy debate on cheating and how it was ruining every aspect of the game of football.

The riddle that popped into Andy's head, as Turner droned on in the background, had kept the two men amused for a couple of hours on one of their last nights out in Bangkok. They tried to list as many "one season wonders" as they could. These were footballers who took the league by storm for a year, sometimes for only a few games, sometimes for only a couple of hours. They'd be lauded by the press, pursued by wannabe models and offered eye-watering sums to wear a certain watch, drive a particular make of car or tell the story of how they made it against all the odds. The national team manager would be interrogated as to why the player was not an automatic choice for his country, and the internet would be awash with stories of an imminent transfer to Real Madrid. By the start of the following season, he'd be training with the reserves and the only people who'd remember his name would be drunks in bars playing trivia games.

A cold chill spread through Andy's gut. Maybe he was a one season wonder, it had all come so easily and now it would all be taken away. His father's words were ringing in his ears, "more luck than judgement." Andy started to wonder whether he'd be selling cars in Romford in three months time. Then he realised… he knew nothing about cars.

"I asked a question. Is that fucking well clear?" Turner's voice brought him back to the present with a jolt.

"Yes James, crystal clear. Absolutely."

The line went dead. James Turner could go to his meeting, certain that Andy knew exactly what was expected of him and Andy could stare at his screen and watch the price of the core holdings in the Emerging Fund drift a little lower as morning trading picked up.

"I'm fucked," he thought.

The only thing that made any sense in his life was his relationship with Caro. It crossed his mind to suggest they chuck it all in and go and live a simple life on Koh Samui or in Hua Hin, but he was realistic enough to know they were still in the foothills of their relationship. A change like that would put them under too much pressure. He needed to get some cash under his belt, then they could think about taking it easy. At the very least they could start their own business. He'd be free of the wrath of the Bull and she wouldn't have some little scumbag lecturing her about value added whilst trying to get a look at her tits. They'd given up trying to keep their relationship secret, which was a huge relief. He couldn't be seen to direct business to her firm any more but she was flying pretty high at Pan Asia again, so there was no need. It gave him a huge buzz whenever they were out together. There were many beautiful, stylish women in Bangkok but Caro had charisma, a presence that drew people towards her. When asked about John F Kennedy, people said the key to his charm lay in his eyes. He developed the knack of making anyone he spoke to feel like they were the most important human being alive. It's an irresistible gift. Andy loved Caro's eyes. She had that same ability to make him feel, with one look, as though he was the only person in the room and she was completely captivated by his presence. He and Tait often dismissed a pretty girl with the line, "the light's on, but there's no one at home." One look into their eyes would indicate that if they could locate a single thought in their head it would be very lonely. For Andy it was a terrible turn off, Tait saw it as an essential qualification to become a victim of The Bet. Caro's eyes sparkled with life, intelligence, wit and mischief. It was truly intoxicating.

As promised, Andy and Caroline lunched with Narong Sunarawani, the legendary Thai businessman. It was reported he'd been a very accomplished sportsman as a young man and he still looked physically powerful. Sunarawani was a little shorter than Andy had expected and carried maybe ten kilos in excess weight. His face was nearly square and his hair almost too black. On a westerner of a similar age, nearly sixty, it would certainly have come out of a bottle. On a Thai, it might be natural, but it was unlikely. His skin was a little rough as though he'd had a bad case of acne as a teenager and the scars were still there. Andy noticed Sunarawani's habit of touching his cheek every so often as though he was aware of the imperfection and it still troubled him.

Sunarawani treated Caroline like a favourite niece and she was the devoted girlfriend, saying little of her own achievements but never missing an opportunity to talk about her man's astonishing success since he arrived in Bangkok. It was clear Sunarawani was weighing up the latest contender for Caro's affections, deciding whether he was worthy of this extraordinary girl, the daughter he never had. Andy knew he was being evaluated and he could not think of another test he was more eager to pass.

Sunarawani was respected throughout Thailand as an honest and decent man, although he had a reputation for being ruthless when required. The losers, when he went into battle, were usually western firms and he was known to have a huge nationalistic streak when doing business. Many thought he should run for political office but he shunned the media and rarely made any form of public statement. It simply added to his mystique. Andy was honoured to be in his presence and astonished the man should be so approachable. Like Andy himself, Sunarawani loved golf and spoke knowledgeably about the sport. The lunch was going better than he could ever have hoped and they were discussing the emergence of some genuinely world-class Thai golfers.

"A friend told me the other day about Thongchai Jaidee," Andy said, referring to Thailand's number one male golfer.

"A wonderful player," said Sunarawani. "I would love to see him win a major tournament."

"I'm sure he will," Andy replied. "I was told he used to be in the army."

"Indeed, he served his country with great distinction."

"Until that incident with the camouflage training."

Sunarawani leant forward and looked distinctly uncomfortable, was this about to be a slight on a national treasure?

Andy pressed on. "I just heard his commanding officer was concerned he spent too much time practicing golf and not enough on military matters."

Out of the corner of his eye, he could see Caro shifting awkwardly in her seat. He was doing so well and now her boyfriend would blow it with a stupid comment about a Thai sporting superstar. Sunarawani stroked the rough skin close to his right ear. The businessman looked deeply troubled and Andy wondered whether he'd pushed it too far.

"His commanding officer called him in and said he'd not seen him in camouflage training that morning… *Kuhn* Jaidee thanked him for the compliment."

There was a pause whilst Sunarawani looked at Andy with his mouth open, he turned to Caro and then back to the Englishman, and then roared with laughter.

"An excellent story, I look forward to sharing it with my friends."

He stood suddenly and a waiter appeared from nowhere to pull back his chair. Sunarawani reached to shake Andy's hand and turned towards Caro.

"I think you have chosen well, Jeab. And a golfer too, he must join me at Siam one weekend, then we can all have lunch together again."

Andy was pretty sure he'd passed the test but glanced at Caro to see her reaction. Sunarawani was on his way to the door with a retinue of bowing waiters trailing in his wake before she smiled and nodded. The invitation to Siam was a real coup, it was such an exclusive club there were rumours it wasn't a golf club at all but a secret military facility financed by the Thai government and the CIA. In an industry populated by people for whom one-upmanship was an Olympic sport, he did not know a single person who dared to claim they'd played there. So little was known about the club, to claim to have been there was a little risky, you might be talking to someone who really had the inside track. Andy was also thrilled to have discovered Caro was Jeab to her closest friends. It's Thai custom to use nicknames and although usually given at birth, they're often surprisingly apt. Caro's name translated as "baby chicken." It appeared that she might not have been such a beautiful baby, however she turned out in the long run.

It had been an amazing day. He wondered what his father was doing as he sipped Cote Rotie, Chateau d'Ampuis with Thailand's most famous and elusive businessman. He suspected Victor might be sitting at his desk with a sandwich, poring over a report that would make him tear his hair out at the latest excesses of the fund managers. There was little chance he'd be looking at Andy's own portfolios; they were in line with all the firm's risk and compliance parameters. Their problem was that when the market fell they fell faster, and when the market recovered they trailed listlessly in its wake. Nothing for the firm's Risk Director to worry about, issues like that went straight to the Bull himself to sort out. That was why James Turner spent thirty minutes of his valuable day making sure Andy was crystal clear about what was expected of him but all Andy himself could remember of the conversation was the last five seconds.

Two weeks had passed since the lunch with Sunarawani and it now felt like part of ancient history. What would happen when the great man discovered Andy was a one-season wonder? That he was in the deepest shit of his life and had no idea which way to dig. Caroline still thought Andy walked on water.

Once their relationship was public knowledge, Andy could no longer place trades with her directly. She'd given him one last idea for an investment in some infrastructure businesses and he placed the order without even looking at what they did.

"Daniel thinks they're a steal. They don't do anything glamorous, they make things people don't really think about being needed for big construction projects. One does traffic cones, another makes those prefabricated buildings the men use between shifts. The best one makes some sort of waterproof sealant, I don't really understand what it does, but Daniel says..."

"Sweetheart, they sound like a great opportunity, how about you knock me up a note and I'll go through it with Simon tomorrow?"

Again it was a pittance in the context of the fund as a whole and she wouldn't stop wittering about what a great idea they were. It was the easiest way to shut her up. Andy was totally consumed with the problems in his biggest portfolio and talk about anything else was a distraction. The following morning he placed orders with Pan Asia for all three stocks without mentioning a thing to Simon Tudor. He simply didn't have the time.

"Don't forget your dinner." Sam appeared in the doorway, clearly on her way home for the evening.

"And James will be here on the tenth of next month, he said he discussed it all with you during your call."

A trace of a smile appeared briefly at the corner of her mouth. Andy could not confirm or deny what was discussed during the call, he was present in body only. The news Turner would be in Bangkok soon after the month end was no great surprise. In the absence of an investment miracle it would probably herald Andy's final day as an employee of the firm. He made a mental note to check his stock of inhalers and put in a bulk order if necessary.

"Good luck with this." Sam dropped a bound report on his desk, once again with the faintest trace of a smile. It was either typical Thai courtesy or sinister German schadenfreude. Andy had little choice but to give her the benefit of the doubt. The cover had the name Ben Worrapon in large letters, underneath were the words, "Quarterly Portfolio Report, presented by Andrew Duncan."

"Oh fuck… when?"

"Now, he's your dinner engagement."

Andy could have wept. The document was a thing of beauty. There were graphs, pie charts, sectoral analysis, competitor comparisons and detailed projections based on the exhaustive analysis undertaken by the Research team in Hong Kong. Only two copies had been produced, one for him and one already in the hands of his client. No expense had been spared in the publication of the document, but its message was summarised in one simple graph that appeared on page three. Markets had been rough, but those who held their nerve and were invested in products that matched the movement of the big markets probably enjoyed a decent return. Anyone invested in Andy's Emerging Fund, would have been better off cashing in at the start of the quarter and putting the money under the bed. Ben Worrapon was not as rich as he'd been three months ago and Andy would spend the next three hours explaining why.

**A rude awakening**

Her face was almost heart-shaped. It was impossible to tell what her eyes were like, they were shut and he had no recollection from the previous night. She was almost certainly Thai, but probably from a wealthy *HiSo…* High Society, Bangkok family. Her skin was too light to be from the poor northeast of the country. That's the point of origin for most Thai girls who end up in the bed of a stranger who has absolutely no memory of what happened the night before. The clothes scattered across the carpet looked like they were straight from the racks of the top designers and the studs in her perfect ears appeared to be real gold and genuine diamonds. She was exquisite and very young. It offered some comfort that Thai women always looked a few years younger than they really are, until around the age of about forty. Then the pendulum generally swings decisively and savagely in the other direction. This girl was one of those cute little things that populated the front page of the magazines aimed at teenagers, or one of the endless TV commercials celebrating the magical effect of the latest skin whitening cream. He stared at her face for at least two minutes but it was like he'd never seen her before. Maybe they met in the hotel bar and she needed a place to stay, maybe nothing happened between them. Then he realised he didn't even recognise the hotel room. The girl shifted in her sleep and a wave of relief passed through him. She'd been so still, she might have stopped breathing. There had to be some prompt that would make him remember, something that would make him recall how he ended up in bed with a young girl he was certain he'd never seen before. As she turned onto her back, he pulled back the duvet. She was naked and he felt a brief stab of guilt at the surge of arousal he felt as he looked at her. The girl was a little more curvaceous than strictly fashionable. Her breasts were large for a Thai girl but perfect, there was a modest fold of flesh around her stomach that might have had a lot of girls reaching for the diet pills or heading for the stairmaster. A soft, sparse collection of dark hairs between her legs suggested this was probably not someone who sold sex for a living. This girl would have thought a razor was for masculine use only.

Outsiders think of Thailand as a hot bed of promiscuity where everyone is at it like dogs on heat. The reality is a stark contrast. Dating amongst *HiSo* Thais has an etiquette that would be considered antediluvian in the West. Sure, you'll still get laid, but you have to put a bit of effort into it first. It's not the inevitable return for a couple of Bacardi Breezers and a bag of chips on the way home. Thousands of men wake up in Thailand, look at the person next to them in bed and wonder why they did it. This was a case of wondering how it could have been possible. She did not look like the kind of girl who'd dive into bed with a man she barely knew and who, in all probability, wouldn't have been able to get it up anyway. He managed to hold the illusion that nothing had happened between them for exactly eleven seconds. That's how long it took to spot the stain on the sheets. The "wet spot" is an endless source of amusement or tension between lovers and whilst there might be the odd argument as to who sleeps in it, there won't have been too many occasions when one will have caused such utter dismay. There was no doubt about the source of the stain on the sheet, it caused his stomach to somersault because it contained rather a lot of blood.

Little snippets of the night before were coming back to him, but still no recollection of where he picked up what appeared to be a dangerously young girl. He headed for the shower and in a matter of minutes was experimenting as to whether boiling hot or icy cold was the best recipe for jogging his brain into some sort of life. Eventually satisfied he had a basic recall of everything that happened up to around midnight, he resigned himself to the fact that only one person could throw any light on the rest of the night. He made a cursory effort at drying his back and legs then threw on a huge fluffy bathrobe that was hanging on the back of the door. He'd barely decided what to say, by way of a very belated introduction to the girl in his bed, as he opened the door.

The bedroom was empty. The girl had gone and the only indication anyone else had been in the room was a stained bed sheet. He was suddenly grateful; otherwise he might have thought his mind had unravelled completely.

"Oh my God, I don't believe it."

Suddenly the pieces all started to fall into place. Someone told him about a mate who picked up a girl in a bar in Bangkok. He thought the night was going perfectly, but woke up alone in his hotel and his laptop, passport, wallet and phone had all disappeared, along with the girl. At some stage she slipped something into his drink. One of his colleagues had tried to top that with the story of a guy who woke up with his side packed in ice and a message from a courteous thief saying she and her colleague had removed a kidney.

Andy had been relatively fortunate. The girl must have fallen asleep herself and then waited for him to go to the shower before she made her escape. He cursed again as he went in search of his jacket and briefcase so he could discover exactly what had been stolen.

# CHAPTER ELEVEN

## Karaoke

"*Chok dee kap.*" The two men raised their glasses and then downed the fine amber liquid in a single gulp. Song had been a generous host, but then he'd made his excuses as usual. The two men were certain he suffered from the Cinderella effect. The fairy tale princess had until midnight before it all went wrong, Song always made sure he was gone by ten p.m. Nobody could recall an evening when he stayed later, nor could you find a single soul who could testify to him ever being drunk. His guests had started with beer, drained two bottles of fine white burgundy over dinner and now the litre bottle of Jack Daniels at their table was half empty.

"Maybe he does the night shift at KFC," ventured Karapong, he giggled but was slightly shocked at his own display of disrespect. He looked at Boonamee to see whether his drinking partner would back him up.

"No, no... he's way too rich for that. At ten o'clock he changes into another being entirely," came the reply.

"My Buddha, what sort of creature do you think he becomes?" Karapong asked in a conspiratorial whisper.

Boonamee leaned forward and pretended to look around to see who might be listening. He belched slightly as he tried to formulate the sentence.

"Maybe he turns into a human being." The two men roared with laughter and Boonamee punched the air in triumph at his joke.

"He certainly wouldn't want anyone to see that happen."

There was a sharp knock at the door and both men jumped. For one second they were certain that Song had returned to wreak a terrible vengeance for their levity. Karapong decided he needed to rescue the situation to be on the safe side.

"To *Kuhn* Song, a fine man and an example to us all." He raised his glass and Boonamee almost dislocated a finger in his haste to reciprocate. A young Thai girl appeared at the door with another bottle of whisky and some fresh ice, she wouldn't meet the eyes of either man but waited until Karapong waved her away before she left the room.

"Pretty girl," said Boonamee. "Are you sure you want to send her away?"

Karapong grinned and tried to manoeuvre his massive frame out of the plush leather sofa. Boonamee came to his rescue and poured another shot of whisky into his glass.

"Only for the time being, I've told Dah to put a reserved sticker on her for later. There are plenty more for you to choose from."

"Tempting, but I'll pass." Boonamee saw it as a badge of honour that he didn't pay for sex. It never occurred to him that many of the girls who went to his bed, did so because they were frightened of him, or because it was the only way they could secure some favour they desperately needed.

"So what do you think of the club?" Karapong was keen to show off his new venture and when Song left them in Bangkok, he called his driver and the two men headed south to the karaoke bar a few miles outside Pattaya.

"Impressive. It's yours?"

"Fifty-fifty with a cousin. It was his until a few months ago, then he got into some difficulty and I bought in. Business has been good and I have *Kuhn* Song to thank for that… and you my friend. I am told it was you who dispatched that tiresome little farmer who got lucky with the lottery."

"Lucky? I think the man himself would disagree. We were happy to help. So where did you get the girls for this place, they're quite special."

Karapong looked quizzical.

"You really don't remember, it was one of your deliveries. Song said you oversaw it all yourself, I was delighted. Our little waitress came in that night. I was lucky enough to sample the goods before our customers got their hands on her but she's still my favourite. Maybe until you make your next delivery." The fat man licked his lips as though he remembered how she tasted and his appetite was reawakened.

The alcohol was taking its toll but Boonamee gradually realised what Karapong was talking about. That night in the aircraft hangar, they made four deliveries and one had been to a karaoke bar outside Pattaya. He remembered how the men sat around looking at the photos and one caught their attention. They all agreed she was the pick of the crop. It was hard to believe she was the same girl who brought the whisky. Pretty for sure, but the girl at the hangar was full of life, the waitress looked like she was sleepwalking, a timid little creature who discovered life was a battle and had meekly accepted defeat. There had been something about her that night that made her stand out from the crowd. The picture on the screen had sparked something in his mind, a memory he tried to blot out. When the bus arrived and she stepped off, he knew from a distance which girl was Nok, which girl was cargo number 97. It wasn't just the face or the body, it the way she carried herself, she had poise, confidence, vitality. It had all been knocked out of her and as he looked at the man seated alongside him, he knew exactly how that happened. Back then it was like looking at a completely different woman, like looking at the girl he'd walked out on back in Korat, Pom, the girl he abandoned because Song decided she was dispensable. Boonamee stumbled towards the door muttering an awkward thank you to his host and headed for the street. He had to get back to his apartment, away from the woman that reminded him of Pom.

The dream did not come until it was nearly light outside. It wasn't the same this time. He was standing outside his apartment when she walked past him. It was Pom for sure. He'd never forget how her hair moved when she walked. Boonamee called after her but she kept going, he ran but couldn't close the gap. She appeared to be in no hurry but the faster he ran, the further away she appeared to get. He tried desperately to think where she was going but she showed no urgency at all, like she was out for an afternoon stroll. Then he realised, she was heading for the bus station. He had to stop her from getting on that bus, if he failed then he knew Karapong would be waiting at the end of the journey and he'd do to her what he did to Nok. He could see the signs for the bus station, sweat poured through his clothes as his legs pumped harder and harder, but Pom was only slightly closer. He knew he was losing her and the entrance to the bus station was in sight.

"No Pom, please don't do it. Don't get on the bus."

He was closing now, her head turned slightly and she paused as though she recognised him. Then she smiled and he was sure he'd get there in time to stop her getting on the bus. His lungs were burning, his heart felt like it might burst inside his chest and it was all he could do to keep his legs moving. She was no more than a few feet from the door of the bus and he was right behind her… he was going to make it.

Boonamee reached out, grabbed her shoulder and she turned and smiled. It wasn't Pom; it was Nok, the waitress from the karaoke bar. But she still let him pull her into his arms, he could feel her hair against his face and the warmth of her body enveloped him. Her full breasts pressed into his chest, the long mane of perfect jet-black hair tumbled over her shoulders and he could feel her breathe deeply. A "sniff kiss" or "*hom khaem*", it felt as though she was inhaling his soul. She was safe. That was when he felt the sharp sting a centimetre below his rib cage. Nok's face still nuzzled against his cheek as he felt the stiletto blade slide deep into his heart. He was falling and the lights around him faded to black. Then he heard the words he'd come to expect.

"Oh my Buddha, so much blood. I've never seen so much blood."

## CHAPTER TWELVE

**The morning after**

"Mr Duncan asked me to call from Berwick Archer, he fears he may have left without paying his bill."

"Not at all. Your colleague asked us to charge the company account when he checked in. There was nothing for him to do when he left."

"He asked me to ensure you reserve the same room for his next stay. Is that possible? Unfortunately he didn't mention which one it was, Obviously you have it on file."

"Of course sir, I'll update his profile and we'll make sure room 716 is requested automatically when he books with us again. Can I help you with anything else?"

"That's fine thanks."

Andy Duncan cut the call and tried to work out whether what he'd heard should quell or feed the advanced state of paranoia he'd developed since waking up. He'd fled the hotel within minutes of realising that the girl had gone. Under the circumstances the last thing he wanted to do was walk up to reception and ask if there was a bill to pay, on the other hand he didn't want to risk the hotel claiming he failed to settle the account. The call allowed him to ask the question without matching his name to the number of the room, the clerk did that for him. She also confirmed he must have had his wits about him to some degree as otherwise he wouldn't have made the request to charge the room to the company account. One of the scenarios he considered as he dressed that morning, involved the girl dragging him into the elevator having paid for the room in cash. Clearly, that hadn't happened, he'd been in charge when they entered the hotel.

Andy thought again about the girl. She was extraordinary, but since he got together with Caro, he never even contemplated sleeping with another woman. When he saw the empty bed that morning, his initial reaction was anger and frustration that he'd been robbed, quickly followed by relief he hadn't willingly cheated on his girlfriend. Clearly he'd been drugged.

Now he discovered that not only had he organised the room, he charged it to the company. He slammed a fist onto the desk in frustration that he could remember nothing from the point at which he bade farewell to Worrapon. The robbery theory was consigned to the bin anyway, so Andy was clutching at straws. Once he realised the girl had left, he made straight for his briefcase. It was on the desk in the corner of the hotel room. The laptop was inside as he left it. His jacket was draped over the chair, his phone and wallet were exactly where he always put them and credit cards and cash were intact. There was only one message on his phone… from Caroline.

"No prob hun - cya tomorrow x"

It was timed at one twenty-five that morning. Immediately before it was the message to which she was clearly responding, "Tough night, v. pissed, crashing with Si." As far as he could remember, he hadn't seen Simon Tudor since he left the office the previous night. When Andy arrived that morning, there was no indication they'd seen each other in the intervening period, let alone a suggestion they were together at the end of a drunken evening.

Andy's last recollection of the night before was of a late night drink at Ben Worrapon's private club. The evening had gone far better than he could ever have imagined. Sam booked a table at the ludicrously expensive Japanese restaurant in the basement of the JW Marriott and the two men spent no more than thirty minutes discussing the investment portfolio. Worrapon appeared to accept, at face value, the assurance that Andy knew exactly what was wrong and could fix it. Charlie's Angels in Hong Kong decreed a switch into infrastructure stocks and out of financials, he'd reduce the fund's exposure to the Euro and they were going to use derivatives to increase the weighting towards the major Asian markets. Worrapon was more concerned about whether the tuna sashimi was fatty enough and whether the service staff had forgotten the order of lobster ceviche. Andy vowed to go easy on the alcohol but once they finished talking business, he was happy to let the wine flow. By the time they were on the way to his client's club, Andy was pretty drunk. Worrapon insisted that as Berwick Archer had picked up the bill for dinner, he should return the compliment with a nightcap. All Andy could remember was a feeling of pure euphoria when he realised Worrapon didn't intend to give him a hard time about investment and a couple of bottles of magnificent Bordeaux only added to his feeling that all might be well with the world after all. The two men shared a love of surfing and as both knew Phuket well, they debated at length the merits of Rawai Beach compared with Karon. Once again, the subject of golf was raised and Andy was bursting to tell his companion that *Kuhn* Sunarawani had invited him to play at the Siam Club. They agreed the next quarterly review should take place over a round of golf, as Worrapon said he was certain that investment performance would no longer be a problem. The only awkward moment all evening was when Worrapon briefly changed tack and reiterated his offer to help Andy out with some inside information from his brother.

"You know you could fix the investment performance issue with a couple of deals, don't you Andy?" Worrapon asked his guest.

"I wish that were true Ben, it will take a little longer, but we will turn it round."

"You know what I'm talking about Andy. My brother is working on a couple of very interesting projects at the moment and they will have a significant impact when they are made public."

"Ben, you know I can't do that. It's completely illegal and even if I was willing, they're pretty good at picking up that sort of thing these days."

"Your call Andy but it's a long road back for that portfolio of yours and I could give you a couple of get out of jail free cards."

"Ben, I think they're more likely to put me in jail, but I'm flattered you've taken me into your confidence."

"I admire your integrity Andy but in a couple of weeks one of your holdings will collapse when the CEO is forced to admit the oil fields they've been drilling in Nigeria are nothing but dust. My brother is working on the refinancing and when it's announced the ordinary shares will be all but worthless."

Andy's stomach tightened, the fund owned two Chinese oil companies and one Korean, it could be any of the three. Worrapon hadn't finished.

"And it would be a shame if you missed out on the biggest telecoms takeover in Asian history. Looking at your Emerging Fund, I'd say you were positioned precisely the wrong way round."

"Please Ben, you know I can't do this, it's a crime."

"I'm sorry Andy, just trying to help a friend. Let me know if you change your mind."

At the time Andy was proud of his resilience, an outstanding display of integrity in the face of overwhelming temptation. His evening with Worrapon was drawing to close, he was elated the meeting had gone better than expected and his father would have been proud, as he stood his ground over the offer of inside information. He had far too much to drink, chances are he met the girl as he tried to find a taxi. If she was drunk too, maybe it wasn't so hard to believe they ended up in bed together. He was pretty sure she came from a *HiSo* family, so when she woke up in the bed of a complete stranger she'd have wanted to make a discreet getaway.

When he rationalised it that way, it wasn't so bad. Of course he cheated on Caro, but it was one mistake. Alcohol and euphoria are a powerful combination and it wasn't the first time he'd woken up with an extremely hazy recollection of what happened the night before. In time it would come back to him, he'd remember bumping into the girl as he left Worrapon's club, maybe they agreed to have one drink. Maybe it had turned into several, maybe they had tequila, that usually did it for him. He really couldn't be held responsible for a single indiscretion if they had a few shooters. On the back of what he'd consumed with Worrapon that would have sent most men into a coma.

Andy picked up the phone to get Sam to send Caro some flowers and to book a table for the two of them at her favourite restaurant, Ruen Malika off Soi 22. It took him three seconds to realise it would save time if he sent his girlfriend a text saying he got pissed and spent the night shagging a stranger he picked up on the street. Classic guilty boyfriend reaction… to be avoided at all costs. Instead he dialled Caro.

"Hi sweetheart, sorry I didn't make it back last night."

"No problem," she replied. "I checked your calendar, when I saw you were with Ben Worrapon, I thought it'd be a late one. How was he?"

"He's fine, we just need to make him some money. We're not doing a great job for him right now."

Caroline sounded shocked; Andy had forgotten he never shared his work worries with her.

"Really, I thought you were shooting the lights out everywhere. If it's not going well, you were lucky, he has a reputation for shredding anyone who underperforms. He must like you."

"I'm a loveable kind of guy." Andy was feeling very good about how the call was going. She obviously didn't suspect a thing.

"I'm amazed you took Simon Tudor along though, Worrapon normally likes to talk to the organ grinder not the monkey. And how come you ended staying with him, I thought you weren't that keen on Simon?"

Oh fuck.

"Oh... he wasn't at the dinner. I met him later." Andy started his defence but had no idea where it was going.

"So he's a drinking buddy now?" Did she suspect something?

"No... no." Then an idea came to him. "I had to call him, Worrapon wanted some analysis and I thought it would look good if I had it hand-delivered. I called Simon and he brought it round. Buying him a drink was the least I could do... then he started to get all maudlin about where his career was going and one thing led to another. You know."

"Oh I know alright. You were a sweetheart when it happened to me, I'm sure you were the same with him. As long as you didn't go shagging any pox ridden bargirls."

"Caro, I swear to you that didn't happen."

"I know, I trust you completely. Dinner tonight?"

"Sure, where?" He choked slightly on the words, knowing the oath he'd sworn was designed to mislead. Hearing Caro say she trusted him took the guilt factor a notch or two higher still.

"Ruen Malika of course."

"Perfect. I'll get Sam to book."

Andy cut the call, with his heart pounding. The last twenty-four hours had been a nightmare. A battering from the Bull about his investment performance closely followed by a potentially awkward meeting with a very important client, then the barely explicable episode with a complete stranger in a Bangkok hotel, concluding with a very tricky call to his recently betrayed girlfriend. On balance he got through it all intact, the only thing that would come back to haunt him was the issue with James Turner. The boss was due in Bangkok the following month and if he couldn't deliver a convincing message on investment performance then he was almost certainly out of a job. Maybe it would be no bad thing, then he'd know for sure how Caro felt about him. Even a confident guy like Andy occasionally harboured doubts about his girlfriend's motives. She could have absolutely any man she chose, that was certain. If she was still happy for them to be together if he was out of work, then there could be no doubt the relationship was for real. Andy had almost convinced himself being unemployed might be a good thing. Then he thought about the invitation to the Siam Club, the sheer opulence of Worrapon's private club, his own sumptuous apartment and the fact he'd shortly splash the equivalent of a couple of hundred US dollars on dinner without giving it a second thought. He went straight from having his father pick up the bills to the insane world of investment management where the rewards were immense. He had no idea whether he could hack it in the real world. What if he did have to sell cars for a living, he didn't even know what that paid, but he was damn certain it wouldn't fund a fraction of the lifestyle he'd come to take for granted. Even his own father was a wage slave for God's sake. He earned great money, but not enough to walk into Turner's office one day and tell him he could shove his job up his butt. That had to be the plan, three or four years of this and he'd be on easy street, then he could quit in dramatic style and he and Caro could slip away and retire with the best part of their lives still ahead of them. To do that, he'd have to hang on to the job, somehow.

"I need a few signatures." Sam breezed into Andy's office with a sheaf of papers. "And Simon asked if you looked at the portfolios this morning, he didn't look happy."

Andy eyed the pile of papers as he reached for his mouse. "Can't they wait?"

"Sure, but the staff won't get paid, the landlord will lock the doors and half a dozen clients will be phoning to ask why you don't respond to their letters. Your call."

That hint of a smile was at the corner of her mouth again. She must have an idea of the problems he was having and she appeared to be enjoying it. Or maybe his paranoia was kicking in again. He'd been a fairly useless boss for the last few weeks and he shouldn't demand respect he probably didn't deserve.

Andy started to sign the papers, as she placed each one in front of him, but he was anxiously waiting for the Emerging Fund portfolio to load on his screen. Sam swept the last document off his desk as the last stock position appeared. He managed to maintain his composure until she closed the door behind her.

"I'm a fucking dead man."

The trades Andy placed the previous week were supposed to be the key to setting the fund on the right track. Each one showed a modest profit but stock markets had risen strongly. Relative to his target, the flagship fund of Berwick Archer's Asian business was off another thirty basis points. The Bull himself was considered to have the "Midas Touch," it's generally accepted these days as being a good thing. Most people have forgotten how the story ended. Basically it's all very well if everything you touch turns to gold, until you decide you fancy a cheese sandwich for your lunch, or your girlfriend turns up feeling frisky. Then it all becomes a little impractical. No-one ever said that about Andy Duncan and looking at the screen it was likely no-one ever would. There was, however, a decent chance that in generations to come, people might talk about the "Duncan Effect." It could be used to describe a situation where every single thing you do turns to crap. Andy was lost; there was nothing he could do to stem his losses.

At first he ignored his phone as it chirped to indicate an incoming text. He stared at his computer in disbelief as to what was happening to the fund he managed. Finally he checked the phone; the message was from Ben Worrapon.

"Dengshu Oil is dust, Alpha buys Omega," The conversation at the club came flooding back, the oil company about to go bust and the imminent telecoms takeover.

Andy scrabbled feverishly for his mouse and pulled up the first of the stocks. Dengshu Oil was his largest holding in the energy sector but everyone expected there to be great news from the company in the coming weeks. Some of that anticipation was already factored into the price, but there'd definitely be another hike when the geologist's report confirmed the size of the oil field. It had never been considered that there'd be no oil at all. Worrapon couldn't be right, could he?

A few more clicks and Andy was looking at Omega Telecoms, a Thai holding company he'd barely noticed before. The fund had a nominal holding in the stock, but the house view was that Alpha Communications, a vast Chinese conglomerate, was about to bid for a Malaysian company called MHP. Andy had been proud to mention the fund's stake in Omega to Narong Sunarawani when they met. Caro's "uncle" thanked him for being so supportive of Thai industry. Andy hadn't wanted to admit he owned a much larger stake in its Malaysian competitor.

Andy felt as though he was attached to some sort of medieval torture device. His brain connected to one end, his entrails to the other. A couple of very large men were turning a wheel at either end and he was being pulled apart in the middle. If Worrapon was right, he had to sell the stakes in Dengshu Oil and MHP and buy as much as he could get his hands on of Omega Telecoms.

It was illegal, immoral, it went against everything he'd ever been taught by his father and at school, but it was the only route left open if he was to save his job.

He picked up his phone and dialled.

# CHAPTER THIRTEEN

**Shakedown**

"I am simply trying to explain there must be a mistake. Please allow me to call my lawyer, I am certain he will be able to clear this up."

"I really doubt that is possible Mr Bezhepov." The policeman appeared to be enjoying himself, although he was hardly giving the Ukrainian his full attention. As he spoke, Inspector Mongkut Tharanyatta appeared to be considering his own reflection in the antique mirror hanging over the bookcase in one corner of the office. It was evident the officer was very satisfied with what he saw.

"My men have established you are clearly the beneficial owner of the Vortex club, you have a large number of foreigners on your staff, both as security and amongst, the… how should I say it… hospitality staff?"

An experienced stage actor could hardly have put more emphasis on the word hospitality, each syllable was enunciated carefully and Mongkut injected a withering sneer, indicating his utter distaste for the sort of people employed in such activities.

"This is just paperwork, I was assured my advisor had taken care of all of this."

"So you don't deny you are the owner of the club and these people are your employees? All of them, yourself included, are on tourist visas. You do not have permission to take up employment of any kind in Thailand."

"My lawyer deals with all that, just let me get him. He will make this right… if you know what I mean."

"No Mr Bezhepov, I don't know what you mean." Mongkut looked at the Ukrainian in what appeared to be genuine astonishment.

"He said you guys were taken care of, it's in the budgets for Christ's sake. This was not supposed to be a problem."

The policeman was clearly shocked at what he heard.

"I think you are suggesting you believe this lawyer of yours, has paid for the complicity of the Royal Thai Police. Is that what you are saying?"

Again the policeman was in theatrical overdrive, spitting out the word "paid", as though it would rid him of the awful taste in his mouth.

"No, I'm sorry… I don't know what has happened here. Only my legal advisor can explain it. Please let me call him."

"In good time Mr Bezhepov, I have another matter to discuss with you. My officers have reason to believe a number of your employees are prostitutes and they operate from this establishment with your full approval. We have evidence your bar may even be benefitting financially from this arrangement. Are you aware that prostitution is illegal in the Kingdom of Thailand?"

Mongkut maintained a completely straight face throughout, although even he occasionally struggled with that part of the routine. The Ukrainian looked as though he'd gone into shock. He shook his head vigorously, as though his brain had malfunctioned and the movement would finally enable him to make sense of the situation. Bezhepov was genuinely unable to believe what he just heard. The two men were standing in the administration office of Thailand's largest go-go bar in the infamous red light district of the most notorious city in the whole of Southeast Asia. There were at least five thousand girls, openly for sale within three hundred yards and the policeman was reminding him of Thailand's strict laws forbidding prostitution. His mouth was wide open and his head was nodding, he looked as though he'd been hypnotised. Finally Bezhepov found his voice.

"I don't believe it, this has to be an April Fool." A quick glance at the calendar made him realise he was about four months too late or eight months early. Then a thought dawned on him.

"OK, I get it, it's a shakedown. How much is it going to take to make it go away?"

The Inspector turned to the junior officer who accompanied him. Bezhepov was certain he was about to ask the young man to leave whilst they agreed a price. Then he could get on the phone, or maybe he'd send Sergei round with a message and a baseball bat. Either way, his lawyer would be in no doubt as to the discomfort this was causing him.

"Officer, cuff him," said Mongkut, nodding towards the Ukrainian. "We'll start with the visa breaches, running a prostitution ring and attempting to bribe a police officer. I'll get the rest of the team to search the premises. I'd be amazed if we weren't adding a few narcotics charges and… let me see, firearms offences would be my guess. You'd have to be crazy to run a place like this without a few guys who are properly equipped."

The Inspector took one last look in the antique mirror and then nodded at the Ukrainian.

"Goodnight Mr Bezhepov, I'll see you at the station."

Tanawat Chanpol had only just checked into his suite at Pattaya's Marriott hotel when Mongkut banged on the door. The lawyer ensured the chain was firmly in place before he opened the door a few inches to establish the identity of his visitor.

"Where have you been? You were supposed to be here an hour ago." The emotion conveyed was a vague disappointment rather than anger.

Mongkut breezed into the room as Chanpol removed the chain and opened the door.

"My dear Tanawat, there is much to do when we undertake an operation such as this, we have to make sure we comply with every letter of the law. It would be regrettable if the case was thrown out because we failed to comply with procedure."

The lawyer had to laugh.

"Yes, it would be a terrible thing if we were to fall foul of the law. I thought you had a small army of subordinates to do all this awkward procedural stuff for you."

"Of course, but amongst your Ukrainian friend's dancers was a particularly enticing little thing from Laos. I decided I should interview her myself and it took a little longer than I expected. She was, however, extremely cooperative, so I released her without charge."

Mongkut stroked each corner of his mouth as though brushing away the crumbs of a recent meal, then appeared to chuckle to himself, without sound or humour.

"Mongkut you are a pig. But I have to confess our work would be so much more difficult without you."

The Inspector took a theatrical bow and smiled broadly. "I'm delighted to be of service. What happens next?"

"I have a buyer for the club already. If you can make sure Bezhepov and his army of Ukrainian goons are thrown out of the country, it could be open again within a month."

"You aren't afraid the Ukrainian will come after you?"

"Not at all, I only met him twice and he thinks I am just a hired hand. He will believe the man who set him up is a Bangkok lawyer called Nitin Wansakul. We met at *Kuhn* Wansakul's office and he was happy to portray himself as my boss in exchange for a small fee."

"So the Ukrainian will go after Wansakul?" Mongkut was impressed.

"It's important to close off all the loose ends, so I intend to make sure the Ukrainian believes justice has already been done. I can't afford to have some of his friends blundering around Bangkok, looking for someone to kill, so we will be doing that for him."

"Excellent. I will set the wheels in motion with Immigration and leave the rest to you."

The two men bade each other farewell and Chanpol picked up his mobile phone and dialled the number of Prem Boonamee.

"Prem, this is Song."

"Yeah, it's on my screen," came the reply. Boonamee wanted to let the call ring out, he was watching a re-run of Bangkok Dangerous on TV, but he did not dare miss a call from his boss.

"That job we discussed, I need you to do it in the next forty-eight hours. And don't forget, it has to look like suicide."

"I'll talk to Kong."

"Prem, I want you to do this one personally. It requires a bit of guile, not brute force. OK?"

"OK you're the boss." Prem's voice was reluctant but there was no doubt the order would be carried out exactly as given.

Tanawat Chanpol, code named Song, cut the call and redialled. It was time to check in with the real boss. The phone rang three times before voicemail kicked in and he could leave a message.

"Nung, it's Song, the Pattaya project is all but complete, but we need to talk about our friends at Berwick Archer."

# CHAPTER FOURTEEN

## Breaking News

Andy could just about get by in French, at least enough for the locals to accept he'd made an effort. They'd let him have a stab at a couple of sentences before nodding in a condescending fashion and continuing the conversation in flawless English. Cultural superiority had been conceded but at least he'd get far better service than his fellow countryman who had no grasp of the language at all. In Thailand, he never bothered to try beyond hello, thank you and delicious. Any *farang* who could deliver those three responses in Thai, would be lauded as a great linguist by locals eager to show off their own grasp of the hapless visitor's mother tongue. Whoever coined the phrase, "a little knowledge is a dangerous thing," could easily have been thinking of the perils of being a student of the minefield that is the Thai language. Even if they can make some sort of fist of the vocabulary, most *farang* will run aground on the tones that completely change the meaning of the word they think they learned yesterday. Watch a Thai girl chatting to a foreigner in a bar; if they're joking and laughing, the chances are they're speaking English. If the girl's brow is furrowed and her face has a look of utter bewilderment, it's probably because the man is trying out a few Thai phrases and she hasn't got the vaguest idea what he's saying. Andy took three one hour lessons before he gave up and decided Sam would be his translator in the office and Caro could do the rest.

It was why he found himself watching the evening news on a ten second time delay while Caroline decided which bits were worth translating. The lead story covered a demonstration on the steps of the parliament building. Andy knew a little about the incessant tension in Thai politics and what sometimes felt like the constant threat of a military coup. More often than not, even when the army was involved, any transition of power was fairly peaceful. But memories were still fresh of bloody street fighting in 2011 and Bangkok appeared to be on the brink of another wave of anarchy. Andy tuned out of the story until Caroline gave a little whoop of joy.

"It's him Andy, look it's Narong."

The story appeared to have switched from political machinations to business, as the film showed the unmistakable frame of Caro's Uncle Narong, dressed in immaculate evening wear. As usual he was waving away the camera crews and the eager journalists, he clearly had no wish to engage with either.

"They want him to run in the next election."

"I thought he had no interest in politics." Andy was simply repeating what he'd read several times in The Nation, Bangkok's popular English language newspaper.

"It's what he always says, but you never know, perhaps he's playing a clever game. If they beg him often enough and he comes to the job without actively seeking it. It could be a very clever strategy."

"Hasn't he told you? You're obviously very close." Andy tried to keep his voice calm, he suddenly realised he was choking back a little surge of jealousy. Narong Sunarawani was every bit as impressive as he'd anticipated when the three of them met for lunch. Caro seemed to be in awe of the great man and now it appeared that he was smarter than even she imagined. He was not simply one of the most successful businessmen in Southeast Asia; he may also be on the verge of winning control of Thailand itself. He didn't even have to put himself up for election, he'd be carried into power on the shoulders of a grateful populace begging him to save their country from a selfish political elite who sought only to line their own pockets. Caro sighed, transfixed by the image on the screen, she clasped her hands together and drew them into her heart.

"Pull yourself together man." Mercifully the voice was only in his head. Andy's paranoia was almost complete. He nearly convinced himself he was about to lose his lover to a man who'd been a family friend since she was a little girl. He was already in no doubt he was about to lose everything else.

Andy was waiting for the news programme to finish so he could explain to his girlfriend that within days he'd be unemployed. There had been a modest improvement in the performance of the Emerging Fund but it still trailed in the wake of its competitors. James Turner's visit to Bangkok was imminent and it was inconceivable he'd do anything other than give Andy his marching orders. Sam mentioned Turner intended to bring an unnamed colleague along and the easy assumption was that the mystery visitor would soon be installed as the new Head of Berwick Archer's Bangkok office.

"Darling, I know you want to talk to me but I have to see the end of the news, then you can open a bottle OK?" Caro was still bouncing with delight at the glowing tributes paid to her beloved Uncle Narong.

The news anchor switched to local Bangkok stories and, had Andy understood a single word, he might easily have gone to bed thinking Bangkok was the most dangerous city in the world. British news is no less voyeuristic but there are far more stringent controls over what can be shown on the early evening news. It always astonished Andy that Caroline, a picture of feminine style and grace, appeared to lap up the grimmer stories.

Dittar Lamnat was a *yaba* addict whose life was never interesting enough to get him on TV. Not until he decided he wanted to share his last six tablets. The days are past when Dittar's last minutes would have been no more than a footnote in a local paper. It was inevitable someone would have their smart phone on video setting when he climbed into the brown bear enclosure at Bangkok Zoo, and tried to explain to its occupant that with a couple of the small yellow pills, he wouldn't look so damned grumpy. In Britain, the news would have cut the film as the man climbed the barrier, in Thailand they're not so squeamish. Andy could not watch, his eyes were fixed on Caroline who appeared to be totally absorbed by the bloody carnage on the screen.

There followed some unnecessary close-ups of the aftermath of a high speed smash on the motorway. Again Caroline looked on with the rapt attention of a medical student observing a surgical procedure. As the anchor switched to the next story, Caro appeared to come out of her trance. The camera was trained on a bright-eyed female reporter standing outside a building where fire crew were clearly in attendance.

"What's this one?" asked Andy.

"Oh it's a lawyer over in Thonglor. They think he killed himself. He must have set fire to the office first but then he shot himself in the head. I guess he must have been involved in some shady deals and was trying to get rid of the evidence at the same time."

The TV crew managed to get close enough to pick out the nameplate of the firm whose senior partner's charred corpse had been transferred to a waiting ambulance. Nitin Wansakul advertised himself as a specialist in property transactions and as Andy turned away a tearful secretary explained to the reporter that she really couldn't believe her boss had killed himself.

"Caro, we need to talk."

The Breaking News banner flashed across the screen once again and Caroline raised her hand to indicate she wanted silence. A senior policeman was in the middle of what looked like an impassioned plea. He was particularly animated as he spoke directly to the camera and the piece only ended when his colleagues shepherded him away. Briefly, Caroline explained the man was making his appeal as a public official but also as a father. Andy was vaguely aware of the story as it received some coverage in the previous days and there was a lot of talk about it in the office, but this was the first time he'd seen anything on TV. Caroline explained the officer's daughter was missing and they were now launching a nationwide appeal for anyone who might have seen her to come forward. A substantial reward was on offer to anyone who could provide information leading to her being returned home safely.

"That'll do the trick," Caroline said. "I can't believe they didn't do it before. She's a nice girl and she's found herself a bad boy. As soon as his friends see the money on offer, they'll let the police know where she is and she'll be back to Daddy in no time."

Andy might have noticed a slightly wistful note in Caroline's voice as though she was recalling a similar event from her own past but he was totally engrossed by the image on screen.

The picture was evidently of Lawan Raksanatra, the seventeen year-old daughter of Police Colonel Pimin Raksanatra, head of a unit of the Royal Thai Police charged with investigating organised crime. More often than not the press managed to dredge up a photo from an ID card or a driving licence or one of those Facebook selfies where the subject has already enjoyed a glass or two too many and is looking far from their best. This was a paparazzi shot taken when the girl had attended a formal dinner in

Bangkok on the arm of her doting father. Caroline explained the girl's mother died in a car accident a year earlier and Lawan was an only child. It was not hard to sympathise with the father, terrified he might lose the one remaining member of his family.

Lawan possessed the flawless pale skin of the Bangkok *HiSo*, her face was almost heart-shaped and although her dress was modest and beautifully cut, it did little to hide her perfect figure. At first there was a vague feeling Andy might have seen her somewhere before, that pale skin and the heart-shaped face. Then came the unease, then nausea as he realised he'd definitely seen her before. He had to imagine her with her eyes closed and the picture was complete. Lawan Raksanatra was in his bed the night he visited Ben Worrapon's club. Then she disappeared.

"So what is it Andy?"

"Errr… what? What do you mean? Nothing." He stumbled over the words.

"What do you mean, nothing? You've been at me all night that we need to talk. What's that all about?"

Andy reached into his pocket for the small blue inhaler and took a deep breath. As the medication hit the back of his throat he sucked it into his lungs greedily. It wasn't an asthma attack, the inhaler had become an adult version of a baby's dummy, giving a small amount of physical comfort but also enough time to clear his head. The girl's face was still on the screen, Andy had not seen her eyes until that moment and now they looked straight at him, daring him to remember what happened.

"It's Turner, he's coming… he's coming to Bangkok…"

"OK, so what's the big deal? He loves you doesn't he?"

"Caro… it's…" Andy was genuinely lost for words. He couldn't get the image of the young girl out of his mind. One of Bangkok's top policemen was appealing for news regarding her whereabouts. Caroline explained she'd not been seen for almost exactly two weeks and he was absolutely certain he woke up next to her thirteen days before. She looked so young and so innocent but once again he felt the stab of guilt as he remembered pulling back the duvet and the surge of desire as he saw her naked form. The only clue as to what happened between them was a stained sheet and, when he returned from the shower, she'd gone.

Andy shook his head, hoping that somehow an explanation would materialise and when it did, it would be one he could share with a now bewildered Caroline. He stared at the TV screen, only because the alternative was to look at his girlfriend, she'd see he'd done something terrible and he wouldn't be able to explain.

The "Breaking News" banner appeared and, once again, the screen was filled by Narong Sunarawani's beaming smile. It was exactly the same piece of footage they'd shown before, further confirmation this was a man who avoided the cameras whenever he could. The expression on Andy's face must have changed slightly as it drew Caroline's eyes to the screen and once again she whooped with joy.

"Oh my Buddha, he's done it again."

"Huh?"

"Everyone thought the Chinese were after that Malaysian group, MHP. They just bought Omega Telecoms and Narong owned sixty per cent of the stock. He's made an absolute killing. That's unbelievable."

Andy was certain every one of his internal organs had made a simultaneous decision to exit his body via his mouth. He knew for sure he was about to choke to death but the pounding in his chest indicated his heart might give out first. The sheer terror he felt at the knowledge he had sex with a seventeen year-old girl on the night she disappeared, was competing with the elation that the Emerging Fund had made a huge profit on the takeover of Omega Telecoms. It was seconds before the joy subsided. Just two weeks earlier he owned a significant position in a company called MHP, confident it was about to be acquired by one of China's largest conglomerates. He'd never cheated on his girlfriend and certainly never laid eyes on Lawan Raksanatra. His job was on the line but otherwise his life was uncomplicated. In the space of twenty-four hours everything had been tossed into the air and only now, two weeks later, were some of the pieces starting to land.

Andy initially resisted Ben Worrapon's offer of the privileged information he possessed in relation to Omega Telecoms, MHP and Dengshu Oil. He ended up in bed with a young girl he'd never seen before but had no recollection of how he got there. By the time he had the chance to ask her, she'd gone. By the following day his resistance crumbled in the face of a further fall in the value of his fund. He placed the orders to sell most of his holding in MHP and Dengshu Oil and invested heavily in Omega Telecoms. It was the equivalent of an unlucky gambler staking his last few chips on a single spin of the roulette wheel. Andy bet on double zero and it came up. He should have been looking forward to his meeting with Turner in the knowledge that one deal had turned his performance around, but there was a single image in his mind and he couldn't shift it. It was the perfect heart-shaped face of Lawan Raksanatra. It was totally still but posed two questions, where she came from that night, more importantly where had she gone? Andy knew the answer to neither question.

# CHAPTER FIFTEEN

**Loose ends**

Song was right, the Korean would never have been able to deal with Nitin Wansakul and make it look like a suicide. It took thought and a fair amount of planning. Boonamee had found the lawyer's office and noted the opening hours were from ten in the morning until midday and then from three until five, every Wednesday, Thursday and Friday. He called and made an appointment for four-thirty. Wanting to be in the office at closing time, Boonamee arrived late for the meeting and was delighted to see that at five p.m. exactly, the lawyer's secretary popped her head round the door and bade a respectful farewell. When their meeting ended five minutes later, the two men exchanged polite *wais* and Boonamee said he'd be happy to let himself out. The men agreed there was little the lawyer could do to help with his visitor's marital difficulties, Boonamee apologised profusely for his failure to understand the services *Kuhn* Wansakul was able to offer. The final pieces of the plan fell into place as Boonamee noted the door to the street was left unlocked, the office suite next door was unoccupied and, unusually for Bangkok, there was no security guard on duty at the entrance.

The following day, Boonamee made another appointment for four-thirty but this time chose his assumed name from a different section of the Bangkok telephone directory. On that second visit, he waited until the secretary left at exactly three minutes past five, before he entered the building. The appointment was simply to ensure no-one else would be with Wansakul at the crucial hour. The lawyer did a double take when he saw Boonamee in the door of his office and glanced quickly at his diary to make sure he'd not confused his schedule. By the time he looked up, Boonamee had donned a pair of thin, white cotton gloves and was pointing a small but deadly looking handgun at the lawyer's head.

"Please stay calm, *Kuhn*......" he couldn't remember the man's name. "I'm sure I can help you with your wife. Just stay calm and everything will be fine."

Boonamee laughed. "Oh *Kuhn* Wansakul, I have no wife. That was simply a small device to ensure we could conclude our business without any surprises. I needed to see the inside of your office and understand its routine."

The lawyer looked puzzled. "Our business? We have no business, I never saw you before yesterday."

"I'm sorry, I should have explained, I'm here on behalf of *Kuhn* Chanpol, you helped him with a transaction in Pattaya, a Ukrainian gentleman… Mr Bezhepov."

"Yes, I met the Ukrainian, that's all. Chanpol told me he needed me to lend a little substance to the transaction, he had no offices of his own and I did the man a favour. Thais stick together when dealing with *farang*, that's all. He paid me a small fee and I've heard nothing since."

"Well the deal did not go well for Mr Bezhepov and tomorrow the police will be here to investigate your part in the transaction. They would, of course, have been here earlier but we have a friendly officer who ensured this line of enquiry was not prioritised."

"I had no part in it… it was Chanpol."

"And that's why we have to terminate our relationship." Boonamee raised the gun once more.

"You're not going to kill me, if you were, you'd have done it by now. You want something, I can give you cash, whatever Chanpol is paying… I'll double it."

"No *Kuhn* Wansakul, I'm definitely going to kill you. There is nothing you have that would convince me to go against the wishes of *Kuhn* Chanpol."

"Then why are you telling me all this? Why don't you just get on with it?" The lawyer tried to sound defiant, but he was on the verge of tears.

"*Kuhn* Chanpol specifically asked me to explain it to you. He said you were an arrogant piece of shit who talked to him like he was the village buffalo. He said it would have been a great shame for you to go to your death without knowing who arranged it."

Every movie fan knows that if they were ever to be confronted with a situation like that, they'd find a way out. Wansakul owned a huge collection of DVDs and considered himself an authority on Hollywood crime thrillers. Action scenes were his favourite but he also loved courtroom drama when it was the sheer intellect of the lawyer that saved the day. Wansakul dreamed that one day he'd mastermind a famous legal victory instead of pushing title deeds around all day, gathering modest fees and trying to ensure some of the cash that helped to oil the city's decision-making machine would stick as it passed through his hands. In the meantime he'd have to settle for watching it all on TV and fantasising that he was the movie hero. He eyed the heavy reading lamp on his desk and wondered whether he'd have the strength to hurl it at the armed man standing opposite. Pan, his secretary, delivered a cup of steaming hot coffee to his desk before she left for the day, he just had to pick it up and throw it into the man's eyes. Or maybe he could launch himself bodily at the young thug and hope surprise would win the day. The look on his visitor's face was of a man who knew exactly what he was thinking, of a man who might even be hoping he would try. When Wansakul watched his DVDs anything was possible, even for someone physically past their prime, the urge to survive would prevail, he was sure of that. Suddenly it did not seem so easy. There was plenty of fight in Wansakul's head, but he was unable to transfer any of it to his limbs. His arms and legs felt like huge lead weights, if he were to be thrown into water, they'd certainly drag him to the bottom in seconds. He tried to speak, to ask if there was anything he could do to secure his life but the words wouldn't come. Boonamee crossed the room and took the lawyer by the shoulder. Wansakul meekly allowed himself to be led to the high-backed leather chair behind his desk. The young Thai was surprised by how easily he capitulated. He turned the chair round so Wansakul faced him and then placed the barrel of the gun between his nostrils and angled it upwards along the line of the bridge of the man's nose before he pulled the trigger. Finally he transferred the gun to the man's hand and allowed the body to slide from the chair onto the floor.

  The drapes Wansakul had chosen specifically, after watching an episode of LA Law on TV, would ensure the fire took hold quickly once it got started. Boonamee entered the office at seven minutes past five, fourteen minutes later he was back in the street. It was five-thirty before smoke could be seen billowing from the office windows and, by the time the fire service arrived, Prem Boonamee was back at his Ekamai apartment taking a long hot shower.

    The girl was sent on her way just before three a.m. Boonamee usually went for slightly older women but this one was probably no more than eighteen. Pretty enough but with short, spiky hair, a little too much make up and an ultra slender boyish figure. Boonamee wasn't even conscious of it, but he'd started choosing women who bore as little resemblance to either Pom or Nok as he could. Both women wore their hair long, had full sensuous figures and keen intelligent eyes. Only days before, Boonamee tried to buy a pair of shoes at Siam Paragon, a vast shopping mall on Sukhumvit Road. As he reached the till, an assistant held out her hand for the goods and automatically switched on the kind of thermonuclear smile only a Thai woman can. She'd noticed the handsome young Thai make his choice and, regretting she'd not moved in earlier, promised the earth to the cashier if she could swap assignments and take over the till as he completed his purchase. Even the plainest girl often has at least one feature that will have men falling at her feet. Women generally agonise over tiny imperfections and can convince themselves that even if everything else is in pretty good shape, it's their asymmetric earlobes which are standing between them and true love. The truth is many men will have stopped looking at anything else if the girl has nice breasts. Tan, the shop assistant, was more pragmatic. She knew she'd never be Miss Thailand, but she had three things going for her. She never tired of people admiring her wonderfully sparkly eyes. Her colleagues reluctantly agreed they'd kill to have firm, full, natural breasts like Tan and then there was her hair. Long and sleek it stretched most of the way down her back. When Tan moved in on a man, she'd pull those endless tresses forward so they lay between her magnificent breasts, then tip her head forward and look up at her prey with eyes wide open. It rarely failed. As Boonamee stepped forward with his purchase, she was in no doubt she commanded his full attention. It only remained to loosen the tie a little and pull her ponytail forward, so her long mane of jet-black hair framed her face on one side and cascaded down the front of her body on the other.

Boonamee's smile became a grimace and then a look of horror. The noise that came from his throat wasn't quite a scream, it sounded more like he was being choked. Then he dropped the shoes and fled towards the escalator and the exit as fast as his legs would carry him. Tan stared after him in open-mouthed astonishment and a bevy of dull-eyed, short-haired, flat-chested shop assistants joined together in a soundless cheer and returned to their work.

Boonamee didn't stop until he reached the Skytrain station and then paused to regain his breath. He'd felt fine right up until he got to the till. The girl smiled at him but it barely registered. Sifting and grading women was an automatic process for him and he had no time for the ordinary ones. Tan would never know, but she'd been swiftly classified as average but with nice tits and then mentally discarded. It was when Boonamee made eye contact that he started to feel uncomfortable, but only when she dragged her hair forward and he could see how long and sleek it was, did he feel the sharp pain in his chest. Then everything descended into a blur until he was standing by the entrance to the Skytrain.

He'd not consciously avoided women since that day at Siam Paragon, but the call from Song meant he had to deal with Wansakul and that took some time and mental effort. The young girl with the spiky hair was drunk when he picked her up and although she'd been diverting enough company for a couple of hours, he was not sorry to see her go. They exchanged more words after he told her to leave, than they had in the whole of the earlier part of the evening. It was Boonamee's sub-conscious that prompted him to pick a girl, as different to Pom or Nok as it was possible to be. It was a defence mechanism, an attempt to ward off the dream.

Boonamee realised the trick his mind was trying to play, but as he lay in his bed after Miss Spiky had gone, he felt his stomach tighten, his muscles tense and the sweat start to ooze onto the sheets and he knew it had failed. The dream would come and it would end in a sharp pain in his chest and a voice that spoke of blood, more blood than they'd ever seen before

# CHAPTER SIXTEEN

**The other Andy Duncan**

Andy Duncan felt as though he was floating, looking down on a forlorn figure sitting at an unnecessarily large leather-topped desk in the huge office that overlooked the Chao Praya river and Thailand's sprawling capital. The man clenched his fists in an attempt to summon all of his energy and in seconds was poring over a detailed analysis of the Emerging Fund, checking back and forth between the summary page and the underlying schedules. Like most businesses, Berwick Archer used a traffic light system, key objectives were listed and readers simply had to see whether the little circle next to the item was coloured green, amber or red. One month earlier and the report on the Emerging Fund was a sea of red. Important clients had lost money, recent purchases had leeched value from the fund, sales were made at a loss, the market had risen but the value of the fund fell and key competitors were in the market with product that outperformed by every conceivable measure. More experienced managers than Andy had received their black bin liner and been told to clear their desk after reports which were not nearly as grim as that. Arguably Andy got off lightly, James Turner gave him a trademark pep talk on the phone and he was told he had one month to turn it around.

As Andy watched the man checking every page of the report, he should have been elated. Every objective was marked with a proud green circle. Much of the credit went to the strategic stuff that came from Charlie's team in Hong Kong, they chose all the right industry sectors to get into, they were absolutely correct about the Euro and they nailed the Asian markets that were about to take off. Those things alone would have been enough to save his skin. He'd still have been on watch from the guys in Hong Kong but Turner would almost certainly have given him another chance. Why sack a manager whose fund is riding high again? It sends completely the wrong signal to clients. The Emerging Fund had, however, done so much better than that. The report showed many of the individual stocks he'd selected had also done very well, but he made two outstanding judgement calls. He sold MHP and bought Omega Telecoms shortly before the announcement of the acquisition of the Thai company by a Chinese giant. He also sold the fund's stake in Dengshu Oil. On the last day of the month, the company's Chief Executive announced a huge refinancing exercise, as the wells they'd drilled in their African concession were declared dry. Andy spread the proceeds across the other major Chinese energy companies and as Dengshu collapsed, investor money flowed into competitors poised to take advantage of the opportunity. The value of the fund's new shares rose on the back of a flood of new investors eager to back the last remaining Chinese and Korean firms active in Africa.

Andy continued to watch as the man completed his scrutiny of the report and pushed it to one side. It was a familiar profile, attractive enough with thick blond hair combed straight back from his forehead. Pale blue eyes and that small scar where the owner had either fallen off a rally bike or walked into a table depending on which story you heard. The face was tanned enough to conceal the dark circles under his eyes but an impartial observer might guess he was a little more than the twenty-five years indicated by his passport. Andy was used to observing himself as though he were two completely different people. He started to marvel at the person who could still make investment decisions, glad-hand clients and make it look like he ran the office when Sam had really taken over. He even made a decent fist of convincing Caroline all was well at Berwick Archer. He would show her the latest report on the fund and make it sound like it had never been any other way. The road to his current glorious position was a steady inexorable advance. The professional side of Andy Duncan checked the report one last time. He'd shortly sit down with James Turner to receive the plaudits for turning the fund around when only days earlier he was certain the meeting would end with his dismissal.

It seemed to Andy that he was watching his professional self from a distance. He'd heard about "out of body experiences", maybe that's what was happening here. Andy reached for his inhaler and took two deep hits of the medication. He smiled grimly as it occurred to him that whenever he read about the phenomenon before, it was in connection with a near death experience. That wasn't too far away from what he now felt. The man he observed had trashed every value his father ever stood for, to hang on to a life he probably didn't deserve and he clearly couldn't handle. And somewhere along the way, he was witness to the disappearance of a young girl, he could remember little and was too scared to own up to what he could recall.

Andy felt as though he was looking on in detached disgust as he heard a sharp knocking and a towering figure appeared in the doorway. Andy straightened his tie, put on his best professional smile and stood to greet his boss.

"Andy, my man, how the hell are you?" James Turner asked as he breezed into the office.

"Couldn't be better boss, things really couldn't be better," Andy replied as he showed his CEO to the small conference table next to the window and its stunning view of the city of Bangkok.

**The unravelling**

"You know her don't you?" Caroline's voice cut through the mental fog that had descended over him, obscuring everything but the picture of the beautiful young girl and her heart-shaped face. The press had found a lot more photos since the first piece of TV coverage. She was almost plain as a little girl, but they showed a couple of pictures of her with her mother and if you believed the old adage about daughters, Lawan Raksanatra was destined to be a rare beauty. They found a few shots of her with her father too, the otherwise hard-faced policeman bursting with pride every time the camera caught him with his daughter. They cut to the latest interview with the father and he looked even more drawn and desolate than before. There must have been some developments in the case, but as usual he needed Caro to translate.

She'd disappeared to the kitchen to find another bottle of Chassagne Montrachet and the report he spent the afternoon poring over with Turner was open on the sofa between them. Andy claimed the outcome of his CEO's visit was never in doubt, as the fund was in great shape. He told her about a couple of flat spots in performance during the previous weeks but he knew all would come right by month end. The day before, he'd received a hand-delivered package that must have come from Ben Worrapon. It contained a series of documents appearing to date back several months. Taken together they'd support the argument that Andy's decision to sell MHP and Dengshu and buy Omega Telecoms was the product of detailed original research and some insightful interpretations of a whole bunch of publicly available documents. Clearly, they were to be used in the event of a visit from any regulator suspicious that Berwick Archer, and Andy specifically, might have been in receipt of inside information. Even with his girlfriend sitting two feet away from him, Andy managed to don his professional mask and trot out a convincing argument that he made the decisions based on his own analysis.

"Bastard," she'd said playfully. "You could have shared it with me, I'd be the toast of Pan Asia if I got us on the right side of those deals. The top guys were in meetings all afternoon when the Omega news came out, trying to work out how we missed it."

"Sweetheart, I'd have loved to do it but with your connection to Sunarawani, you'd never have been able to do anything with it, you know that." Andy hadn't even practiced that lie, it just popped into his head.

Caro had switched the news on as she headed for the kitchen and the first story up was Lawan Raksanatra. As he'd bragged and boasted about the way he handled Turner, Andy managed to push the other stuff to the back of his mind. He was so immersed in his story he began to believe he worked it all out for himself, that there was no text from Worrapon and no illegal trades. He even rationalised what had happened to the girl. Caro was right, Lawan Raksanatra was a *HiSo* girl who liked bad boys. She'd been fine when he left the bedroom, she must have sneaked out while he showered and he couldn't be held responsible for whatever happened to her after that. The girl would turn up and he'd have to keep his head down for a couple of weeks and stick to his story if there was an investigation into the profits he'd made. It would all be fine. A glance at Caro's perfect smiling face assured him that it couldn't be any other way.

As Andy stared at the TV screen, however, the certainty began to fade and the practiced bluster was about to elude him. It was Caro's voice again.

"I said… you know her don't you?"

"No… no why should I know her? How would I have met a policeman's daughter for God's sake?"

"Every time you see her face on TV, it's like you're seeing the face of someone who's haunting you."

"For Christ's sake Caro, it's an awful story. That girl is so young and her father so devastated… it's just heart wrenching, that's all. I swear."

Andy desperately needed his inhaler, but frantically scanning the room, trying to see where he left his briefcase, only made him look more deceitful.

"It was the night you said you stayed with Simon Tudor."

"What was?" Andy sensed where this was going and his mind raced trying to think how he could answer her questions.

"She disappeared the night you didn't come home."

"So?"

"So you didn't fuck her?"

Caro stood over him and, as she asked the question, he could feel specks of her saliva spatter on his cheek. He'd never seen her lose her temper before, but it looked as though she was going to beat him to death with her bare fists.

"What are you asking me? Why do you think I fucked her?" His answer sounded desperate and he racked his brains for a way to calm her down.

"I'm asking you if you fucked her, and then left her to die in an abandoned office block on the outskirts of Pattaya. Because someone did… was it you?"

"Jesus Christ, what happened?" Any shred of composure had left him and panic surged through his addled brain.

"They found her body, that's the breaking news. She's been dead for a long time, they're already guessing she died the night she disappeared, the night you stayed with Simon Tudor… or so you say."

"Oh no… please tell me that's not true. It can't be true." Andy wept and, as he spied his briefcase on the dining table, scrabbled across the floor on hands and knees to get to his inhaler.

"Was it you Andy? Did you kill her? Because that policeman says the city forensic laboratory is confident they have enough genetic material to identify the perpetrator. All they need is a suspect and they'll have a match in no time."

"Caro, I swear I didn't kill her."

"So you did fuck her."

"She was fine when I went to shower and she'd gone when I got back. I didn't kill...."

Andy never got to finish the sentence. Caroline launched herself at him, raining punches onto his face and body. Her nails raked his face and her fingers sought out his eye sockets. Andy covered his eyes with his arm but otherwise made no attempt to defend himself. It felt like an age before she was spent and sobbing next to him on the floor. Her hands were covered in blood from his face and arms and his ribs and chest were raw and bruised.

"I told them it couldn't be you, I told them you wouldn't harm a fly, I told them you loved me and you'd never cheat on me. They laughed."

"What are you saying? Someone told you I did that?"

She sounded totally resigned and deflated, as though her attack on Andy had drained all the anger and spirit out of her body.

"Not exactly. They said they saw you with her the night she disappeared and you were all over each other. Then it's on the news she's missing and they assumed you were already helping police with their enquiries."

"Who are these people anyway? Who told you they saw me with the girl?"

"Daniel, my boss at Pan Asia and his boyfriend. They love gossip and they couldn't wait to share this one with me."

"And you believe them? Why didn't you tell me what they were saying?"

"I saw how you reacted when the story came on the news before. They only told me today and I wanted to see your face when you heard she was dead. I was sure I'd know whether you killed her."

"And you think I did kill her?"

"What else should I believe? You hid this whole thing from me, even after you saw the girl had disappeared. If there was an innocent explanation... you could have told me... we could have gone to the police. You behave like a guilty man, what else should I believe?"

Andy sat up and tried to wipe some of the blood from his face, he winced as he felt a click in his chest and recognised a feeling he'd not had since he came off worst in a rugby scrum at school. At least one cracked rib for sure. Caroline still lay on her back staring wide-eyed at the ceiling, all the fight long departed.

"I'll tell you what happened and I'll try to explain why I thought I couldn't tell you. All I can say is I never set out to cheat on you and I definitely did not kill that girl. She was alive the last time I saw her. I have no idea how she ended up in Pattaya. After I've told you my story, I'm in your hands, if you want to turn me in to the police then I'll go willingly, I promise."

Caroline sat up, searching his face for something on which she could start to rebuild the trust he'd shattered.

"Talk to me."

It took over an hour for Andy to go through every single recollection he had from the one and only night he met Lawan Raksanatra. He started with the dinner with Worrapon and ended with the confession he used the inside information his client offered him to do the deals in Dengshu Oil and Omega Telecoms. Caro had a whole bunch of questions, some of which were necessary because Andy hadn't explained himself that well, others were clearly to get him to repeat a piece of the story out of sequence to make sure he told it the same way the second time around. It was standard practice for anyone with police interrogation training, or someone who watched a lot of crime movies. Once he finished, they sat in silence for at least half an hour. Then Caro stood and disappeared into the bedroom. It was no more than ten minutes before she re-emerged wearing chic cut-off jeans, sneakers and a long Chanel t-shirt that ended at the top of her thighs. In her hand was a set of car keys. Andy's heart sank; they only used the car in the basement when they went on long journeys.

"You're leaving?" he failed to keep the helplessness out of his voice.

"I have to see Daniel and he left for Hua Hin this afternoon. I called him from the bedroom and he agreed to meet me, we can't have the discussion on the phone."

"What discussion?"

"He thinks you're already helping the police, when he finds out you're not, there is every chance he'll tell them you were seen with the Raksanatra girl. I've got to beg him to give us some time to find out what really happened to her."

"Why would he do that? And what makes you think we could ever find out? We're no detectives."

"I'll call Narong, I'm sure he'll help and I'll be telling Daniel the request to keep his mouth shut is from the man himself. He'll do as he's told, everyone is in awe of Narong."

"So you believe me?" Andy made a feeble attempt at a smile.

"There are two possible scenarios; Narong will help me prove which is correct. Until then judgement is suspended."

She sounded pompous and formal but there was the faintest hint of the old loving Caro in her eyes. For the first time in many weeks, Andy felt like someone was on his side. The door slammed shut and she was gone.

Andy had barely righted the furniture when the door flew open again and his stomach lurched. Instinct told him he should throw himself to the floor and beg for mercy. It was Caro.

"Car keys," she said, picking them up from where she dropped them for a second to unlatch the apartment door.

"You should have called me, I'd have brought them down."

"I tried but it's impossible to get a signal in that basement. I'll see you tomorrow."

This time she pursed her lips gently in what could easily have turned into a kiss to be blown in his direction. She stopped herself but, for a hopeful Andy, it meant what they had together was still there beneath the surface. The door closed as he kissed his fingers and opened his palm in the direction of his departing girlfriend. Maybe things were going to be OK after all.

## The Price

The doubts started to creep in minutes after she left. Why hadn't he offered to go with her? What would he do if Daniel had already gone to the police? And what about Narong? If he didn't agree to use his resources to find Lawan's real killer then where did that leave him? There was nothing he could do until Caroline returned.

An hour passed before Andy could bear it no longer. He tapped out a short, urgent SMS saying he hoped she was safe and begging her to get in touch. Hua Hin is nearly three hours from central Bangkok by road and there was no chance she'd have any news from Daniel, but he was desperate to make contact. No reply.

At ten-thirty his phone buzzed and there was the message from Caro.

"Driving before – no time to reply. Seeing Dan now."

Anger surged in his gut as he saw how she referred to her boss. His rational side understood it was an abbreviation because she was texting, but the use of the short-form name still felt like a betrayal. How could she be so familiar with a guy who held their future in his grubby little hands? It didn't help that Andy had never liked the man, he gave her a tough time along the way, mainly because she was a woman and he was a bully. It was easy to imagine him in school, the kid everyone else picked on, now he had some authority he thought it was payback time. Maybe it was just as well he'd not gone with her, it wouldn't have taken much provocation for Andy to have his hands round the bastard's throat. He couldn't go to the police if the life was choked out of him. Andy shook his head in despair. He'd become accustomed to the out of body experiences, the feeling his true self looked on from a distance as "professional Andy Duncan" went about his daily routine. He now realised these two personas were in a verbal battle in his own head.

"Why's she calling him Dan? This guy is screwing with my life."

"It's a text and she's in a hurry. Get over it."

"Why didn't I go with her? I could have explained it myself."

"Yeah right, and what would have happened if he said the wrong thing?"

"I'd have strangled the little bastard, that's what?"

"And you think that's a smart move?"

"I'm an innocent man, I've done nothing wrong."

"Well you wouldn't be innocent any more if you strangled her boss would you."

"I suppose. What if we can't get Narong to help? Why should he do anything for me? Why should he believe me? I barely know him."

"He's not doing it for you, he's doing it for his beloved Jeab. Caroline wants the truth, so he'll help her get it."

"Are you sure?"

"Course I'm sure. Fancy a drink?"

"Don't mind if I do."

And so the night passed, slowly, agonisingly and ultimately in a haze of Tanqueray Gin and the remnants of an old bottle of tonic that had long since lost its fizz. "You and me both mate," Andy said as he tossed the empty bottle into the trash. He checked his phone at least every five minutes and each hour placed a call from the landline to make sure his mobile really was working. His texts got increasingly desperate but there was no reply from Caroline. He racked his brain for any recollection of a hotel she might have mentioned when she said Daniel was in Hua Hin. At four a.m. he started dialling the number of each of the top hotels, they were all very helpful but confirmed they did not have a guest of that name. Then it occurred to him the room was probably booked in the name of Daniel's boyfriend, but Andy had no idea what it was. He started to go through the list all over again.

"Two gay guys, have you got a couple of gay guys… *farang, kao jai mai?*" The operator terminated the connection and Andy hurled the phone against the living room wall.

Andy woke with a start. It was nine-fifteen and he should have been in the office at least an hour earlier. His mobile was where he left it and he had one received message.

"You have a ten o'clock. Where are you?" It was Sam. Andy didn't bother to reply, he let the phone slip from his hand to the floor.

"Where the fuck was Caroline and what had happened with Daniel?" The argument raged once again in his head. She was simply supposed to convince her boss he was victim of a terrible coincidence and they needed time to prove it. She held the trump card of Narong to twist the little bastard's arm if necessary.

Andy picked up his phone and tried Caroline's number again. It went straight to voicemail. He knew he had to clear his head and made for the bathroom. Ten minutes under a steaming hot shower should do the trick. It was fifteen before he dried himself and found a t-shirt and a pair of shorts. The office was the furthest thing from his mind and Sam's second text asking if he would make his ten o'clock meeting also went unanswered. Andy was searching for a fresh inhaler when the door to the apartment opened. It was Caroline and she looked deathly pale.

"Jesus Caro, where the fuck have you been? Why haven't you answered my messages? What's happened?"

He started across the room but she raised her hands, closed her eyes and shook her head almost imperceptibly. She looked traumatised. He stopped in his tracks.

"Andy don't… it's bad. Really bad."

He walked slowly towards her and held out his hand, after a few seconds, she reluctantly allowed herself to be led to the sofa.

Andy tried to sound calm and soothing, but his voice cracked.

"Tell me what happened."

Her voice was weak and tremulous. "I saw Daniel."

"And he thinks I killed the girl?"

"No… not at all. He knows you didn't kill her."

Andy couldn't stop himself from smiling. "That's great… isn't it? So what happened?"

"Andy, he knows you didn't kill her because he knows who did it. He's always known."

"What? So why hasn't he gone to the police? And what was all the shit about me being involved? Jesus Caro, why didn't you call me?"

"I couldn't use my phone. Andy, you have to hear something first then it will start to make sense."

Andy had the look of a man who didn't believe he would ever get his head around what was happening, but there was nothing he could say. Caroline produced a small audio recorder and clicked play. The voices were instantly recognisable as those of the two people facing each other on the sofa.

"Caro, I'll buy the stocks that are causing the problem."

"Andy, you can't. Where would you get money like that?"

"I don't mean me, I mean the Emerging Fund. Five million is loose change, nobody will ever notice and it will get you off the hook."

"You'd do that for me. It's your career on the line." Caroline's voice sounded vulnerable and bemused.

"It's nothing. At that size of deal, no-one at the firm will even notice it. But that's not going to solve your problems."

"It's not?"

"You need a sure-fire investment winner. I've got one for you."

"How can you be certain?"

"Because I'm about to invest one hundred million dollars into each of Dao Kin and Samaran so the prices are going to fly. You need to get your clients into them before I do. Keep it sensible, in line with what you usually do then it won't be on anyone's radar screens."

"Andy that's front running. It's illegal, we could both get into a lot of trouble."

"Only if we get caught and we won't."

Andy remembered the conversation. It had taken place at the depths of Caro's despair about her own job. It was his way of saving her skin. Using the sheer size of the Emerging Fund to bail her out in a way that would almost certainly never be noticed. The recording was still running but had gone silent, Andy remembered what happened next and to his dismay, it was all there. They both listened to only three or four seconds of what was about twenty minutes of very noisy and passionate sex. Caro hit the stop button

The room fell silent for what felt like an age until Andy found his voice.

"How the hell did that get recorded?"

Caroline looked devastated, her lips moved but no words would come.

"And what's it got to do with a murdered girl? Please tell me what's going on."

"Andy, it's Daniel. It's… blackmail."

"About a couple of dodgy trades and a girl he knows I didn't kill. He can fuck himself."

Andy was up and heading for the door, he would see Daniel himself and sort this out once and for all. Grabbing the car keys, his hand was on the front door before he realised he was barefoot and wearing only a singlet and shorts.

"Andy there's more… much, much more. You have to listen."

She handed over a portfolio report; it was in the standard form Pan Asia Securities would issue to one of their own private clients. The name of the client on the front cover was Andrew Duncan.

"It all started with that oil stock. East African Resources, the one where you told the company they should buy back all the B shares."

Andy looked flabbergasted. "You're joking, I was a fucking white knight. I was only invested in the A shares, my fund would have made nothing if they bought back the B shares. The company didn't even take any notice of me. It was a bit of PR."

"Daniel set me up to get you to do it. I had no idea what he was planning, but when your request was made public, the price of the B shares rose. They made a load of money on the price rise."

"Well you can't pin that on me. I got nothing out of it and neither did my fund."

"They can. They opened an account in your name and bought a load of B shares on your behalf. Anyone looking at it now would say you made that announcement for personal gain. And it's not only the African thing, the account's got loads of trades your firm would never have approved. They started small but now there's nearly two million dollars in there."

Andy's inner fire was extinguished by the realisation he was on the verge of going out in what appeared to be underwear. He walked back to the sofa, never taking his eyes off the crumpled face of his distraught lover.

"Andy, don't say anything. Just listen, you have to hear it all."

He didn't trust his voice, he nodded.

"I couldn't call you because they bugged my phone. That's how they got the tape of us talking about those deals."

"Who's they?"

"Please Andy, listen, there are bits of this I don't know or understand. The only person I know for sure is involved is Daniel."

He nodded again and dug his fingers into the palms of his hands.

"They have this recording that shows you did the deals to help me out. They also know about the other ones you did later. You bought some shares I recommended."

"Yeah, construction stocks. Traffic cones, prefab buildings and some sort of sealant stuff... that was peanuts. What could possibly be wrong with those trades? Apart from the fact you recommended them."

"I'm sorry Andy, Daniel badgered me all morning to get you to do it, I didn't even look at the stocks. They were shell companies, they've got no assets, no business, it's just a way of routing cash to the Thai mafia. He said anyone looking at the deals would see you were funding organised crime."

Andy was desperate to ask questions, what did any of this have to do with the girl? He could see that Daniel used Caroline to set him up with some dubious trades for the Emerging Fund, it was bad but none of it was earth shattering. It would cost him his career and all of a sudden that didn't seem to matter. He opened his mouth to speak, but Caroline raised her hand.

"They must have bugged you as well, probably your phone. You don't even have to be using it for it to work."

There was another recording and she pressed play. It was the conversation he had at Worrapon's private club, the night Lawan Raksanatra disappeared. They'd selected one segment, the part where Worrapon told him about the dry oil wells in Africa and the imminent takeover of an Asian telecoms firm. Twenty-four hours later Andy acted on those tips and the Emerging Fund made a huge capital gain. He could contain himself no longer.

"So Worrapon is in on this too. He set me up."

Caroline looked utterly bemused.

"Andy, that's impossible. He's a highly respected businessman, there's no way he's involved in something like this."

He gave her a knowing look. Most of the richest men in Thailand were supposedly "highly respectable", but cocktail parties generally buzzed with tales of their shady deals.

"Andy, if Worrapon was involved, he'd have a minion do the dirty work. He'd be crazy to implicate himself. This is Daniel's work, they taped you to get access to information, they used me to encourage you to do deals you'd never have done otherwise. I'm so sorry."

"So they ruin my career, I'm past caring. What's the worst that can happen, they sack me and I never get to work again. Fuck it. I've had it anyway."

"Andy, they put you in jail for this sort of thing. It's not just your career. And anyway… they haven't finished yet. They're going to make it look like you killed the girl."

He slumped forward, unable to get his head round why this was happening to him. Why anyone would go to so much effort to destroy him.

"You don't remember anything after the club, do you?"

"Nothing, until I woke up with a naked girl in my bed, in a hotel I don't remember checking into."

"Was there a taxi outside when you left the club?"

Andy thought for a moment, he desperately wanted it to come back to him but it wouldn't. He shrugged.

"Daniel says they had a car outside. You were drunk and the driver helped you into the back seat and offered you a bottle of water. It was drugged. They did much the same to the girl and they got you both into the hotel via a service elevator. One of his associates took the room, posing as you. Whatever they gave you was enough to dull the memory but not the senses apparently."

Caroline bit her bottom lip and a tear rolled down her cheek, she looked away from him and her shoulders slumped.

"What do you mean Caro?"

"You had sex with her, they showed me the tape. You looked like you were almost out of it for sure, like you were really high on something but I saw it." She buried her head in her hands.

"Caro, I swear. I have no recollection of any of this. It wasn't me… or if it was, you saw for yourself I was drugged to the eyeballs."

"I know… I know, but still, watching that… and knowing what happened after. It's just so…"

Andy reached for her, but she pulled away.

"Caro, I don't know what to say. You've heard it yourself; it's all been a set up. They planned this from the start and we've both been victims. They've used both of us." He paused, but there was no response. "I don't get why anyone would go to this much trouble to destroy me. Why?"

"Andy, they want something from you. They say if you give it to them, they will give you your life back. No-one needs to know about the deals, they can destroy the evidence."

Andy started to laugh, it was inconceivable he had anything that would make all of this worthwhile.

"What do they want?"

"One billion US dollars."

**The trade**

As Andy Duncan watched the traffic of the Chao Praya river hundreds of feet below, he dreamt of a time machine. One that could take him back to Rawai Beach, the surf school and the most perfect sunset he'd ever seen. It never occurred to him to return to the time when his mother was still there, or to his teenage years when he could have changed so much of what happened in his life. He just wanted to expunge the last four years, his time at Berwick Archer, the things he'd done and the person he'd become.

He thought again about the dinner at the Savoy and the offer he got from his father. Three months at Berwick Archer and then enough cash to travel the world for a year. Maybe his time machine could take him back to that dinner and he could look his father in the eye and say, "No thanks Dad, I'll pass." Or the fateful day when Brad Tait lost the firm twenty-three million dollars and Andy found a way to shift the blame onto someone else. His reward was a job as a trainee fund manager, apprentice to a man with neither morals nor scruples. A phrase he heard his father use a hundred times fought its way to the front of his mind, he was pretty sure the origins were biblical. He normally tuned out when Victor did his impersonation of a Presbyterian minister but, as he looked out onto the Thai capital, he could imagine his father standing in the pulpit wearing a starched collar and frock coat, peering at a cowering congregation over tiny steel-rimmed glasses. His sermon was building to a crescendo and he punched the air as he delivered the line.

"When you sow the wind... you will reap the whirlwind."

Andy never really focused on what that meant before. He and Tait joked about being alchemists, turning base metal into gold. It was an unduly flattering interpretation of their achievements, encouraged by the boundless generosity of their employers. Sowing the wind sounded like an equally improbable challenge and it felt like that was indeed what Andy had attempted to do. Now, as his father predicted, the whirlwind was here and he was slap bang in the middle of it.

More than twenty-four hours had passed since Caroline delivered Daniel's ultimatum. As the story unfolded, Andy was incredulous at the effort that had gone into snaring both of them. Daniel and his associates held his life in their hands. The share deals would be enough to guarantee that he'd never work in the investment business again and, in all probability, he'd be sent to jail. That would be enough to force the hand of any man. Nonetheless, they decided to organise the murder of an innocent girl and ensure the evidence could point in only one direction. Forensics and Andy's own silence, once the girl went missing, would be considered conclusive in any court in the world.
"Why did they have to kill someone, didn't they have enough on me with all the work related stuff?" He didn't really expect Caroline to have the answer.
"I asked Daniel the same question."
'What did he say?"
"They never intended to kill anyone. When they planned all of this, they were going for a few million dollars and were pretty sure you could cover up the loss somehow. That's why they tried to put your career on the line. Then they got greedy. The problem was, the more they planned to ask of you, the more they thought you might walk away. They decided they needed more leverage."
"So they just picked some innocent girl?"
"Oh no, they chose very carefully. She was the only daughter of one of Thailand's toughest policemen. He'll leave no stone unturned to find out who killed her and he'll want to get to them before any of his colleagues. Raksanatra will want vengeance not justice. Killing her was all part of the plan. If you run away, you'll be looking over your shoulder for the rest of your life."

"So I'm fucked anyway. Why should I do anything they want?"

Andy hurled his glass across the room and watched it shatter against the wall. An appropriate metaphor, it briefly occurred to him, for his life with Caroline.

"Andy, they have put a huge amount of resource into this and the rewards are enormous. They told me what's in it for you if you play ball."

"I'm listening."

"We get twenty million US dollars and a couple of genuine Hong Kong passports. They're not copies, they have someone who can issue the real thing. We'll have new identities."

"We?"

"Of course it's we. We're in this together and I want us to get out of it together."

"What else?" A wave of relief washed over him.

"There's a policeman. He isn't the top guy but he's supervising the forensic side of the investigation. Once they have their money, he'll switch all the samples they have. A few days after that, a body will be found that matches the forensics in every respect. The police will find their murderer and the case will be closed."

"Great, someone else gets killed. How do I know it won't be me?

"It won't be. I think we can trust them to keep their side of the deal."

"Why should I trust them to do any of this? What if I get them their money and they leave me to my fate. That's what happens in the movies, the criminals tie up the loose ends, that means they kill anyone who knows what they did."

"Andy, I'll be at your side. It's our chance to make a lot of money and get away from all of this. If they come for you, they have to come for me too. I've already explained to Daniel that if anything happens to me, then Narong will hunt him down. It will all be in a letter I leave with my solicitor. It's not a chance he can take. Anyway, what could we do to implicate them in anything? When this is done we'll have broken every securities law there is, we'll have stolen a billion dollars and helped to cover up a murder. Who are we going to run to with that story?"

Andy weighed up what he heard, trying to work out the options open to him, then he punched the air.

"Caroline, we can go to Narong now. He loves you like a daughter; he'll do anything for you. He can help us with this right now. Then we don't have to face this on our own."

She took his hands in hers and gave him a weak smile somewhere between reassuring and condescending. It reminded him of the time he told his father he was the best swimmer in his nursery class.

"Next time we go home to England Dad," he explained. "I'm going to swim." It appeared there was more chance of him making that journey than of Narong Sunarawani coming to their assistance.

"Andy, you're a wonderful man and I love you to bits, but sometimes you can be so dumb," she even patted him on the hand just like his father had done when he was four. He cocked his head on one side and waited for her to continue.

"Narong was a huge investor in Dengshu Oil, he lost a fortune when those wells were declared dry. It was also him who started Omega Telecoms. He built that company up from nothing with his own money."

Andy still couldn't see why that had anything to do with the trouble he was in.

"If I ask for his help now, I'll have to tell him what they have on you. I'll have to explain all the dodgy deals. He couldn't sell his stake in Dengshu like you did, you used privileged information to bail out and leave investors like Narong to take the loss. And you bought into Omega right at the last minute, he built that from nothing and you made a killing with a single illegal trade that took you two minutes. You can't expect him to come running to your aid right now."

Andy nodded, she was right of course. Narong said little in public but it was known he had little time for the wheeler-dealers who made money without ever producing anything tangible. His companies produced oil and made cars, telephones and machinery, they employed thousands of people and were a cornerstone of the real Thai economy. Why should he help a financial speculator who made money with information he had no right to possess?

"So why should Daniel be afraid of him?"

"Daniel knows he can't hurt me. If he does, Narong will go after him, whatever the circumstances."

"So this way, Daniel makes a fortune, we get twenty million dollars and Narong is none the wiser."

"What the eye doesn't see. Isn't that one of your English expressions?"

"And there's one other thing," Andy said, pressing his fingers into his forehead.

"What's that?"

"What choice do I have?"

As the evening news began, Andy reached for the remote control and turned off the TV. In seconds the face of Lawan Raksanatra would inevitably be on screen, they'd have found a few more photos of her, or there'd be another interview with a friend or a teacher lamenting the tragedy of a young life cruelly extinguished. Had Andy watched the broadcast, he'd have seen the place where the body was found and an interview with the senior police officer in charge of the forensic investigation. He explained how the manner in which the girl was assaulted ensured there was a great deal of genetic material and man-made fibre they were confident could be linked to the perpetrator. He stated that an initial screening had been completed and it was unlikely the girl's murderer had a record of offences in Thailand. Further detailed analysis would be undertaken but to date there had been no match with the database of known offenders. The policeman went on to say that science had advanced to the stage where they could use the material they recovered to undertake physiological profiling and they'd certainly be able to identify whether the person they sought was Thai or foreign. If the latter, they may even be able to establish roughly where the person had come from.

The interviewer was impressed and in response to a direct question, Inspector Mongkut Tharanyatta of the Pattaya police was happy to say he was confident they would find the person who killed this beautiful young girl. Indeed the net was already closing.

# The Plan

"You can't be serious. They really think this will work?" Andy shook his head in disbelief.

"Andy, I know nothing about this side of the business, they told me to give you this document and said you'd know what to do. I've never got involved in how the money actually flows."

Caroline looked as though she was about to cry. Andy had spoken to Daniel only once on the phone since Caroline returned from Hua Hin and they agreed she should be the conduit for any instructions. His effeminate little squeak was always irritating, under these circumstances, Daniel's voice brought Andy to the brink of an uncontrollable rage.

"I'm sorry sweetheart, but they have controls to stop people doing this sort of stuff. There's a whole bunch of ways the people at Berwick Archer will stop it in its tracks."

"Daniel said you'd react like that. What's the problem?"

"This whole thing relies on me liquidating nearly a fifth of the portfolio and then delaying the purchase of new stocks so the sale proceeds can sit in a bank account for nearly a week. Then we're supposed to open a deposit account with a bank no-one's ever heard of and pay the money over. And that's when your mates tap their wizard's cane and make the money disappear. Who thought this up for Christ's sake? Harry fucking Potter?"

"They're not my mates Andy, I've got plenty to lose here too."

"I know, I'm sorry. It won't work and when the bells go off, it's me they'll be coming for and Daniel and his mates will hang me out to dry for Lawan too."

"Why won't it work? Daniel was pretty certain they'd thought it through."

"As soon as I try to sell that much stock, the trades get blocked until both my father, as Head of Risk, and the goddamn Bull himself sign in to the system and give them digital authorisation. There's no way that will happen and that's not all."

"Sounds like it's enough. What else?"

"We can only use new deposit takers with the same approval. This says we are depositing the excess cash with Cathay

Bank. Never heard of them and neither has anyone else." He paused to think for a second, he was certain the plan was doomed to fail. "First Independent is one of the biggest banks in the world, it looks after the assets of the fund, they won't allow us to place a deposit with a new counterparty without the same digital approval. Even if you could get round that, they'll have someone looking at transfers of that size and they'll stop it manually. You'd need someone on the inside at First Independent to make sure the money goes across. I can't make that happen."

Caroline was holding something in her hand. "Daniel said to give you this."

Andy looked at the plain manila envelope as though it might be contaminated. He reluctantly took it from her and ripped it open. There was a very simple message inside.

"We will have access to the digital passwords and we have someone at First Independent who will approve the deposit. Now get on with it."

Andy could not help but look around to see who might be watching them. It took a second to realise Daniel could hardly have listened to their conversation, considered his reply, had it typed up then placed in Caro's hand within a few seconds, all without Andy seeing a thing. Whoever he was up against was several steps ahead and genuinely had thought it all through. They even knew the objections he was likely to raise. There was nothing left for him to do but to execute the instructions he'd been given to the letter.

The trades were to be made on Wednesday; the cash would be available on Friday and by close of business that would disappear into the bowels of the banking system. Daniel clearly had an expert, with a detailed understanding of corporate structures and the labyrinthine complexities of international finance to route the money round the system so it would be all but untraceable by the middle of the following week. It would be that long before Berwick Archer noticed the money was missing. The deposit with Cathay Bank was supposed to be repaid to the firm on the following Wednesday. Only when it failed to arrive would alarm bells start to ring. He and Caro were due to fly to Hong Kong as soon as Cathay Bank received the cash. Later that night, as Mr and Mrs William Ward, they'd leave for Santiago in Chile. There'd be stopovers in Tokyo and Dallas but when they arrived in South

America, they'd have full access to the twenty million dollar share Daniel promised. If they failed to contact Caro's lawyer each Friday thereafter, a letter would be on its way to Narong, and Daniel and his associates would be marked men.

    Andy was instructed to work as normal and stay at his desk until Daniel confirmed the cash had been received. He and Caro would then head for the airport and freedom. An accomplice was in place inside First Independent, the bank that would pay out the billion dollars on behalf of the fund. He'd advised they might be required to call the Bangkok office immediately before the payment was processed. It was essential for Andy to be at his desk in case that happened. Daniel also wanted him to wait until the cash moved, in case anything went wrong. The young Englishman could already imagine the torture he'd go though right up to the point the cash transferred. Every knock on his door and every ring of his phone could be Turner, the Thai Securities Authorities or the Royal Thai Police, telling him the game was up. He shivered at the prospect, knowing he wouldn't be able to focus on anything to do with his job for the remainder of his time as an employee of Berwick Archer. There was little point in actively managing the Emerging Fund. In less than a week, there'd be a billion dollar deficit in the assets and the firm for which he worked would be holed below the water line. He could almost hear the theme tune from the movie Titanic, and suddenly he had visions of that final scene, except it was he and Caroline clinging to a piece of driftwood as the mighty liner gave up the struggle and disappeared beneath the waves. Andy racked his brain to recall whether their fictional equivalents both survived.

    Desperate for something to take his mind off what lay ahead, Andy thumbed through the DVD collection gathering dust near the TV. There was also a small collection of books, most of which came with the apartment. It was never anticipated that anyone would read them; they were simply intended to convey the right impression to visitors. Most had won some obscure literary award or suggested an interest in a trendy branch of the arts. There were books on Buddhism, Taoism and Macrobiotic cookery. Andy smiled as he tried to remember the last time either he or Caroline attempted anything more ambitious in the kitchen than toast. Exclusive restaurants and gourmet take-outs had fed the couple since the day they met. It was yet another symbol of how superficial and fake his life had become. Only two of the books were his own purchases. One was the work of a journalist who climbed Everest. The main reason people die on the great mountain, he explained, is because they failed to consider that when they reach the summit, they're only halfway to their objective. There are far more deaths on the way down than on the way up, as many climbers have nothing left once they make the peak. Andy was resigned to what he was about to do, but the parallel wasn't lost on him. In truth, he got nowhere near the top of his trade but there was a very real chance he wouldn't make it back to base camp.

One other book was familiar and it now seemed ironic that that was a detailed instruction manual for the aspiring fund manager. It had been his bible as he tried to make his way at Berwick Archer but he'd got barely three-quarters of the way through when his first serious bonus cheque hit his account. It wasn't a conscious decision but he never read another page after that day. Subconsciously, he decided that he had nothing left to learn. As he picked up the book once again, he turned to the last few pages he read before it was discarded. It was revelatory stuff at the time, setting out the strategies that could be pursued to control risk. The word "hedge" has only negative connotations for many people. The funds that bear the name are allegedly run by unscrupulous scoundrels bent on lining their own pockets regardless of the consequences for the man in the street. In reality, a genuine "hedge fund" uses complex techniques to allow its investors to take risk, for which they will be rewarded, but to ensure they are protected if Plan A doesn't go as expected. A lot of fund managers get so excited about the rewards available on the upside they never really bother to ensure there's a Plan B. In minutes Andy was immersed in what he was reading, he should have had it painted in man-sized letters on the wall. Risk is fine, if the rewards are there to be had, but always make sure you have some protection in case it all goes wrong. Wise words indeed.

He checked his contacts list and was relieved to see that he had the number he sought, it was a question of whether the person he wanted to speak to had changed their mobile phone.

**The Execution**

The police were called to James Turner's house on Hong Kong's Peak Road at four minutes past midday on Friday. The man himself stumbled into the road and narrowly avoided being struck by a passing taxi. Inevitably, the driver chose not to stop, he didn't have a fare-paying passenger in the back so it would have been an awful waste of valuable time. At first, his neighbours failed to recognise the bedraggled, unshaven character trying to attract the attention of anyone who might stop and listen. There was blood on his hands and face and his white monogrammed shirt was torn at the neck. Passers-by anxiously moved to the other side of the road as Turner weaved his way through a line of parked cars trying desperately to find someone who'd come to his aid.

"Help me please, they killed her... Jesus Christ they killed her."

David Madigan had lived three doors away for nearly five years but even he did a double take before he could be sure the down and out screaming in the street was the same man who'd sipped vintage cognac in his dining room a few nights earlier.

"James, what on earth...? What's happened?"

Turner slumped to the ground as he realised he'd found someone who'd listen.

"David, they killed Milly, they fucking shot her right there in my living room. I did everything they asked but they shot her anyway." James Turner was crying like a child. His chest heaved and the challenge of speaking and breathing at the same time had overwhelmed him. He sucked air into his lungs in huge gulps and tears flowed down his face.

Madigan put his arm round the man and felt him rock back and forth in his arms like a baby.

"James, where's your family? Where are Kate and the kids?"

Madigan tried to sound soothing whilst gesturing to a woman who stopped next to them to call the police. He mimed the word a couple of times and touched the thumb of his right hand to his ear and the little finger to his lips.

"They're inside… they're fine. It's Milly… they killed Milly."

Three hours passed before the Hong Kong police established a coherent account of what occurred in Turner's house in the previous two days. They noted the bags stacked neatly in the hall. Turner explained the doorbell rang as he phoned for a taxi to take the family to the airport. They were due to head for Phuket for a long weekend and the businessman cursed the fact he'd given his own driver the weekend off. Had they been collected by his chauffeur, the alarm would have been raised and the horrors of the subsequent forty-eight hours could have been averted.

A package had arrived from Berwick Archer's office in London that required a signature. Such a delivery was a regular event and Turner had no reason to be suspicious. As soon as he opened the door, the deliveryman placed a TASER on his chest and pulled the trigger. Turner was thrown across the room as the charge tore though his body. By the time he came to his senses there were two men in his home and one already had his arm around Kate's neck. Both intruders wore light, blue silk bandanas over their mouths and thin woollen caps on their heads. Only their eyes were visible and all Turner could say with any confidence was they were foreign. As the family housekeeper appeared in the doorway, the shorter of the two men pushed Kate towards her husband and grabbed the Filipino maid by the hair. The taller intruder covered Turner and his wife with a high calibre handgun.

"Children?"

Milly looked in panic at her employer but said nothing.

"Children." The man screamed in her ear and pulled hard until a handful of hair separated from her scalp. She roared with pain.

"Milly, find them."

Turner knew the men would search for the kids if Milly didn't get them and the consequences could be far worse. Before she could turn to the staircase, Edward and Sophie appeared at the living room door. Turner's son was barely fifteen but he instantly stepped in front of his sister trying to shield her from what was going on. Sophie was a year older but generally deferred to her younger sibling.

"Not hurt… if you obey." It was hard to know if the man was struggling with his grasp of English or if his staccato delivery was a deliberate attempt to hide an accent.

"My wallet is in my jacket. There's twenty thousand US in the safe. I'll give you the pins for all my cards. Just leave us alone."

Turner had never been in a situation he couldn't buy his way out of before. He sounded remarkably calm, totally confident that cash was the answer. The man laughed, but showed no interest in the wallet or the safe.

"Laptop."

Turner looked confused, they couldn't be there just to steal his computer, it was inconceivable. The man took the hesitation as defiance, he pointed at his colleague.

"He like to fuck." He gestured towards the females in the room. "Maid maybe… or wife... or daughter?"

Kate tried to make herself as small as possible as the taller man stepped forward, Sophie shrank back still further behind her brother.

"No... no… you can have it, laptop, money, anything. Just leave them alone."

The shorter intruder, clearly the leader, appeared only to grunt but, in response, the second man's shoulders slumped and he backed off.

'My briefcase." Turner nodded in the direction of the luggage stacked in the hallway. In seconds the laptop was open and Shorty had also located a small plastic box that was no more than four centimetres square. He swiftly connected it to the USB port of the machine and reached out to grab Turner by the wrist. Having pushed his captive's index finger down onto the perspex top of the box, a dialogue box appeared on the screen.

"Password… office system."

Turner responded with a nine-digit code, praying his mind wouldn't go blank. In seconds Shorty was expertly navigating his way through the icons on the laptop. Finally he turned the screen towards Turner. He was looking at the office trading system. There were two outstanding alerts both of which stated they required his urgent attention, the originator for both was Andrew Duncan.

"Authorise them." The man spoke softly but the menace in his voice was clear.

The first alert was headed "trading limits" and showed that the fund manager wanted to sell one billion dollars worth of stock owned by the Emerging Fund. There were some matching purchases that reinvested every penny of the proceeds, but these were not due to settle until the following week. The fund would still have the required level of stock market exposure, together with a huge cash balance for nearly a week. The second alert was a request to open a new deposit relationship with Cathay Bank in Shanghai. Obviously that was where the excess cash would be deposited. Standard procedure required informal consultation with the Chairman of the Group Credit Committee and courtesy demanded a call be made to Timothy Clarke, the Group CEO. Berwick Archer's operating manuals had been lovingly crafted by Victor Duncan, and he believed he'd thought of everything. A scenario in which two armed intruders held the CEO and his family hostage had not been considered. James Turner looked up from the screen, his imminent, flagrant breach of procedure being the furthest thing from his mind. The image that burned into his brain was the taller of the two men staring longingly at his sixteen-year-old daughter. Without hesitation he hit the button marked "authorise." When yet another dialogue box appeared, he typed a second password. The cursor was transformed into a rotating red blob that turned for what felt like an age, then the screen went black. Turner's heart was in his mouth. Then the first page appeared again, both the alerts were shown in green and next to each was the word "authorised."

"OK, that's it." Shorty seemed to be satisfied.

"I've done what you asked, please leave us alone," Turner begged.

"We will."

"You will?"

"In forty-eight hours." Shorty slammed the laptop shut, dropped back into the armchair next to the desk and kicked off his shoes.

Prem Boonamee's assignment was simpler on one level. No family to worry about and the maid had the weekend off. She left the night before when she got the call to say her mother was sick back in Manila. They originally worked on the basis she'd be there. Her absence made it simpler from a logistical perspective but it meant he'd have less leverage. The threat of pain is a powerful incentive for anyone to behave in a way that they'd normally refuse to consider. If someone you care about is likely to be the victim, one's resistance level will be lower still.

Boonamee wasn't too concerned either way, his target would do as he demanded. Getting into Victor's Hong Kong apartment was the easy part. Song arranged for a significant cash sum to fall into the hands of the building's Head of Security. Boonamee rang the bell and was admitted to the man's ground floor office, as arranged, at six that morning. The key would have to be returned when Boonamee left, that would also be when he would slice through the man's carotid artery. Song hated loose ends.

His two accomplices were not due to enter Turner's house for another three hours, but they'd agreed Victor Duncan might not give up the crucial password so easily. Boonamee needed time to work his dark magic. They also knew the Risk Director was out of his apartment by seven each day, had they left it later he wouldn't have been there.

By eight o'clock, Boonamee realised they misjudged Victor in one very significant respect. The Thai's brief was to obtain the password and deliver an authorisation for the two alerts requested by Andrew Duncan in Bangkok. What was to follow would mirror exactly what was planned for Turner's house just ten minutes away on foot. Berwick Archer's Risk Director would have to be held for forty-eight hours until it was time to physically transfer the proceeds of the sale to the Cathay Bank. There was also an outside chance he'd receive a call from First Independent, the bank responsible for the assets of the Emerging Fund, to double check the transfer of such a huge amount. That would not happen for two more days and Boonamee was to keep him company in the meantime.

The plan did not allow for the fact that Victor was not nearly as healthy as when he visited the offices of Berwick Archer in Bangkok. Song was known to him as Tanawat Chanpol, the man who made the Bangkok office work. The Risk Director reported favourably on the remarkable efficiency of the lawyer, and Song remembered a man who looked to be hard pressed but otherwise in the best of health.

In the intervening weeks, Victor visited his doctor on several occasions but told no-one he'd shortly need time off for a cardiac procedure. The man facing Boonamee that morning was a shadow of his former self. As a consequence it took the young Thai only thirty minutes to extract the password. The alerts had barely reached Victor's screen on the trading system when Boonamee was ready to have them authorised. It was an unexpected bonus, which would quickly be followed by the first hitch in Song's carefully orchestrated plan. When Boonamee turned to explain he'd be around for another forty-eight hours, he was staring at a man who had a familiar look on his face. The young Thai had seen that look before, each time on the face of someone whose heart had stopped beating.

Boonamee had long since lost any compunction about the acts Song asked him to undertake. He bullied, he cajoled, he organised and occasionally he killed. Once in a while he would get some idea of what was at stake, how much money flowed in as a consequence of their deals. He never really focused on it, just on the cash Song regularly dropped into his hand. Song wanted it that way, he said Boonamee shouldn't be distracted by the business side. In truth he didn't want his enforcer to dwell on how much money they were making because then he might realise he was getting a relatively small cut.

This time they had no choice, he'd know exactly how much money was being stolen. Although Boonamee had secured the initial authorisations, he needed to stick around until Friday. Only then would the final cash transfer be approved and, if the bank called for a verbal confirmation, Victor would have to do that in person. Song's plan considered several scenarios which Boonamee might have to handle. None of them allowed for the possibility that Berwick Archer's Risk Director might be dead.

Boonamee had nowhere to go and no idea what to do next. He'd obtained both passwords more easily than expected; he'd have to use the second on Friday to give the digital authorisation of the cash transfer. If the bank called for a verbal approval, then Song's plan was in ashes. In all probability he'd blown the whole deal.

As night fell, Boonamee sat in the darkened living room of Victor Duncan's apartment. The body of the owner was wrapped in a shower curtain and lay in the bath. The only light came from the blaze of neon that would keep Victoria Island bathed in a bright white glow until dawn. Boonamee desperately wanted to sleep but was still racking his brains for what to do next. Should he call Song and explain what had happened? Or pray that on Friday the transfer would proceed without a hitch? That was part of what kept sleep at bay, the other thing was the absolute certainty he'd dream of a girl, a knife and blood. So much blood.

One hour before James Turner emerged onto the street outside his house, shirt torn and hands covered in blood, Cho Wan Kei was gnawing the last few millimetres of his fingernails in his splendid office overlooking Hong Kong harbour. He'd spent twenty-three years with First Independent Bank but, as a Chinese, never rose to the heights he felt he deserved. The organisation was based in Boston so it was unsurprising the very top guys were American, but there'd been way too many slights, too many bonus payments that barely met his worst expectations and too many appraisals that gleefully detailed his failings while ignoring the dedication and skill he brought to his role. Senior positions became available regularly in the Asian business and he applied every time. Within weeks they'd announce another import from the USA. In the previous five years he'd reported to seven different bosses, all of whom were younger, less qualified and mono-lingual. Cho was fluent in Mandarin and Cantonese as well as English, yet it meant nothing to his superiors. They mistook Asian courtesy for timidity and convinced themselves a local could never survive in the cut and thrust of global finance. Most of the new arrivals from Boston had only ever eaten Chinese food from a carton in their homeland and paid lip service to local culture. In his first few years he was grateful a huge multi-national enterprise gave him a chance.

Two decades later he despised his bosses and was comforted only by the certain knowledge it would only take a couple of decades for China to replace the USA as the only genuine superpower. There were rumours of a new round of cost cutting and endless speculation he'd be on the list. There'd certainly be a bean counter somewhere in Head Office working out how to pay the minimum severance, to screw him on his pension and to make sure he never cashed those share options they told him would be the road to riches. Cho was at the end of his tether, if they weren't going to give him what he deserved then he planned to take it.

When his assistant knocked on his door at midday, Cho nearly soiled his trousers. He'd spent the morning thinking of how he could renege on the promise he made to the Thai lawyer. He tried vainly to recall that stupid English expression about stable doors and bolting horses as he realised there could be no going back. Cho had already done enough to get himself arrested, if he didn't go through with the final part of the plan, there'd be no escape. In the early years of the twenty-first century, the big banks appeared to compete with one another as to which could be the most profligate, reckless and out of control. Even so, most insisted on knowing something about the creditworthiness of the other financial institutions their clients used. For Berwick Archer to deposit a billion dollars with Cathay Bank, a detailed report had to be prepared by one of Cho's staff and approved by both he and his immediate superior. He was pleased but not surprised at how easy it was to falsify the documents and get the details of the organisation loaded onto the bank's system. Head Office was certain to notice the irregularity within a couple of days and if he stayed in Hong Kong, his world would come crashing down around him.

At nine that morning a small package had arrived containing details of an afternoon flight to Thailand, together with a passport in the name of Wu Fo Chin. He'd compared it with his own genuine document and could see no difference. Also in the package was a Platinum Amex, an ATM card and a statement showing there was a bank account waiting for him in Bangkok with five million US dollars to its credit. He could earn all of that in less than ten minutes, starting with that knock on the door. The pretty young clerk passed him a standard form showing one of the bank's clients, Berwick Archer, had instructed the transfer of one billion US dollars to Cathay Bank on term deposit on behalf of its Emerging Fund. Cho was required to call the CEO and Risk Director and ask for their coded confirmation of the transfer. A date stamp and the initials of the young clerk indicated she'd already put in a call to Andrew Duncan, head of the firm's Bangkok office. He'd given the necessary confirmation that the transfer was genuine. Cho was required to speak to the two senior men in Hong Kong and ask for the third, fourth, eighth and ninth characters of their password. His task was to ensure that the numbers he was told over the phone matched those that appeared on his screen, then he could confirm the bank's authorisation.

The transfer flashed red in front of him. All he had to do was make the calls. The first number he dialled was his wife of ten years. They both recognised it was a huge mistake after only eighteen months, but neither could muster the courage to quit. He told her he'd been called away on business and had no intention of coming back. The second call was to the only restaurant whose number he'd committed to memory. Cho did not need a table and had no intention of turning up for the booking he made. His office partitions were only half-frosted glass and for the moment it was important he appeared to have made two phone calls. As he terminated the second call, he signed the document confirming both Berwick Archer's senior employees had authorised the transfer with the correct codes, then he clicked on the small red dialogue box on his screen. It asked for a password, which he typed into the space indicated. The cursor whirled and for a second he expected an alarm to go off, for metal shutters to slide down securing the exits from his office and for armed guards to appear from nowhere. It vaguely occurred to him that the metal shutters would be overkill if the guards were really armed, but then he was jolted firmly back into the real world. The cursor stopped spinning and there was a single phrase on his screen. It said, "Transfer Authorised."

Turner's family hadn't washed or changed clothes in two days. The female captives quickly decided that although they were allowed to eat and drink they'd do so as little as possible. The intruders made it clear they'd not be allowed to visit the bathroom unaccompanied and they were anxious to avoid the need.

Just fifteen minutes before Cho gave the trade it's final approval, James Turner dealt with the alert on his screen, exactly as he had two days before. Once again it was in response to a request from Andrew Duncan, this time to transfer the cash proceeds of the securities sold two days earlier.
"What now?" The question was directed at Shorty.
"All done." Shorty had not communicated with a single complete sentence in two days and it was still impossible to tell whether this was the limit of his linguistic talents or a ruse to hide his identity.
"You're going to leave us alone now." Turner tried to make it sound like an instruction but there was no authority in his voice.
"Sure."
The men were clearly preparing to leave, but then Shorty paused.
"One thing," he said, nodding to the taller man who grabbed the neckline of Milly's dress. As she was dragged to her feet, the fabric ripped and she reached up to protect her modesty. In doing so she lost her balance and crashed back to the floor. That's when the taller man shot her three times in the chest and that's when Kate and Sophie Turner started to scream.

"Charlie, you're in charge for God's sake. You have to deal with this, I think there's something wrong here."
"OK, but take me through the detail again."
Charles Maybury had been with Berwick Archer's Asian business for twenty years. As Head of Research, he hired clever, beautiful women and his team effortlessly guided the investment strategy of the firm. When he heard people describe his team as Charlie's Angels, he'd shake his head in feigned disapproval and launch into a well-rehearsed speech about their professionalism and expertise. Then he'd sift through the latest batch of applications and discard anyone who was male or unattractive, without a second glance at their qualifications. In all his time at the

firm, he'd never been confronted with the sort of issue facing him at that moment.

Standing in front of him was the firm's legal counsel in Hong Kong. Heather Cox was easily attractive enough to make it into Charlie's own team, but was always so damned aggressive. He'd never have been able to put up with that sort of crap. Charles tried to focus on the document she put in front of him and the explanation she gave as to why there might be a serious problem with the Emerging Fund. Heather was anxious for him to call the Group's Chief Operating Officer in London but first, he had to get the story straight in his head. It was bad enough that both Turner and Victor Duncan were out of the office at the same time, leaving him in charge, but there was another pressing issue. Heather Cox was leaning over his desk, pointing at the relevant paragraphs on the offending document. Her shirt had come open and he could see the edge of a very lacy bra that was fighting a losing battle to keep her breasts in check. There was also the tiniest hint of a bump under the lawyer's skirt close to the top of her thigh. In Charles' experience that could only mean one thing... stockings. Berwick Archer's Head of Research was not used to being confronted with administrative issues, they normally fell to either the CEO or the Head of Risk. That was not his main problem. As Heather Cox became more heated in her argument, his main concern was to conceal a growing erection.

"Charles, I've never heard of Cathay Bank but now First Independent has sent over this list of our deposit relationships and there it is."

"OK, so how much have we placed with them."

"Nothing."

Maybury winced and pulled his chair a little closer to the desk. "So what's the problem? How can you get so worked up about an empty deposit account?"

"The account was only opened on Wednesday and I checked what else went on in the Emerging Fund on that day. Andrew Duncan sold a billion dollars worth of stock and the proceeds clear today. I think the account is going to be used to deposit that money."

"Have you talked to James or Victor about this?"

"I can't contact either of them. It's the first time I've ever known them both to be out at the same time. That's why I'm talking to you." All the emphasis in her voice fell on the word "you".

Charles felt like he'd been slapped and in an instant the pressure on his trouser zipper eased a little. Drinking with his friends, he liked to share his observations about how people interact. Amongst his favourite was the idea of the "implied sentence ending." It's not about what you say. It's how you say it. Heather Cox said, "That's why I'm talking to you." Charles heard, "That's why I'm talking to you, you useless disgusting little pervert." He was getting irritated and really wanted to get her out of his office, but he had to hear her out.

"Heather, are you telling me James and Victor know nothing about this account?"

"I can't get hold of them to find out. They must have authorised it on the system otherwise it wouldn't exist, but they're not here to confirm what it's for."

"Hang on." Charles tapped his fingers on his desk in frustration. "You're saying they authorised this already, so what on earth is the problem?"

"I usually get a draft contract before we open an account with a new bank. I've seen nothing on this one and neither James nor Victor is here to explain what's going on. Something is wrong; I know it and I need you to raise it with London. I've tried but they're all in meetings and nobody will interrupt them for someone of my lowly level."

There she goes again, thought Maybury, she hadn't used the words, but he definitely heard "the sexist bastards" at the end of that sentence.

"Let me get this straight. If James or Victor were here to explain this, you'd be happy. You're just suspicious because they're both out."

"I guess so. The account looks odd. I can't find Cathay Bank anywhere on the list of regulated financial institutions and now neither of them is here to explain it. It's not stacking up."

"I'll deal with it." Charles Maybury sounded like he was convinced. "I'll make the call."

Heather Cox smiled for the first time since she entered his office and went to pull up a chair at the side of his desk. Maybury shook his head.

"I'll call you when I've sorted it out."

The lawyer retreated reluctantly and the door closed behind her. Maybury decided, as he watched her leave, he'd made a significant error of judgement. Heather Cox was definitely the sort of girl who wore pantyhose not stockings. How could he have been so stupid?

Maybury had never heard of Cathay Bank, but new institutions were springing up all over Asia, as China emerged still further as a capitalist powerhouse. Although the account had been authorised by both Turner and Victor Duncan, Heather Cox hadn't seen the paperwork she expected and wanted to hear the rationale from the horses' mouths. Neither was available to explain.

Most of the employees knew Turner was in Phuket for the weekend but expected Victor Duncan to take his place. Victor had recently confided in Maybury that he had a heart complaint and might have to check in with his doctor from time to time. Maybury was therefore not surprised that both men were unreachable. Working on separate floors, he had no way of knowing Victor had not been in his office since the previous Tuesday evening. He was certainly unaware that as Heather Cox explained her concerns, Victor Duncan lay dead in the bathroom of his apartment.

For Charles Maybury, the situation was not nearly as disturbing as the lawyer believed, but he'd been in the business a very long time and when things did go wrong they tended to do so with catastrophic consequences. He'd have to make one call to check all was as it should be, to make sure there was a sensible explanation for the opening of a new account with a bank he'd never heard of before. He picked up his phone.

Storm clouds had gathered on the horizon and the mist was thick enough to virtually obscure the view of the Chao Praya river many floors below. Andy Duncan had just sent the authorisation to transfer one billion dollars to the new account set up in the name of the Emerging Fund at Cathay Bank. Within hours Daniel, and his associates, would ensure that the money was split and moved on through a chain of other accounts so it wouldn't be traced until it was too late. Twenty million dollars should find it's way into an account in the name of Mr and Mrs William Ward, and he and Caroline were due at the airport shortly for the first leg of their convoluted escape. Andy had to wait for one call. He was desperate for the phone to ring, knowing it could be the signal that he could flee, but equally terrified it could be First Independent saying they'd blocked the transfer or Daniel saying the money had not arrived. When the phone did ring, he barely suppressed a scream.

"This is Andy Duncan." His voice cracked as he forced the words out.
"Andy, it's Charles Maybury in Hong Kong. I need to check something with you."

It took only a few minutes to deal with the call from Hong Kong but it left Andy feeling even more nervous and unsettled. He had to remain at his desk until Daniel confirmed the money had been transferred, then he could leave for the airport with Caroline.

When the call finally came it was Caroline on the other end of the line.

"Andy, it's me. Daniel sent me the confirmation; it shows the twenty million in our account. It's over. First Independent transferred the billion dollars, everything worked like clockwork."

"Seriously? I got a call from Hong Kong but it was Charles Maybury, someone there got suspicious but Charles called me to make sure everything was OK. That was the only check they did, I can't believe it."

"Andy, that's great isn't it? It all went precisely as Daniel planned. Now you need to get out of there. I'm waiting for you downstairs. Get down here as quick as you can. We need to get that plane." Caroline was getting impatient; this was not a conversation they needed to have on the telephone.

"But Caro, I don't get it. If someone picked up on the fact it was suspicious, why wasn't my father on the other end of the phone? Why didn't Turner himself call?"

"Did you ask Maybury?"

203

"Yeah, course I did. He avoided the question. Like he had a secret. If this was picked up in Hong Kong, then it would have been Dad's department that chased it up."

There was an uncomfortable pause as Andy tried to make sense of what he'd heard and Caroline racked her brains for a way to get Andy out of his office and into the lift to make his way to the basement.

"Caro… you said Daniel would get hold of my father's password. How did he do that?"

"Andy, I have absolutely no idea how he got the password. These guys are techno-wizards; they found a way into the system. Like that little dyke you used to hang around with, whatever her name was. She showed you all that stuff about back doors. Maybe they did that… maybe she did it for them."

"No, she definitely didn't help them. I'm certain of that."

Caroline was getting really desperate.

"Andy please, we can talk about this in the car. Get down here now, we have to get out of here."

"Where are you?"

"I'm waiting by the car, where we always park it. It's what we agreed Andy, remember?"

"OK…OK I'm coming. So you're calling from there now?"

"Andy, I'm in the driver's seat, the engine's running. Should I go without you?"

"No, I'm sorry. I'm just not used to this sort of thing. I'll be there, give me five minutes."

"Three." That was an order.

"Yeah, three. I'll be there in three."

Andy could make no sense of it at all. It was clear from the call he got from Charles Maybury that someone in Hong Kong was aware the new deposit account was suspicious. Victor Duncan would have been onto it in an instant, the call should have come from him. When Andy asked why his father hadn't dealt with the query, Maybury sounded less than convincing. 'He's not around right now,' just didn't sound right. Daniel never explained how he'd get hold of his father's password. Perhaps that was why Victor was unavailable, maybe he too had become a victim. Andy had called his father several times since he got off the phone to Maybury. Victor's mobile and office number both went straight to voicemail. There was something wrong. If only his father could be reached.

Andy looked at his watch; he promised to be in the car in one hundred and fifty seconds. Caroline was waiting for him. That was the second thing he couldn't get his head around. Images of the night she left for Hua Hin flashed through his brain. He thought she'd left, but then she was back, saying she'd forgotten the car keys. He'd have brought them down, had she phoned, but she couldn't. There was never even the faintest of mobile signals in that basement. Pressing a couple of buttons on his office phone called up the last calls received. One minute and forty seconds earlier he was talking to Caroline and she'd called from... her mobile. Wherever she was when she made that call, it couldn't possibly have been the basement. If she'd called from somewhere else, there could only be one reason why she was so eager he went to the basement as soon as possible. Caroline wasn't waiting for him, but someone else was.

**The Spoils**

In the days after Berwick Archer lost one billion US dollars of client's money, the fraud was never far from the front pages. Some papers dredged out the video of Brad Tait and India Clarke and claimed it was just a portent of the famous firm's spectacular fall from grace. The investment community generally closed ranks around such issues, even local regulators and governments are keen to settle things quietly so confidence is not lost in the financial system. It was never an option in this case. James Turner's own captivity and the brutal slaying of his housekeeper was the headline story by Friday night. Victor's body was found in the early hours of Saturday morning, once the police established the motive of the two men who attacked Turner's family and were unable to locate the Risk Director anywhere else. By Monday morning teams of accountants from one of the world's top four firms had moved into Berwick Archer's offices in Hong Kong and Bangkok, to establish exactly how one billion dollars had been mislaid. There was no chance whatsoever the company could keep the issue under wraps. By the middle of Monday morning the word on everyone's lips, across the global financial community, was FRAUD. Trading in the Emerging Fund was suspended and the share price of Berwick Archer fell like a stone. On the Tuesday morning, an ashen-faced James Turner appeared briefly in front of the TV cameras at the entrance to the IFC building in Hong Kong. His attorney would read a brief statement but informed the assembled journalists that Mr Turner was still under the care of his doctors and would be unable to take questions. The lawyer began to read.

"It is now clear that a criminal gang was able to gain unauthorised access to the systems of Berwick Archer last week. In collusion with a member of staff at the company's bankers, they were able to steal one billion dollars from the accounts of the largest fund managed by the firm. Whilst James Turner is not directly responsible for the security of the company's systems, he has to take full responsibility for the overall activities of Berwick Archer in Asia. It is with deep regret that he has decided the only honourable thing to do is to relinquish his role as Chief Executive of the Asian business. He is standing down with immediate effect."

The lawyer stepped forward trying to make room for Turner to escape the crowd, but the route was blocked by rows of eager reporters thrusting microphones in his direction and screaming questions.

"Please… please…" the lawyer said. "Mr Turner has made his statement, he has nothing more to say."

It took nearly three minutes for the beleaguered businessman to cover twenty yards to the limousine parked at the side of the road. He looked totally shell-shocked.

In London, Timothy Clarke wrung his hands as he watched the interview on TV news.

"The fucking bastard. Honourable thing? What the fuck does he know about honour? This happens on his watch and he's like a rat deserting a sinking ship. Who told him he could give an interview like that? We're fucked with the regulator, fucked with the press and now I'll have the insurance company on my arse saying we shouldn't have said anything in public. I'll fucking have him if it takes me until my dying breath."

Clarke's par five office played host to three senior executives and the boss of their PR agency. All four were aghast at what they were witnessing. Timothy Clarke once called a retiring colleague a "daft old bugger", shortly after a party in the man's honour. Staff close to the Chief Executive expressed profound shock at the uncharacteristic display of bad language. What they heard that morning was an extraordinary outburst. Regrettably, they'd later agree, it was entirely in proportion to the scale of the problem they now faced.

Timothy Clarke resigned twenty-four hours later when the board agreed to recommend that shareholders accept an offer for the entire share capital of the beleaguered group from a rival fund manager. The takeover had been proposed by Declan Riley, Chief Executive of Mayo Partners, and he made it a condition of his offer that Clarke relinquished his post as Chief Executive. The collapse of Berwick Archer had taken six working days since Andy Turner set the whole thing in motion by selling one billion dollars worth of shares.

It felt like a lot more than a month had passed as James Turner sipped an ice-cold Bombay Sapphire gin and tonic in a sheltered corner of the terrace overlooking the Andaman Sea. He'd borrowed the same house for the weekend it all started, the weekend his family was terrorised and his maid murdered. Of course he never made it to Phuket on that occasion, but this was the third week of his break and he was almost ready to face the world again. It was handy an old colleague was there to refresh the ice in his glass and pass the plate of rice cakes the maid left on the table.

"James, it must have been a terrible shock."

"You have no idea. I'd just given them the password for the final transfer. I thought that was it, they'd leave and I'd call the police."

"So they shot her, just like that."

"It was unbelievable, Kate and the kids will never get over it. Milly's blood was all over Sophie's face, she was that close. I thought the bastards would kill the lot of us."

"Why did they kill her? It was all over by that stage. They had what they wanted, I guess they were just a couple of psychos."

"No… it was calculated all right. I screamed at Chanpol when I finally got him on the phone. I told him nobody was supposed to get hurt. We agreed they'd lock Kate, the kids and Milly in a room with access to a bathroom. They wouldn't even have to see the blokes with the guns, I'd take them some food three times a day and they wouldn't be exposed to any of it. Then they'd rough me up a bit before they left. That was the plan, that was what we agreed."

"So what did Chanpol say, when you talked to him?"

Turner pulled the blanket the maid had placed carefully around his knees, up over his chest and arms. The sun had dipped below the horizon on Karon beach and there was the slightest of chills in the air.

"The little bastard laughed. He told me the whole family had to look genuinely terrified and the only way to do that was to make sure they really were. He said the police would never have bought it if we'd come out of there looking like we had house-guests for the weekend. Every member of the family had to be credible. Then you'll never believe what he said."

"So tell me."

Brad Tait finished half his drink and casually put both feet on the glass table in front of him.

"He said I should be grateful to him."

"Grateful? He's got to be joking."

"He said they discussed it, I had to look as though I'd been terrorised, I had to be scared, angry and bent on vengeance and the police would spot it straight away if I was faking it."

"So, what's there to be grateful about?"

Turner closed his eyes; it looked like he was really struggling to find the words.

"He said they argued over how to get me into… the right frame of mind. He was in favour of shooting Milly, the other two… wanted Sophie… you know." Turner looked like he could barely believe what he was saying.

Tait nearly turned the table over as he sat up and leant forward.

"You have to be fucking joking. Did he forget who gave him this deal, did he forget who's the boss?"

"He was typically Thai, very apologetic but reassuring me he only had my best interests at heart. He was certain the police would have seen through it otherwise and we'd not have got away with a cent."

"But we did, didn't we?" Tait was smiling, he was anxious to get Turner off the subject of his maid and what the intruders had been hoping to do to his daughter. As far as the Australian was concerned, Milly was just another casualty, there'd been plenty of others, he couldn't see why this one was any different.

"I reckon we did. Nobody's looking in our direction so I'd say Chanpol was right. The police are chasing their tails and the money is as clean as a new pair of Calvin Kleins, straight from the pack."

"What about Andy Duncan?"

"They lost him on the day of the transfer but Chanpol reckons they're close to tracking him down. He's the last loose end. I can't see him going to the police and, if he did, he knows nothing that points to us anyway. He was the perfect combination of smart and stupid to make this possible. Almost credible in the job, but innocent enough to fall for every trap we set for him."

"To Andy Duncan." Tait raised his glass and Turner followed suit. "I can't tell you how upset I was when you explained how I was supposed to get myself sacked. Take a load of coke, do a lousy job and shag the CEO's daughter. I was gutted." Both men laughed at the irony.

"Well," Turner said, "I had to give you a role you wouldn't screw up and that suited your talents."

"So what were you really after? Was it the cash or were you just squaring your account with the boss in London?"

Turner eyes turned to ice.

"A bit of both. Those bastards made up their mind about me years ago, everyone at the top of the firm. I was the rough diamond who could make them money but only Timothy fucking Clarke was to be trusted with running the company. He was the safe pair of hands they so desperately craved. Well they were right about me, I'm great at making money, but I wanted to prove them wrong about Clarke. I wanted to take their precious fucking firm out from under them and all on his watch. He's ruined and watch this space, I might make a comeback."

"You're kidding."

"Who knows? Declan Riley's a big mate of mine from rugby days, we played for Happy Valley together when he was in Hong Kong. As the proud new owner of Berwick Archer I reckon he might need some help."

Tait shook his head in awe at the man opposite him. Turner was clearly shaken by the events of four weeks earlier but appeared to be invincible. Tait would have run off a cliff had Turner asked him, instead the request was to find a smart but innocent trainee fund manager and to play his part in the destruction of one of London's premier investment names. In return he'd be paid one hundred million US dollars. Tait might have done it just for the fun and because Turner asked… but the cash was a nice bonus.

"So how do we get our hands on all that dough?"

"Chanpol is coming here any time now. He has all the paperwork; we need to sign a couple of things. He's bound to try to rook us when it comes to expenses but who cares? There's plenty to go around and he's done an amazing job."

On cue the sound of helicopter blades cut through the calm of the night and in minutes both Chanpol and Sam from Berwick Archer's Bangkok office were standing on the terrace. Pleasantries were exchanged and the two visitors were ushered towards their chairs.

"Tanawat. You've done a great job, but I'll never forgive you for Milly. She didn't need to die. And killing that policeman's daughter, are you sure that's not going to come back to haunt us?"

"*Kuhn* James, these things are in the past, we are simply here to complete our business with you."

"Sure, I guess. The money. I won't fight you on every last penny but we agreed a budget for this. How much have you got for me?"

"In a moment *Kuhn* James. First I would like to introduce you to some of the team who delivered this project." An exquisitely beautiful girl of Asian descent emerged from behind the screen at the edge of the terrace. "You know Caroline Chan already. We really couldn't have done any of this without her and she was very keen to see you both again."

The two westerners bowed graciously.

"Fuck me Caroline, you look fantastic. It's great to see you again, especially as we have something to celebrate." It was Tait, once again unable to suppress the excitable puppy reaction that had become his trademark.

"Brad, James, it's nice to see you both. I insisted on coming tonight, I wouldn't have missed it for the world."

Very little of what Chan had said to Andy Duncan in their time together was true. That she never slept with Brad Tait, in spite of his near constant begging, was an exception. The Australian was determined to put that right. He opened his mouth to speak again but Chanpol cut in.

"I'd also like you to meet the man who runs my organisation, he wanted to conclude our dealings personally."

Turner shifted nervously in his seat, he could sense things were taking an unexpected turn. "Your boss? What the hell are you talking about? I thought you were the boss."

"No *Kuhn* James, I am known to my associates as Song, the Thai word for two. You already know Sam, it's not her real name but it is Thai for the word three. Allow me to present Nung. Number one."

From the shadows, an immaculately dressed Thai appeared. Turner was sure he'd seen him before but could not place the face. Maybe it was the gin, or the residual shock from four weeks before or the inescapable feeling that his carefully engineered plan was unravelling before his eyes. He glanced around the terrace, there were staff who should be checking that everything was to his satisfaction, there were armed security guards patrolling the perimeter of the house. Where were they when they were needed? Then the realisation dawned. The house had been borrowed from Chanpol himself, so everyone there was an employee of the lawyer. Turner turned back towards the Thai who was offering a large, perfectly manicured hand. Although not tall, the man was certainly physically imposing, a little overweight perhaps but with the build of a rugby player. When Turner failed to respond to the outstretched palm, the man stepped back and raised his hand to his face. His skin was rough and a little mottled as though he was suffering from a mild case of eczema. Standing about three feet behind Nung, was a young, athletic, smartly dressed Thai, who'd have been delighted to know, Turner thought he looked a bit like the bloke that starred in Bangkok Dangerous alongside Nicholas Cage.

"Mr Turner…" Nung said, "my name is Narong Sunarawani. I'm genuinely delighted to meet you. You already know my daughter Caroline and this young man is…"

"Boonamee, sir, Prem Boonamee." Chanpol filled the awkward gap, realising his boss had no idea who he'd chosen as security for the night.

"Yes, of course… Prem." Sunarawani smiled apologetically at the young Thai as though his brief lapse of memory would haunt him until his dying day.

Turner regained his composure. "You must be joking, Narong Sunarawani, I know you. Thai nationalist, saviour of the country's industry, friend of the poor and, if you fancy the job… Thailand's next Prime Minister. You're one of the richest men in Asia let alone Thailand, what the fuck are you doing running around with a two-bit gangster and a bent lawyer?"

Chanpol had heard it all before. There were few things that might dent his customary calm and the opinion of a *farang* was not on the list.

Sunarawani gave an avuncular smile, pointed to an empty chair right next to Turner and raised an eyebrow. Turner nodded, indicating the Thai should sit.

"Mr Turner, I am simply here to conclude our business relationship. Name calling is really quite unnecessary. I thought you might like to know what happened to all the money."

"What happened to ALL the money?"

"Indeed… all the money. After expenses your share is quite small."

"So it's an old-fashioned sting is it? The guilty meet to share the spoils and we get cut out of the equation. I don't get it, why would you get involved in shit like this?"

Turner was astonished at how calm he felt, he desperately hoped it was because somewhere deep in his sub-conscious a plan was forming that might save the day. He feared in reality it had more to do with the gin and the painkillers.

"I'm so glad you asked me. I love to tell the story."

"I'm sure you do."

"Mr Turner, you are aware I am a very successful businessman. I have built several businesses from scratch and some are quoted on the Stock Exchange of Thailand. Regrettably, they are then at the mercy of people like you, interested only in short term profits, I have a bad quarter's results and you sell my shares, the price falls and if I need to go to my bank for working capital it is more expensive or they turn me away, pointing to the fall in my share price. This makes my job harder and if my share price does not rise, you encourage a competitor to make a bid for my company. All in the name of… what is that ridiculous phrase? Ah yes… shareholder value. And who do you employ to do this? People like Andrew Duncan who is barely out of short trousers…" Sunarawani jerked his head in the direction of Brad Tait, "…and people like him, who is more of a slave to his bodily functions than a new born baby."

The Australian wanted to reach out and grab Sunarawani by the throat but his survival instinct told him that would be a major error of judgement. Instead he shrugged, suggesting that he'd weighed the case against him and couldn't really argue. His mind was ready to fight his corner; his shoulders had said "fair call."

"Capitalism's worked pretty well for centuries, if you don't like it… butt out," Turner replied.

Sunarawani roared with laughter.

"Oh Mr Turner you misunderstand. I love capitalism, but I play by my own rules. Let me give you an example. I have a successful business, it employs many people across Thailand and delivers a very good product that is popular with millions of customers."

"Yeah, sounds like the capitalism I recognise."

The Thai was irritated by the interruption.

"But there is a problem. A competitor emerges; he manufactures across the border in Myanmar and can afford to sell his product more cheaply. Unless I respond Thai jobs may be lost and my company might fail. What should I do? Reduce my margins, cut costs by making an inferior product, spend millions of baht on advertising or maybe I should hire some overpriced advisors and attempt to take over my competitor. What do you think?"

"That's the power of the market, you have to give the customer what they want. If you can't respond then you deserve to fail."

"I responded Mr Turner. I hired a man to follow my competitor's car on a motorbike and then kill him with a machine pistol. Luckily his penchant for ladyboys became known and with a little financial encouragement, the police and the press never looked beyond his dreadfully betrayed wife as the perpetrator. His company failed, mine prospered. That, Mr Turner, is my version of capitalism."

"You're a crazy man. You do this because you enjoy the mayhem. We asked Chanpol to put Duncan in an impossible position, where he'd have no choice but to place those trades and transfer the cash. We did not tell him to kill the daughter of one of Thailand's top cops. What the fuck was that about? It's got nothing to do with business, it's because you like screwing up people's lives."

"Mr Turner, once again you are wrong. Ms Raksanatra was very unlucky but we chose her carefully. Her father was an extremely stubborn man and was close to making life very difficult for us. We had to discourage him. The car accident we organised for his wife threw him for a few months but he came back at us with renewed zeal. Since his daughter's most regrettable death he has been on indefinite leave from the police force. We were able to deliver an outcome for your project that helped us with our other business objectives. A perfect example of the synergies you investment people keep banging on about."

"That's insane, that's not business, you're a gangster."

"It's business Mr Turner, I choose not to be bound by the rules that the financial community seek to force upon us. You contribute nothing but expect vast rewards."

"So that's why..." Turner interjected.

"Don't flatter yourself Mr Turner, this is not about vengeance on the investment industry, I'm merely explaining the drawbacks of being a man who wants to run a business, rather than simply leech off it financially as you do. You think you understand finance and business but you know nothing and when greed takes over, your judgment disappears. You manage billions of pounds of other people's money but were duped by a lawyer, his assistant and a very accomplished but as yet undiscovered actress." He gestured towards where Chanpol, Sam and Caroline were now standing.

"Actress?"

"My darling daughter, she never worked a day in the financial services industry before we gave her this role. Yet you accepted her as an experienced professional after one lunch and a twenty-minute meeting. Perhaps that's all it takes in your business. Her ambition was always to act, and you must agree her debut performance has been a sensation."

Caroline nodded modestly as all eyes fell on her and she gave a tiny little curtsey. Turner fought the image in his mind but it was irresistible, Caroline Chan accepting an Academy Award for her role in "The Fall of Berwick Archer." Sunarawani appeared to have lost his train of thought as he looked proudly at his daughter, or he was waiting for Turner and Tait to step forward and ask for an autograph.

"Where was I?" Sunarawani continued. "Oh yes, of course. Life as a conventional CEO is not for me. And as you know there are many who think I should make a career in politics, but it has many of the same drawbacks."

"It has?" Turner was trying out his voice to see if it still worked, his chest was getting tight.

"There is not a single country in the world that could not solve all of its problems if it only had the will but there are two major obstacles. One is the greed of feckless, useless politicians who know that they have a short time to fill their pockets until they are found out."

"And the other?"

"Democracy, Mr Turner. Difficult problems require tough solutions and democracy does not permit its politicians to do anything that is remotely unpopular. You simply choose the least unpalatable compromise. Your press will squeal if they can find just one person disadvantaged by government policy and the lives of the politicians are placed under the microscope. A single indiscretion and they are vilified. The only people who pursue public office in the west are retarded publicity seekers who couldn't get a proper job. They've never done anything tangible, they never intend to, but they love seeing themselves on TV talking about it. This is not a role I would desire."

"Based on that description, I'd say you'd fit in fine."

"You do me a disservice. I have my business plan and I pursue it relentlessly. Politicians are nothing more than opportunists with an eye on the lecture tour and the odd backhander. Your own Prime Minister declared war on Iraq as a favour to the Americans and having bombed the Arabs to bits, is now paid to advise them on how to achieve peace. It's beyond irony. In Thailand we have soap operas with more believable plots."

"You can dress it up anyway you want. You're a common criminal. That's your choice."

Sunarawani looked genuinely hurt.

"Mr Turner, I am a very uncommon criminal and I really do not think the word does me justice. I am a businessman, I've decided that some of the constraints that would be placed on me, if all of my activities were through public companies, are inappropriate. You must be aware that my businesses bring employment to hundreds of thousands of people across Asia but in Thailand in particular."

"But you don't feel you are subject to any rules at all."

"The people who make your rules are idiots, to govern you have to understand the human condition and your society is ruled by pathetic weak-willed liberals. I think it was your own Prime Minister who said people are basically good and just need to be given the right opportunity."

"And your point?"

"It's a dreadful error of judgment. People are venal, greedy, shallow and lazy. Give them an opportunity and they will rob you blind. The only thing they understand is fear. Until your politicians understand that, your society will continue to wither and die."

"So you decided to create your own set of rules." Turner tried to catch Tait's eye, hoping that the younger man would give some indication that he'd worked out how they could make an escape. Tait was staring blankly at Sunarawani.

"Mr Turner, I have only one. Thais must always win and foreigners must always lose. It is the only way my country and its people can achieve the prosperity it deserves."

"So what's the plan? How are you going to turn this fucking cesspit of a country into a great success? You're dying to tell me."

Turner sneered at Sunarawani, fighting with the only weapons at his disposal. Unable to hurt the man physically, verbal jibes against his beloved Thailand was all he had left.

Sunarawani was briefly rattled. Glancing at Boonamee it looked like he might ask the man to deal with Turner there and then, but he regained his composure.

"I'm so glad you asked me that. Song here runs most of my businesses. On the face of it they are the usual combination of gambling, money lending and trading in valuable commodities such as drugs, precious stones and… women. We also have a little investment business in Chiang Mai. They bring prosperity to thousands who would otherwise be working the fields. Where possible we focus on taking the property of *farang* who have come to our country to prey on our economic weakness and we find a more deserving owner. A Thai owner."

Turner could barely believe what he was hearing.

"You're an old-fashioned gangster and you claim that you do it for the benefit of your countrymen. How many Thais get totally fucked up by your drug running and prostitution rings? That's just bollocks to make you feel better about what you're doing."

Sunarawani chuckled. "It is true that some of my fellow Thais will suffer along the way, but this is a long term project to bring wealth to the masses… and to me of course. We are Buddhists. These people will receive their reward… in another life. In any event, Mr Turner, I don't think I will be taking any morality lessons from a man who hired *Kuhn* Chanpol to destroy his employer because of a grudge… and then pocket a billion dollars of stolen money."

Turner opened his mouth to respond but quickly closed it again. It was true that the moral high ground was pretty hard to occupy in this particular debate.

"Anyway Mr Turner, we were discussing how my enterprises seek to redistribute wealth in an easterly direction. Mr Song here used to do it in a small way, helping bargirls buy property fully financed by a westerner whose mind ceases to work as soon as he gets an erection." Tait was sure that the man paused to look in his direction, but then Sunarawani continued. "We've moved upmarket since then. For instance, we were delighted to help a charming Ukrainian professor build the largest entertainment complex in the whole of Pattaya. It was even more satisfying to relieve him of the burden of running it and turn it over to an ambitious young Thai entrepreneur. But you have been the crowning glory, we thought it would be years before we could make a strike like this one, but a billion dollars. Even I'm impressed with that."

"Looks like you missed a trick to me." Tait had decided to assert himself on the conversation.

"Mr Tait, I'd quite forgotten you were still with us. Please tell me, what trick was that?"

"So you get a billion out of Berwick Archer, if your plan is to steal western assets why didn't you go for the whole business? It was on its knees after this but it got snapped up for pennies by Declan Riley, another of those *farang* you so despise."

Sunarawani looked thoughtful for a moment. To the two westerners it appeared that he was contemplating a missed opportunity. He was merely deciding how best to tell the next part of the story.

"I don't despise Mr Riley at all. I feel a little sorry for him and I am grateful that he is less cautious than he should be about his… appetites. You see, I finance all of Mr Riley's acquisitions and have done so since I discovered he is a member of a rather disreputable club."

"You're not serious?"

"Deadly serious. You see, Mr Riley is very close to a gentlemen called Mr Shin. He has a large house on the outskirts of Pattaya. A number of influential people go there for parties or just for a few hours break from their stressful lives. They all like the company of young girls… very young girls. And I have the video evidence to prove it. Mr Riley is the public face of Mayo Partners, the new owners of Berwick Archer, but it is my company."

Turner was gradually piecing together how the Thai had hijacked his idea to destroy his employer. He desperately wanted to find a flaw in Sunarawani's plan.

"So it was you who delivered the inside information on Dengshu and Omega, Worrapon was a front. If you're so smart, how come you took such a huge hit on Dengshu, everyone knows you lost money on that one."

"Oh Mr Turner, once again you underestimate me. Ben Worrapon is Caroline's brother, albeit by a different mother and my oldest son is indeed a banker with access to the information we gave to young Mr Duncan. They were certainly part of the plan but Dengshu was a triumph for our family."

Turner was vaguely aware that it was unlikely that Sunarawani planned on letting him go, having told him so much, but he was transfixed. The man was deluded, possibly insane but Turner had to hear where this was going. He certainly did not expect where it went next.

"Mr Turner, have you seen the Producers, the movie by Mel Brooks?"

Turner nodded, he didn't trust himself to speak.

"And you know all about Winston Churchill I'm sure." There was an intensity in Sunarawani's eyes, it was like one of those crazy messianic preachers from the Midwest of the USA, or possibly like the star performer at Nazi Germany's Nuremberg rallies.

"Mel Brooks and Churchill inspired our idea for Dengshu. You will recall the Producers, a film-maker had taken a great deal of money from some gullible old ladies, the only way he could get off the hook was to deliver a box office failure. His investors would understand their money had been lost in a brave but ultimately unsuccessful commercial venture. They would never know that each share had been sold over and over again. The perfect fraud."

He paused as though Turner might offer hearty congratulations for his wit and invention. "I'm sure you are wondering where Mr Churchill comes in."

Turner nodded, he was wondering... in spite of himself.

"In the run up to D Day, it is claimed that Churchill completely fooled the Germans by building a cardboard invasion force in the south of England. It looked like he had many armoured divisions poised to strike in Calais. From a distance it looked genuine… it was not. We simply combined the ideas."

Turner nodded his head as he realised what Sunarawani was saying.

"You take a bundle of money off investors thinking they're cashing in on the African oil rush but you don't drill a single well. You just put a huge fence round the site, ship in a few bits of kit but never do any of the really expensive stuff. The cash gets syphoned off into your offshore accounts and then you announce that the wells are dry and you strike camp and leave it to the natives to graze their cows on it."

Sunarawani applauded. "Mr Turner I'm delighted that you have grasped the essence of our plan so quickly. But, as I expected, the punch line has escaped you. The money was handled exactly as you described. Investors across the world have invested huge sums. We made it look like we were drilling, then paid for a report to say that the wells were dry. The investors shrug and move on. It's wonderful."

"So where's the punch line?"

"There is oil in those fields for sure, but for the next decade or so, we will station guards at the wire. We will explain that there are health and safety issues, that there is a dispute about the ownership of the land. Eventually the board of Dengshu will reluctantly throw in the towel and recommend a takeover bid from one of my companies. Then, in say fifteen years, we will announce a vast oil reserve. This is something that you westerners are incapable of comprehending but it is second nature to an Asian. We plan decades ahead, it is not about this quarter's profit."

Turner laughed. "You'll never get away with that. They'll realise that the oil was there all along."

"But nobody will ever trace it back to me Mr Turner, remember I am one of the investors in Dengshu who has been wronged. No-one knows my role in running the company." Then he paused and looked Turner in the eyes. "Except you and Mr Tait, of course.

"So Sunarawani, is it greed or just the fact that you hate westerners so much that drives you?"

"I don't think hate is the word Mr Turner. Despise captures it so much better. I have neither affection nor respect for your people."

"Bad experience when you were a kid was it? Some big white boy stole your teddy bear?"

"You can't provoke me Turner, your opinion of me is of no consequence. I just wanted you to know why you will get nothing from your plan to destroy Berwick Archer."

"I'm interested really, why do you hate us so much?" Turner was playing for time, without any real idea how that would help.

"Your ancestors enslaved dark skinned people all over the globe, claiming it was to spread Christianity, when in truth it was to plunder their resources. Now your societies are in decline and you have neither the wit nor the courage to reverse the trend. Half your children get worthless qualifications and are then astonished that it does not pave the way to a glittering career, the other half turn to indolence or crime, or dream of being pop stars or footballers. You pander to the lazy and feckless by paying them not to work. Only people like you prosper in a society like that and only for a short time."

"So our politicians are crap and our kids are a bit spoilt, that's the sign western civilisation is crumbling?" Turner asked.

"Mr Turner, it's much worse that that. *Farang* have ceased to evolve. Do you understand the concept of survival of the fittest? Weak strains die out and each remaining generation becomes stronger than the last. You use medicine to save those who nature intended to die and allow people to breed who should make no further contribution to the gene pool. You are using science to reverse a process that has taken millions of years. That is why you will fail, you have become too soft to survive."

Turner couldn't believe what he was hearing.

"I owe you an apology Mr Sunarawani. I called you a gangster and a crook. I was wrong, you're a twenty-four carat gold Nazi psychopath and if people like you ever get to run a country then God help us all."

There was no reply. The Thai wasn't listening; he'd obviously got carried away with his own rhetoric and was staring into the distance as though entranced. Chanpol coughed gently to attract his attention.

"Where was I?" Sunarawani asked of no-one in particular. There was an uncomfortable silence; the evening was about to take a critical turn. Neither Turner nor Tait could see how they would survive. The Thai beckoned the two Englishmen to join him as he took in the view of Karon Beach in the distance. Sam and Caroline had disappeared and only Song and Boonamee remained. Sunarawani addressed both men.

"Gentlemen, you will have gathered that I am a devoted fan of Hollywood movies. I've even been known to use them as inspiration in my business dealings. The Producers... things like that."

Turner and Tait exchanged a glance, wondering where this could possibly be going.

"I love James Bond, what young boy didn't want to be just like him?"

There was no reply.

"Well, you know that bit where the villain has Bond at his mercy and he can't resist explaining his whole plan to 007. It's got to the point where he can't let the secret agent live. There's that wonderful line... in Goldfinger wasn't it? What does he say again? 'No Mr Bond I'm not expecting you to talk. I'm expecting you to die'. Something like that anyway, I can't quite recall. Now... where was I? Oh yes. That's pretty much where we've got to gentlemen. I've told you everything, so I'm supposed to jump back in the helicopter and leave young Boonamee to deal with you. Of course once I'm gone, you somehow overpower him and in the closing scenes of the movie, I get my come-uppance and you get the girl. That's how it's supposed to go right?"

Turner appeared to have lost the power to move, he stared at Sunarawani as though in a trance. Tait knew that he had to do something or this was the end. Sunarawani wasn't finished.

"That's definitely what would happen in the movies. Right?" He screamed the final word and Tait responded automatically, it was only the slightest nod of the head but it was all Sunarawani wanted, an acknowledgement that he'd been understood.

"The thing is gentlemen... this is not a movie."

Sunarawani turned towards the helicopter at exactly the same moment that Boonamee fired for the first time. Turner and Tait both took two bullets in the chest. Their executioner stepped in and shot each of them between the eyes from close range. The three Thais moved quickly to the helicopter. A clean-up team would arrive within fifteen minutes of Song's call. The bodies and all the possessions of both men would disappear, never to be found again.

**Payback**

Boonamee had barely arrived back in his apartment in Bangkok when word came through that they'd located Andrew Duncan. The Thai landed in Hong Kong around two-thirty the following afternoon. Pier Four is where the fast ferries embark for Lamma Island, one of Hong Kong's offshore jewels. Boonamee arrived forty-five minutes before the agreed time to ensure that he was completely comfortable with the meeting place. The informant was told to wear a white cap and a red Liverpool football shirt. He too was at the rendezvous early, but only by ten minutes. Arriving by motorbike, he looked completely at ease, leaning against the saddle of his bike smoking a roll-up cigarette. Boonamee was always cautious but, if this was a trap, it was being sprung by a very cool character. More likely, the guy had done what was asked of him and was there to hand over the information and collect his cash.

At exactly three a.m. Boonamee moved to a spot around twenty metres from the entrance to the pier as arranged. He leant against the railing and stared down at the water below, it was deeper than he imagined but then this was where the ferries came in, so it made sense. The man in the white cap took a last draw on his cigarette and dropped the butt next to his bike, then ambled over to the railing as though he had all the time in the world.

"Yip?" Boonamee asked.

"That's me," the man looked relaxed and appeared to be enjoying the subterfuge.

"What have you got for me?"

"Cash first."

Boonamee pulled out an envelope stuffed with Hong Kong dollars. The man grabbed it and flicked through the contents. There was no time to count all the notes but he was clearly impressed by the number he'd been given.

"Steven Lancaster, Room 1314, Mandarin Oriental Hotel."

"And you're sure it's Andrew Duncan."

The man handed over a photo; it was clearly the Englishman on the steps of the famous hotel. Boonamee smiled and nodded, he was impressed. The messenger slipped the envelope into his back pocket and turned to go back to his bike. Boonamee produced the knife and severed Yip's spinal cord with one fluid movement. It was a straightforward task to fold the upper half of the man's body over the railing while Boonamee retrieved the cash from his pocket. From a distance it looked like Yip had enjoyed a few too many beers and was emptying his stomach into the water below. Boonamee was the attentive friend, helping his drunken buddy… right up to the point where he grabbed the young man's feet and tipped him into the water.

Boonamee took a moment to find his bearings and then headed back to the walkway that would take him past the entrance to Berwick Archer's Hong Kong office and across Connaught Road to the entrance of the Mandarin Oriental Hotel. It would be a few hours before the lobby of the hotel was busy enough for him to enter without being noticed but he had all the time in the world.

Sally Peng reluctantly admitted that she'd never worn a bikini before. It was a terrible waste, her companion told her… she looked fabulous. Neither had she stayed in such a luxurious hotel and a week of unrestrained hedonism was completely new territory. She had lovers before, but quickly grew tired of men who could not keep up with her intellectually or physically. Work was her abiding passion and her idea of a treat was to take a day off and go hiking in the New Territories that mark the boundary between Hong Kong and China proper. Suddenly, and rather unexpectedly, she had a new man in her life and it was going very well indeed. It felt like an age since she'd run the IT systems at Berwick Archer. Her ideal role, until James Turner chose his scapegoat when the video of Brad Tait and India Clarke appeared on YouTube. Since then she'd found it impossible to get another job in Hong Kong. Employers tended to believe Turner's story that she was either involved in the leak or negligent. Her pleas that she had no control over the video conferencing facilities in Bangkok fell on deaf ears. Briefly, she stayed with her parents in Beijing but quickly tired of the smug look on her mother's face. The message was clear, they always told her she'd never make anything of herself in Hong Kong and they were right. She failed, but as loving parents they'd help her pick up the pieces of her shattered life. They'd even introduce her to some nice men. There was a wonderful young lecturer at the university where her father worked, or a fascinating new recruit at the Space Centre who, inexplicably, could not find a girlfriend. Sally would be perfect.

She left a note, not unlike the one she'd written the last time she left home and set out for the New Territories once again. When the phone call came, her first instinct was to call the cops. Instead she listened and, by the time she'd heard the entire pitch, was certain this was a once in a lifetime opportunity. She'd been asked to use her detailed knowledge of Berwick Archer's systems to steal a very substantial sum of money. It went against everything she'd ever been taught, it was contrary to every moral principle that guided her though her working life. As she looked around the small shabby hotel room she made her base for the latest hiking trip, it crossed her mind where those principles had got her. People like James Turner were riding high and had wealth beyond her dreams, she was frozen out of a job she loved and of the opportunity to find another. The voice on the other end of the phone cut through her musings.

"Can you help me? It's totally illegal but there's a lot of money in it for you."

"Yeah, I'll do it. Why not?"  A little over a month later, it was looking like one of the best decisions she'd ever made.

Andy Duncan poured her another glass of iced lemonade and started working some more sunscreen into the tops of her thighs. She didn't need any, he just enjoyed doing it. Sally was a revelation. Initially he'd asked her how someone might access passwords at Berwick Archer. Andy was anxious about how Daniel might get hold of his father's access codes. Nonetheless, he made it sound like it was an abstract concern rather than part of a genuine issue. They spent two hours on the phone and he started to realise how much Sally hated the people who ran Berwick Archer and all the other investment firms on the island. Andy had been reading the book he found in his apartment about controlling risk and hedging his investments. He began to worry about what would happen if Daniel went back on his word and didn't pay the share he promised. Encouraged by her complete antipathy for Turner and Tait, he opened up to Sally that he was being blackmailed. Unaware that Turner was behind the planned fraud, she was thrilled that the man who ruined her career might be about to get his just desserts. That was when Andy made the suggestion. He wanted an insurance policy in case Daniel reneged and Sally could name her price for services rendered. The plan was simple. She would hack into the company system and create an instruction to liquidate the whole of Ben Worrapon's thirty million dollar portfolio. At the same time she would change Worrapon's client record so that the proceeds would go to an account on a remote Caribbean island, wending its way through a complex chain of banks domiciled in a variety of offshore centres. Sally's family had used the technique for years to ensure they could keep their cash away from the prying eyes of the authorities. When you work for the Chinese Space Agency, America's CIA is an eager customer for any insights on offer. Doctor and Professor Peng had invested a lot of time and effort in protecting the value of their pension.

    The plan was for Sally to take half and the balance would allow Andy to make his escape, regardless of whether Daniel paid up as promised. He hadn't told Sally that Caroline was part of the deal. At least she was until she called claiming to be in the basement. He knew that was impossible and the scales fell from his eyes. How could he have been so stupid? Caroline had been in it all along. More than a month had passed since the day the money transferred. He laid low in Hua Hin for two weeks before finding his way to Hong Kong to meet with Sally. She took to a life of crime with great gusto, and presented him with travel documents in the name of Steven Lancaster. The ease with which she sourced the counterfeit passport initially sent Andy's recently acquired persecution complex into overdrive. It briefly occurred to him that, she too might be part of the plan to destroy him. He strained to keep his voice light and full of humour when he asked the question.

"So how does an unemployed IT guru get her hands on forged ID then? Is there a Microsoft Wizard for this that I never spotted?"

Initially she looked embarrassed and uncomfortable, which only served to feed his paranoia.

"Well... can you keep a secret?"

"If I can't, then I reckon I'll be in jail pretty soon."

"I've got some very dodgy friends, and I don't just mean you. Hacking became a bit of a hobby and I joined a group on-line. There were a few nutters who wanted to stop capitalism in its tracks and the odd crazy who thought they could bring government to a halt. Then there were a few like me who just did it for fun or to make a little extra cash on the side. There's a really nice guy who calls himself Pimpernel who works in the Passport Office."

Andy's suspicions were fading. "Like Scarlet Pimpernel, that bloke in the French Revolution with the secret identity."

'Exactly, it's fiction but that's the idea. Pimpernel sells identities and for the modest sum of ten grand he turned you into Steven Lancaster."

Andy was impressed. He thought they'd go their separate ways but, having discussed what they'd done late into the night, they slid into bed together. Andy and Sally had not been apart since. It was a little over-confident to check into a high profile hotel like the Mandarin and it took a couple of days to realise they should still be lying low. The couple checked out the night before a young Chinese taxi driver was found dead under Pier Four of the ferry terminal. Initially Police thought that might have been the body of a senior officer of First Independent Bank. Cho Wan Kei disappeared the same day that James Turner emerged from his house on the Peak, screaming that his housekeeper had been killed. The body in the harbour was quickly identified as being too young to be that of the banker. When Mrs Kei finally received a call to say her husband's body had been found in the boot of his car, at a shopping centre car park, she decided not to mention their final conversation. There was a nagging doubt in her mind. If she admitted he was leaving her, she feared she might not get her widow's pension.

Sally had sourced two more perfect sets of fake papers and by nightfall they were home as far as Andy was concerned, on the terrace of a luxury hotel room, overlooking Karon beach in Phuket. Andy had basked in the euphoria of his escape and the fact that he and Sally had more money than they could ever have imagined, but he knew that they were not yet in the clear.

"Sally, you've been amazing these last few weeks, but there are things we haven't talked about yet."

"It's OK, I know your dad's death hit you pretty hard. When you're ready. I've suddenly got all the time in the world."

"I don't think that's sunk in yet. If I hadn't got into all this, he'd still be alive."

"I don't think so Andy, they were going to get the money anyway. It was just bad luck that you happened to be the guy in the middle. They'd still have needed to get to your dad, even if they'd found another way to do the trades."

She held his hands between hers and kissed him softly.

"I guess you're right, but that's not it."

"So tell me." She sat upright and put on her most serious face.

"I told you they were going to make it look like I killed Lawan Raksanatra, but I never explained how they'd do that. I did spend the night with her, but I was drugged, I remember nothing, then this terrible story appeared on TV."

"And you're afraid they'll tell the police to cross check the forensic evidence with your DNA." It was a statement not a question.

"Absolutely, if they do that, I'm finished."

Sally thought for a moment, it looked as though she was weighing up all the things that could happen to Andy if the police got word that the DNA belonged to him.

"No, don't worry about it. It's not going to happen."

"How can you be so certain?"

"I checked with your old girlfriend. You remember, Caroline. The one you were going to run away with until you realised she was part of the plot and you had to make do with me." The look on her face said sad and hurt, but Sally managed to hold it for only a few seconds before she started to laugh. "You really thought I didn't know about her?"

"Well I... well I... ummm."

"And does that conclude the case for your defence?" She was really enjoying herself. "Andy, everyone in Berwick Archer knew you were an item. People still mailed me with all the gossip, when you didn't even mention her right from the start I got a bit suspicious."

"You say you... that you... ummm, you talked to...?"

"Well not exactly talked. I hacked her e-mails. You really cared about her didn't you?"

"Well I thought... you know it was..." Andy wondered if he'd ever construct a coherent sentence again.

"I'm teasing you. I dumped most of the stuff but there were a couple of mails I knew you'd want to see, and... hang on a minute, I think this is Exhibit A." She tapped away at her keyboard while she talked and as an e-mail loaded, she turned the screen so Andy could see.

*To: DanPan*
*From: Jeab*
*D. What's the plan with the forensic stuff? Think you should destroy, no point in going after AD now. What you think?*
*To: Jeab*
*From DanPan*
*Sweet that you're still concerned... must be love. Forensic got lost weeks ago. It never belonged to AD anyway - one of S's mob did the dirty deed. And even if it had been his – don't think there's mileage in opening that up again."*

Andy read the message several times before it sank in. He'd never touched the girl and any forensic evidence connected the crime to someone else. A wave of relief rushed through his body, the last piece of the jigsaw had slotted into place.

"I think she still cares about you." Sally was trying to pout but the look did not come naturally.

"Who?"

"Caroline."

"Who? Don't know anyone of that name."

"Are you sure?"

"Never been so certain of anything in my life."

Sally smiled and closed the laptop.

"Hungry?"

"Starving, let's go."

Sally picked up the small blue inhaler he'd left on the bedside table and tossed it gently towards him.

"Don't forget this."

Andy caught it and weighed it carefully in his hand before dropping it onto the bed.

"No, I don't think I'll be needing that now."

"So what's the plan for tomorrow?" Sally asked as they headed for the elevator.

"We're meeting my friends. Steve, Fah and Yoyo."

"You made that up right?"

"Not at all," he replied. "We're going to teach you to surf."

As Sally and Andy made their way to the hotel terrace for dinner, a flight landed at Suvarnabhumi. It took off from Kiev's Boryspil airport nearly nineteen hours earlier. The stopover in Dubai took longer than planned and the passengers were eager to disembark. Aboard was a young Ukrainian who looked like he'd seen military service. The haircut, the posture and the air of physical confidence were a clear signal that this was not a man to be taken lightly. He travelled under the name Roman Lenakov, and his passport indicated that he was a consultant. That was true in a manner of speaking. His employer was based on the border of Afghanistan and Pakistan and his job was to train new recruits in everything he learned in eleven years with the Russian Army's Special Forces. His latest mission was more personal. His father was a respected Ukrainian professor who'd recently been the victim of a fraud that drained all his financial resources and put him in grave danger with respect to his business associates in Kiev. Alexei Bezhepov was on his way to avenge his father and on his phone was a picture of the man he sought... Tanawat Chanpol.

As Alexei Bezhepov cleared immigration at Suvarnabhumi Airport, Mongkut Tharanyatta answered an emergency call to an exclusive apartment block off Third Road, Pattaya. The task was way below his pay grade, he expected junior officers to get their hands dirty, only getting involved later if it suited him. The request for a response was routed to his phone because of the address. An automatic flag on the Pattaya police system meant anything related to 26 Malako Towers off Soi 3 generated a personal alert. The apartment belonged to Tanawat Chanpol and was often used by his associates when they were on business in Pattaya.

As the car turned into the last street on his journey, Mongkut's eyes were drawn to a young woman standing on the corner, staring at the entrance to the block. She had very long hair and an extremely good figure, closer examination would have revealed beautiful intelligent eyes. Mongkut only managed a fleeting glance but he was impressed, she was a hell of a good-looking girl. His car screeched to a halt outside the apartment but it was clear that another police vehicle was already in attendance. Mongkut recognised the junior officer.

"What have we got?"

"Nothing to worry about boss. It's a gang killing for sure. We know this guy, he's a nasty piece of work."

"Name?"

"Boonamee, Prem Boonamee. Someone skewered him like a chicken and just left the body in the doorway of his apartment." The young policeman was enjoying himself. It made his job so much easier when the criminal classes killed each other. One less villain to catch and nobody really cared if they found the perpetrator. Mongkut looked less happy with what had occurred.

"Do we have any witnesses?"

"Yeah, there's an old lady who lives on the same floor as Boonamee. Seems like she arrived soon after the guy got cut. She reckons we should be looking for some girl who was coming out of the lobby as she arrived. Wouldn't mind interviewing her based on the description, 'big eyes, long hair, nice tits,' from what the old lady said. But there's no way someone like Boonamee is going to let a girl like that get the better of him. Reckon it's a coincidence and anyway the old woman's ranting and raving."

"What's that supposed to mean? What's she doing?"

The young officer shook his head, then raised his eyes to heaven, or to indicate where Mongkut should go to see for himself.

"Boss, she's lost it. She's wandering around the top floor mumbling to herself. The same thing over and over again."

'What's she saying?"

The officer bent his back and started to shamble aimlessly around the sidewalk, it was a passable impersonation of a little old lady. Then he looked up at Mongkut with what was supposed to be a crazed expression on his face.

"Oh my Buddha, so much blood. I've never seen so much blood."

## THE END

## Also by Matt Carrell

### Thai Lottery… and Other Stories from Pattaya, Thailand

If you want to find out more about Pom, the girl Prem Boonamee abandoned in Korat, Thai Lottery is the first in this series of short stories. It tells of what happens when a debt becomes a matter of life and death.

### Thai Kiss

Matt Carrell's first novel tells the story of Paul Murphy, on the run from a British drug dealer he flees to Pattaya, Thailand. As he starts to rebuild his life, there are many who want to share in his new-found success, but who can he trust?

### Something Must Be Done

"When bad guys have guns, the answer is to arm the good guys." If you've made up your mind about gun control, this short story, set in the UK and in a US High School, will make you think again.

**All available from Amazon.**

Please visit my website at www.mattcarrellbooks.com

Printed in Great Britain
by Amazon.co.uk, Ltd.,
Marston Gate.